MIDLAND MURDERS

By Dick Stodghill

ISBN: 978-0-6151-3604-2
JLT-Charatan Publications

First Printing

JLT-Charatan Publications

For Jackie Stodghill, who helped so much with these stories. And in memory of Eleanor Sullivan and Cathleen Jordan, two gracious editors now deceased.

The first eight stories in this collection were originally published in the following issues of **Alfred Hitchcock's Mystery Magazine.** A Debt To Be Paid appeared in **Ellery Queen's Mystery Magazine.**

Driscoll's Box Score (October 1979)
Driscoll's Big Story (August 1981)
Class Reunion (November 1981)
Meaningless Murder (July 1982)
Missing Melinda (January 1983)
Kickback (May 1983)
The Town Club Murders (January 1984)
Vigilante Law (June 1984)
A Debt To Be Paid (June 1980)

Some stories have also appeared in anthologies.

CONTENTS

INTRODUCTION

The Midland series featuring newspaper columnist Hal Blinn and reporter Grady Driscoll evolved in an unusual manner. It began with Driscoll as narrator in a first person, past tense story. But Driscoll was a little too brash and impetuous so I decided to tone him down a bit and remove him from the starring role.

That's where Blinn entered the scene as narrator, but in first person, present tense. I used that method because I wanted to set the series apart from others running at the time.

After one story was published in that style, Cathleen Jordan succeeded Eleanor Sullivan as editor of Alfred Hitchcock's Mystery Magazine. I received a call from Cathleen urging me to change the series to past tense. That seemed like too many changes, three in just three stories, so I said no. Although refusing to make another switch, I would have liked to because I was already weary of the present tense way of telling a story. But that's how it remained until I gave up on Blinn and Driscoll after eight stories even though I enjoyed working with the characters.

In reading them again after twenty years, however, I decided I liked the stories better than I had believed all that time.

Anyone familiar with Muncie, Indiana knew at once that Midland really was Muncie. They also knew that the *News-Banner,* the paper where Blinn and Driscoll plied their craft, was in reality the Muncie *Evening Press.* That's where I, like Hal Blinn, was writing a daily column. The resemblance ended there.

Horner's Tavern was modeled after Frosty Miller's, which at that time was on the corner of Main and High streets a block from the *Evening Press.* The Delaware Hotel, Hal Blinn's home, was the place where I stayed overnight while applying for the job of reporter at the paper. In real life it had been torn down before Blinn came along.

The only character modeled on a real person is City Editor Jake Richards. His prototype was Jack Richman, who had retired as *Evening Press* city editor a decade earlier. Jack was the best city editor I ever worked for. Crusty and demanding – but not as much so as Jake Richards – he exemplified a newspaperman of the old school, a breed that seems to have vanished. That, like so many other changes, is unfortunate.

The final story in this collection is not part of the Blinn-Driscoll series. Unlike the others, *A Debt To Be Paid* was published in Ellery Queen's Mystery Magazine. Eleanor Sullivan, who edited both magazines at the time, decided she didn't like it and marked it to be returned to the writer. Then Ellery Queen himself, whose real name was Fredric Dannay, told her he wanted it for his magazine. Eleanor said she ran down the hall to the mailroom to retrieve it before it was sent out.

Fredric Dannay and his cousin, Manfred Lee, collaborated on all the Ellery Queen stories. One did the plotting, the other the writing, but they never revealed which of them did which job. I later was fortunate enough to meet Dannay in New York.

There was one more unusual twist to the story. It appeared in an anthology featuring a story from each of the fifty states. Among the other stories selected were ones by Edgar Allan Poe and Jack London. The story, originally slated to be rejected, proved to be quite an ego booster.

DS

DRISCOLL'S BOX SCORE

Jumping to conclusions is bad business for a reporter. Editors, other reporters, friends and even casual acquaintances have warned me against it for years with a single word: don't. Remembering the advice, I waited a full five minutes before deciding the police arrested the wrong man for the murder of Linda Rogers.

I pegged it on the evidence. It was overloaded against John Raymond Prewitt. What kind of a murderer hides his victim's billfold, ring and bracelet behind an old four-legged bathtub in his own apartment along with what appeared to be the murder weapon and then tells the police to go ahead and search without a warrant?

A stupid one, maybe, but it would have to be the dumbest character to come down the pike in a long while. Or a guilty one. The kind that breaks down quickly and admits it, sobbing that he didn't mean to do it. Prewitt wasn't one of them. From the first he claimed to be innocent and stuck to his story. That didn't rule out stupidity, of course, so I was anxious to get a look at John Raymond Prewitt.

I had been in Midland about a month, covering the criminal courts for the News-Banner, when I discovered on a Wednesday that Prewitt's trial was scheduled to begin the following Monday. It was the first case of any consequence since I'd taken over the beat so I asked Jake Richards, the city editor, how he wanted it covered. In Cleveland or Akron we'd have given it five or six inches on page forty, but murder, even a routine one, isn't that

11

common in a town of eighty thousand so Richards said it would be page one every day. That meant spending the morning in the courtroom, waiting until the last possible minute and then rushing back to the paper and banging out an hour's worth of copy in twenty minutes to meet the noon deadline.

If we were going to play it like another Lizzie Borden trial I wanted to know more than the name of the defendant when I walked into Circuit Court Monday morning so I pulled the file on the case, took it to my desk and began reading the clips. There weren't as many as I expected. A long one when the body was found, a couple of more when Prewitt was arrested and about a dozen shorter ones on routine court matters.

After reading them all I skimmed over the arrest stories a second time, pushed the clippings to the back of the desk, lit a cigarette and relaxed. That's when I thought about it for five minutes. Most of the three hundred seconds were spent wondering if I was trying to make something of nothing because the early symptoms of boredom with the town and the job were setting in. I expected it in a year or two but hardly after a month.

Midland is a decaying industrial city in the heart of Indiana's corn, tomato and soy bean belt. It's dirty, hot and flat. You can drop a marble anywhere in town and not have to walk twenty feet to pick it up. The temperature had fallen below ninety about three times since I'd arrived in town and then only at two in the morning. If anything interesting goes on in Midland it's a well-kept secret. After so many evenings of reading, attending movies or bar hopping, restlessness begins to take over.

I dropped the clippings in the brown envelope, took it back to the library, returned to the newsroom and locked my desk. I was getting up to head for Horner's Bar when there it was again, that damn reflection of a round-faced, short-necked, thin-haired Irishman I've come to accept as Grady Driscoll at thirty-three, staring at me from the glass partition separating my desk and the rest of the newsroom from the hallway. I've got to cover the glass with a poster or get my desk changed.

Stopping at Horner's for the first beer at the end of the day was already a habit. It isn't much; a few booths, a long bar, a back room with four tables and a couple of pinball machines. The back room is a hangout for newspapermen, several lawyers with caseloads that allow ample time for drinking, and a few employees of the stark, prison-like courthouse across the street. The courthouse is only ten years old but already is a landmark of ugliness. One wag described the gray-white, L-shaped monstrosity as the world's biggest public outhouse.

Horner's is the place to go if you want to find Jake Richards any afternoon between two and five. He usually shuns the back room in favor of a seat at the bar so I eased onto the stool next to him and said, "Jake, I don't think Prewitt did it."

He had no idea what I was talking about. He turned his slim, stoop-shouldered body around and squinted at me with watery gray eyes. Jake has never learned to drink and wear glasses at the same time so the deep lines at the corners of each eye are evidence of forty years of peering around barrooms, eyes narrowed in a usually unsuccessful attempt to see what's going on around him. When spectacled, Jake has a prim look more mindful of a schoolteacher than a hard-bitten city editor. His voice modulates in the medium ranges and seldom is raised in anger, but when he speaks the reporters listen. I've worked for some good ones, but Jake is the best, even if he has spent a lifetime on a paper with a circulation of twenty thousand, give or take a thousand. It took him awhile to zero in on Prewitt. Finally he said, "Oh, you mean the guy that goes on trial next week. Why don't you think he did it?"

"Just a hunch, I guess. It's too pat. Everything adds up so neatly I don't trust the answer. That probably sounds foolish coming from the new guy in town."

"Not at all," Jake said. He spoke loudly because he was making a fearful racket banging his empty glass on the bar. When a full one was set in front of him he continued, "You'd be more likely to see something that doesn't fit right than those of us who've been around from the start. We've seen it fall into place day by day like a jigsaw puzzle and accepted it, but you digested the whole thing in half an hour."

"Maybe you're right," I said, but I really didn't understand his reasoning.

"Of course I'm right. A reporter should never accept anything until it's been proven to his own satisfaction. Have you ever covered baseball?"

"Lots of it."

"What's the first thing you do after the game? I'm not talking about interviewing the managers or players."

I thought about it and said, "Add up your box score, I guess."

"You prove your box score." He emphasized the word prove. "The times at bat, walks, sacrifices, and batters hit by a pitch or sent to first because of interference have to equal the runs scored, men left on base and the other team's putouts."

"Right."

"Well, a reporter should look at every situation like a ball game. If his box score proves out he knows exactly what took place. If it doesn't, he keeps going back over it until everything adds up."

I signaled for another beer, laughed and said, "I think I get you, Jake, but maybe I shouldn't have another one. One beer and you're starting to sound profound."

"I am profound," he said without smiling.

"Okay. In my mind this case doesn't add up so I'm going to do a little checking until it does."

"Fine," Jake said, turning back to the bar. "Just don't do it when you're supposed to be covering the courts. That's what you get paid for, remember."

I walked three blocks, climbed the stairs to my third floor furnished apartment, tossed a TV dinner in the oven and, while it heated, sat in the only comfortable chair mulling over the case. The story wasn't a pretty one but it was similar to many I remembered from the dozen years I worked for big-city newspapers. Linda Rogers, thirty, exceptionally pretty judging by her photo, was an unemployed cocktail waitress, divorced, the mother of a six-year-old son, and had come to Midland from Louisville ten years before her death.

John Raymond Prewitt was thirty-three, a construction laborer separated from his wife and a native of a small town in Tennessee that sends half it's native sons to Midland. His only previous arrests were alcohol related. He was charged with the murder of Linda Rogers three days after her body was found by two boys hiking in a park seven miles from town. She had been beaten to death. Her throat was cut, but according to the autopsy report, she had been dead for some time when it was done. Apparently an amateurish attempt to throw the police off the track.

Prewitt had been drinking at the tavern where Linda Rogers was last seen alive and left shortly before she did. The tires on his ten-year-old car matched tread marks found near the body. That, along with the articles found in his apartment, was the evidence against him. His arrest resulted from an anonymous tip by telephone.

The next morning, Thursday, I called Murray Townsend, the public defender representing Prewitt. "Your client," I said, "is either innocent or stupid."

Townsend chuckled, said, "Personally I think he's innocent, but making a jury believe it won't be easy. As far as being stupid, he's actually illiterate. He can write his name and that's it, but he isn't dumb. Discounting education he's as smart as either of us."

"What's his story?"

"Swears he didn't do it. Says it was the first night in weeks he wasn't drunk. He's certain he didn't black out and is positive he didn't put the woman's belongings behind the bathtub. He also claims he never owned a straight-edge razor in his life."

"Mind if I talk to him?"

He didn't, but Townsend reminded me the trial was to begin in four days. He was afraid I might write something prejudicial, something that would hurt his client's chances. At that point, though, nothing could have made the outlook more discouraging for Prewitt. It was the old story: give him a fair trial and then hang the guilty bastard.

The sheriff, always a politician, had Prewitt waiting in a small interrogation room when I arrived at the jail. Anything to oblige the press. Before I went in, the sheriff took me to the kitchen, poured two cups of coffee, handed them to me and said, "Be sure to tell Prewitt I sent one for him." I laughed inwardly. No harm in covering all the bases, I thought. You never know, Prewitt might be acquitted and vote in the next election.

John Raymond Prewitt stood up when I entered the interrogation room. It was my first look at him and he was just what I expected. He was small, about five-eight and one-fifty. His hair was straw colored, his blue eyes watery. He looked like a man who had led the hard life, one who drank often and long, but he smiled, introduced himself and extended his hand.

"Your lawyer says you don't remember anything about it," I began.

"I don't remember nothing about killing nobody but I remember the night. I had a few drinks, sure, but not as many as usual and besides I'm used to it, I drink every night." He laughed at his own words. "Before I got in here, that is."

"Could you have blacked out?"

"Naw, I remember that night real clear, even the girl – Linda – coming in Don's Place. I was surprised to see her there."

"You knew her?"

"By sight. I seen her before In the Backstage Bar. I don't usually go there, the prices are higher, but it was one a her regular places. I never seen her in Don's before that night. It ain't the kind a place she'd go."

"What do you mean?"

"It's a rough place. No fights or nothing, least not very often 'cause Don won't stand for it, but the people are rough. She'd go to the Backstage or the Green Door, places like that. A little nicer, I mean. Don's is for, well, you know – workers, people like that."

"Did you talk to her?"

Prewitt shook his head, groping for words. "She . . ., well she wasn't the kind I'd talk to. She wouldn't a had nothing to do with me."

He had difficulty expressing the thought but I knew what he meant. Prewitt was awed by a woman that pretty, afraid of a rebuff. He would admire, but only from a distance.

"What did she do when she came in?" I asked.

"The only empty stool was next to me so she took it. I knowed something was wrong or she wouldn't a been there. You could tell she'd been crying. Her face was kind a puffy, too. It might a been from crying but she looked like somebody slapped her around."

"How long was she there?"

"I don't know. I finished my drink and went home. Maybe I had one more after she come, I ain't sure. I didn't know about her being killed till I went in Don's the next night."

I lit two cigarettes, handed one to Prewitt. "Why weren't you drinking that night?" I asked.

"I'd been out home. My wife's home I mean. We're separated – my drinking and all. It happened before a couple a times. It was my fault, but we always got along okay when I was away. I had dinner there that night and we talked about me maybe coming back. That's why I didn't drink much, I was at the house till the eleven o'clock news went off. We was watching television, me and my wife and stepdaughter."

16

"Has she visited you here?"

"Both of 'em, every visiting day."

"Did you lock your car when you got back to your place?"

"I doubt it, I hardly ever lock It. It's just an old junker. That's why I was surprised when it was gone the next day."

"You mean it wasn't where you left it?" I was surprised too. That hadn't been mentioned in the stories I read.

"Naw, It was gone. I figured kids took it for a joyride and left it somewhere so I looked around. I found it about six blocks away over on Main Street. It was outta gas so I got some and took it back."

"Did you report it stolen?"

Prewitt laughed. Calling the police would be the last thing he'd do. He said, "Naw, It wasn't worth It and I figured I could find it."

"Did you tell the police about it when you were arrested?"

"I don't think so. I don't remember they asked me that. They didn't ask me much except why did I kill her and I told 'em I didn't."

"Did you tell your lawyer about it?"

"I doubt it. I hardly remembered it till we got talking here. Why, you think it's important?"

"I don't know," I said, but I sure thought it might be. "Where exactly on Main Street did you find it?"

"Half a block this side a the East End Tavern parked on the opposite side a the street."

I caved in under the rays of the early afternoon sun when I stepped outside the air-conditioned jail. Beer time, I thought, and decided it would be a good opportunity to pay my first visit to Don's Place even if it meant a six or seven block walk right past Horner's. It was too early for Horner's anyway. A city editor can drink there at two o'clock, but not a reporter.

During the hot months in Indiana the heat reflects off the pavement in shimmering waves so the sun gets you coming and going. I cut across the courthouse plaza, a huge expanse of bare white concrete, and found out how it would be at noon on the Sahara. The reflected light is blinding and the humidity gives you the sensation of drowning when you try to draw a deep breath. Even Don's Place looked inviting when I saw the sign in the distance.

Not really. Don's is a couple of blocks south of the business district in a shabby, desolate area bordering the railroad tracks.

17

It occupies the corner of a decrepit, two-story brick building that is vacant, aside from the tavern. The exterior of Don's – a door flanked by two large uncovered windows containing fly-speckled beer signs – doesn't overwhelm you with desire to enter. It isn't much better inside, but at least Don provides air-conditioning.

I ordered a beer, gulped half of it at one swallow and asked the large, surly woman behind the bar if Don was there.

"In at six," she snarled.

I lit a cigarette, watched the traffic through the dirty front windows and decided it was time to check in at the paper. I asked the lovely lady where the phone was. She jerked her head toward the door and said, "Booth around the corner." A colleen to warm the heart of any Irishman. A real way with words, too, although she was a bit conservative with them.

I'd had enough of her so I walked back to the paper, found everything was quiet, went out again and walked three more blocks to my old VW. The News-Banner charges employees six dollars a month to park in its lot. No real newspaperman would go for that, so I park free on the street. The walking is good exercise, too.

The humidity was so high the VW seemed to float to the East End Tavern. I parked across the street, walked a block toward town and knocked on doors as I worked my way back. It's an old neighborhood on the downgrade. The houses are big and all have large front porches. It was a long shot and I drew blanks at the first five houses.

An old man was sitting on the porch of the sixth. Before I reached the steps he raised a hand, shook his head and said, "Don't want any, sonny." When I convinced him I wasn't selling anything he relaxed and was glad to have company. Sure he remembered the old white car parked in front of his house in May.

"Got rheumatism, boy," he explained. "Never sleep more than two hours at a stretch. Hell, if I do I can't get up again. That's why I was looking out the window when this fella pushes it over to the curb."

"Pushed it? What did he look like?"

"One thing at a time, sonny. He pushed it 'cause it quit running back a ways up the street and this was the first empty space."

"Could you see what he looked like?"

18

"Street light down at the corner helps some. Couldn't see his face but he was about six foot and had dark hair. Wearing a light colored raincoat and gloves. Thought that was odd because it wasn't that cold."

"What did he do after he got the car to the curb?"

"Walked away – fast, like he was in a hurry. Down to the corner" – he pointed toward downtown – "then south. Figured he'd come back or send a tow truck, but the next day a different fella come and tried to start it. Couldn't so he got a can outta the trunk and went and got gas. That's all that was wrong, outta gas."

"You're sure it was a different man?" I asked.

"Sure I'm sure. The one that come for it was a little guy, lots smaller. Sloppy, too. The one that left it was dressed better. Neater, if you know what I mean."

"Did the police ever talk to you?"

"What for? Did the little guy steal the car? Didn't look worth stealing to me. I was surprised the first guy was even driving it. Borrowed it, I figured."

The old man probably figured right, I thought while walking back to the VW.

I returned to Don's Place a little before six. My girl friend was off duty, but her replacement wasn't much of an improvement. He was a pugnacious individual with a squared-off head, no neck and slits for eyes. He slapped a beer down in front of me like he was trying to start a fight.

Don himself – last name Zelinski – came in about five minutes after I did. He was in his mid-forties with thinning black hair combed straight back, a hook nose and a fresh shave that didn't get rid of the blue cast to his cheeks, neck and cleft jaw. He was wearing a tight maroon turtleneck shirt that displayed bulging arm and shoulder muscles. He took a thirty-eight out of his pocket and put it under the bar.

Sizing me up with flinty gray eyes, he jerked his head at my empty glass and said, "Have another?" I nodded. "New around here, aren't you?" he said when he brought the refill

"Right. Grady Driscoll with the News-Banner. Were you working the night the girl was killed after leaving here?"

"I figured you were here about that," Zelinski said with a chip-on-the shoulder attitude. "Yeah, what about it?"

"Did you notice her?"

19

"Hell yes I noticed her. She never came here, thought she was too good for a place like this. It could have caused trouble so I kept my eye on her."

I took a long drag on my beer. "Did you know her?"

"I knew who she was."

"Was she a hooker?"

Zelinski snorted. "Hell no, her kind are a hooker's worst enemy. They give it away. Not to everybody, just their friends, but they always got a lot of friends. She called one that night, probably was on her way to see him when she got jumped."

"Any idea why she was here?"

"Naw, except something was bothering her. She looked like hell, like she'd been crying. Probably needed a drink but didn't want to go to one of her regular places looking like she did."

"Had she been roughed up?"

"Could have been. Not bad, but she might have been slapped around a little. Hard to tell."

"What about Prewitt?"

"He's been coming in for years, off and on. He was quiet, kept to himself most of the time, never caused trouble. Sometimes when he was broke I'd let him go to the grocery for me and then give him a couple of drinks."

"Anybody follow Linda Rogers when she left?"

"Ask Joe," he said, nodding toward the pug. "I was back in the kitchen when she left."

Joe had been listening. "I don't think nobody left in the next fifteen minutes," he said.

I had a hash-house dinner and then headed for the Backstage Bar. It's not a fancy place, but compared to Don's it's luxurious. The Backstage caters to lawyers, bankers, businessmen, a few courthouse people and at certain seasons those connected with a civic theater next door. I had been there a few times and knew the bartender, a bright young college graduate.

I ordered a Bushmills and said, "Tom, tell me about Linda Rogers. I'll be covering Prewitt's trial."

"Linda was okay," he said. It was early so customers were scarce and he had plenty of time for talking. "She was here about every night. She'd leave for awhile, come back, leave again. She waited table off and on but usually was just hanging out. She was a damn good-looking woman so she didn't have to pay for many of

20

her own drinks. She usually was quiet – had a reticent, little girl air about her – but she could get wild when she drank too much. I liked her, I think almost everyone did."

"She wasn't a hustler, a prostitute?"

Tom grinned and said, "Not really, but I'm sure there were times when she took money from men. I know she spent more on clothes alone than she ever earned."

"Any particular men in her life?"

"Sure, lots of them but not the same ones for long."

"Know of any who were upset when she broke off with them?"

"It usually was the other way around; the men broke off with her."

I ordered another Bushmills and asked, "Why was that?"

"Some were married and some the kind that drift from one woman to another. Linda wasn't too bright, didn't have much to offer aside from her looks. Men would lose interest after awhile."

"Who were her latest admirers?"

"Let's see," Tom said, thinking about it. "There was Manny Gallen, the lawyer. He was sneaky, tried to play it cool because he's married. He's one guy I don't like and I don't think Linda did either. I think she was afraid of him."

"Any idea why?"

"I wouldn't be surprised if he has some kinky habits. I could tell Linda was leery of him but she left with him once in awhile. She left with him the night she was killed but it was early, say nine-thirty or ten."

I lit a cigarette while Tom took care of another customer. When he returned I asked, "Any others beside Gallen?"

"The only one at the time was Greg Staley, the detective. He was pretty serious about her."

"How do you mean serious?"

"Well, he's a serious person. Nice, everybody likes him, but very quiet. He started coming in about six months before Linda was killed. He had just been divorced, was at loose ends and took to her right away. He talked to her a lot. She was a good listener even if she wasn't much of a conversationalist. I had the feeling Staley would have married her if she'd have gone along with the idea. I don't think it bothered him, the way she was with men, I mean."

"Does he still come in?"

"Sure. Not as often as before and he doesn't stay long. He was really broken up about it. Still is, I think."

Back in the apartment I fixed a drink, kicked off my shoes, flopped down in the good chair and reviewed the day. It wasn't Prewitt, I decided, he's being framed. The only candidates I had to replace him were Gallen and Staley. Probably Staley, I thought. Tom was wrong; he didn't accept her way with men as casually as it seemed.

The courts were busy Friday morning but I found time to take a look at Prewitt's file in the prosecutor's office. A month before the murder he was arrested for drunk driving when a police cruiser was forced over a curb to avoid his oncoming car. Officers Oliver and Staley were in the cruiser. The case was still pending, but Manny Gallen represented Prewitt at his arraignment so both of my candidates knew Prewitt, knew his car and knew where he lived.

The most interesting information came from Steve Granger, the News-Banner's police reporter. I asked him to check Staley's schedule the night of the murder and he briefed me over lunch. Staley had gone on duty at eleven that night and was alone in a cruiser most of the shift. The thing that settled it in my mind, though, was the fact Staley took the next three days off because his eye was badly scratched when he arrested a woman lying drunk along East Main Street. She clawed his face, Staley reported, but the woman later filed a charge of police brutality, claiming Staley slapped her around and she was defending herself.

Convenient timing, to say the least, for someone whose girl friend was beaten to death the same night. I wouldn't have even bothered talking to Manny Gallen if I hadn't already made an appointment to see him at four o'clock.

I disliked Gallen the minute I stepped inside his office. His chubby pink face had a built-in smirk and he had a distracting habit of brushing back a lock of brown hair that kept falling in front of his forehead. He was in his mid-thirties and medium in height and weight.

I didn't waste time on preliminaries. "Where did you and Linda Rogers go when you left the Backstage Bar the night she was killed?"

I thought the question might shake him up, but it didn't.

22

"To her place," he said without hesitation. He gave me a knowing leer, was almost boastful in saying, "It wasn't the first time."

"What happened?"

"Come on, Driscoll, you're not naive enough to ask that. I left early, too, no later than eleven-thirty."

"Why was she upset when you left?"

"Was she?" Gallen's smirk was expanding. "Well, frankly, for a woman of her kind she was a little on the prudish side." The way he said it made me like him even less.

"Wouldn't go for some of your weird ideas so you slapped her around, right?"

"Why you —" Gallen said, rising halfway out of his chair. He thought better of it, sank back down and said, "Okay, so I hit her twice. Not hard, either. She wasn't hurt a bit. She went out again later, you know that."

"You didn't see her again?"

"No, I went home. Even if I wanted to see her, which I didn't, I didn't like her boyfriend nosing around."

"Boyfriend?" I said, trying to sound surprised.

"Greg Staley, the cop. He was always watching her. When I left that night he was hunched down in an unmarked cruiser half a block away. It made me nervous."

Just one more thing against Staley, I thought while driving from Gallen's office to a restaurant I'd heard about in the northwest section of town. I'd been trying for a month to find a good steakhouse, but was destined to fail again. I decided to wash away the aftertaste at the Backstage. Midland is a Friday night town – everyone who can possibly leave for the weekend does so on Saturday morning – so the bar was already crowded at eight o'clock.

I thought about my next move. I had accumulated a lot of information but no solid evidence against Staley. The only thing to do was confront him, hope he might break down and confess when he realized I had pieced together what he had done. The confrontation came sooner than I anticipated.

I had drained a Bushmills and half a beer when I became aware of someone standing behind the empty stool to my left. I was sitting near the front door, the only area that wasn't crowded. I swiveled a quarter turn on my stool. The man was about six feet tall and weighed around one-eighty. He was wearing a conservative, well-tailored gray suit. His features were sharply chiseled and the paleness of his blue eyes was emphasized by jet-black hair.

"I'm Greg Staley," he said, extending his right hand. "I hear you're looking into the Linda Rogers case." News circulates as fast in a town of eighty thousand as it does in a village of five hundred.

No point in pussyfooting around, I decided and didn't bother to shake his hand. "That's right," I said. "Tell me, why did you kill her?"

I was hoping to shock him and couldn't have been more successful. He stood still a moment, the color draining from his tanned face, and then climbed clumsily onto the stool. His voice was low and quivering when he said, "Why would you think a thing like that?"

"Because everything, and I mean everything, points to you."

Staley looked around to see if anyone had overheard. I had made certain no one could.

"Let's go someplace where we can talk," he said.

"My place," I said. "We can walk it in three minutes." I had made up my mind at the beginning that getting into a car with him would be foolish. The bulge under his arm gave him all the cards and I didn't intend to end up like Linda Rogers.

When we reached the apartment I waved him to the comfortable chair, went to the kitchen, washed a couple of glasses, put in ice and poured bourbon for Staley and Irish for myself. Back in the living room I handed him his glass and said, "You loved her, didn't you?"

He nodded, took a drink and said, "So why do you think I killed her?"

"You couldn't stand her carrying on with other men. She promised you she wouldn't, didn't she?"

He shook his head from side to side this time. "I didn't ask anything of her. She was okay with me the way she was. I worried about her, though, tried to watch out for her, especially when she was with certain people, but I wasn't around at the right time. I thought she'd stay home once she was there that night , but she didn't." He took another hearty drink, looked at me and said, "You must have more reason than that to think I did it."

I told him in detail what I'd uncovered. As I went along he perked up, became more interested. He cursed under his breath when he heard that his fellow detectives hadn't even gone to the trouble to find out Prewitt's car had been stolen. When I reached the end of the story he finished his drink, helped himself to another from the bottle and said, "You've done a thorough job, better than the department. You made one mistake, though."

"What's that?" I asked, becoming wary, edging forward on my seat and watching his hands.

He stared straight into my eyes for a minute and then quietly said, "I didn't do it."

I finished my own drink, muttering to myself. Damn it, I believed him

"Okay," I said after a lengthy silence. "Who did then?"

"You believe me?" Staley asked.

"I believe you. I believe Prewitt, too. So who did it?"

"Manny Gallen, maybe. It had to be someone who knew Prewitt, knew where he lived, knew his car, even knew he had gone home and wouldn't have an alibi."

"No," I said, "it wasn't Gallen. It was someone at Don's Place or someone watching through the windows from outside. That's what I thought you did because the bartender said no one left for fifteen —" It hit me suddenly. I had forgotten Jake's advice, had overlooked something that didn't add up.

"Damn it," I said, "Don told me she called somebody!"

"That's right, she called a friend, Mona Grant. Told her she needed to talk, was going over to her place. It's in the file; Mona reported it after she heard what happened."

"Okay," I said, "but don't you see, Staley? There's no phone in Don's Place. There's a booth outside around the corner, but it can't be seen from inside. That means Don had to be outside to know she made a call. He told me he was in the kitchen but hell, he'd gone out the back door!"

We talked it over for a while. Staley didn't realize it, but I was stalling for time, keeping him from going to see Don Zelinski too quickly. If anything was going to happen, I wanted it to be after the Morning Sun's deadline.

We decided it happened almost the way the police reconstructed it. They had quit too soon, though, instead of going on digging so they arrested the wrong man. Don had seen Linda was getting ready to leave and decided to make a play for her. He went out the back door, saw her make the phone call and then made his move. She rebuffed him and he lost his temper, hit her a few times and she probably struck her head against the brick wall. In any event, he found she was dead and he had to do something to keep from being arrested for murder.

It was only an hour until closing time so he hid her body somewhere, probably in his own car, went back inside and no one realized he hadn't been in the kitchen the entire time. Somewhere along the line he remembered Prewitt and after everyone was gone he carried out the frame-up.

Staley worried me. His voice was too level, too controlled when he said, "Let's go see Don."

Zelinski saw us coming, walked to the end of the bar and said, "I don't have time to talk to cops or nosey newsies."

"Take time, Don," Staley said. The words were spoken quietly, but the pitch of his voice put Zelinski on guard, made him realize he'd better do as Staley said. He looked around the crowded barroom, jerked his head in the direction of the kitchen and said, "In there."

We followed him through the swinging door. I had warned Staley earlier about the gun. Zelinski stopped just short of the door to the alley, wiped his hands on a towel and said, "Now what's so important?"

Staley, standing ten feet from him said, "We know about it, Don. You killed Linda and set Prewitt up to take the fall."

"You know nothin'!" Zelinski snarled.

"We know everything. You gave yourself away when you mentioned Linda making a phone call. Now Driscoll's found a witness who saw you pushing Prewitt's car when it ran out of gas."

Zelinski blanched, looked at me and stammered, "You nosey – " He grabbed a meat cleaver and drew his arm back to throw. I ducked behind a table but it wasn't necessary. The sound of Staley's gun was ear-splitting in the tiny kitchen. Zelinski spun to his right, cried out, dropped the cleaver and grabbed his shoulder.

I called police headquarters from the phone booth. The first cruiser arrived by the time I reached the door to go back inside and within five minutes there were two more and an ambulance.

"You could have killed him, you know, " I said to Staley when things quieted down.

"Sure," he said, "but that would have been too easy. For him and for me."

Saturday was my day off but the phone woke me at six in the morning, "Great story," Jake Richards said. "Found it in my basket when I came in. How'd you get it so fast?"

I mumbled something, still half asleep, and then Jake said, "Why didn't you wait and come in this morning and write it? That way I could have put you in for overtime."

That woke me up fast. "Overtime?" I said. "Nobody told me that."

"Well, you'll know better the next time."

I remembered the meat cleaver and laughed. "Jake," I said, "I hope there ain't gonna be no next time. You and your damn box scores. The next time I prove one it's going to be in a nice, comfortable press box."

DRISCOLL'S BIG STORY

After hearing Driscoll's story I regret having asked whether he knew of anything exciting in the offing. It wasn't exciting, merely depressing. Nevertheless I'll use it.

Column material has been scarce so it isn't a time to be choosy. I'd prefer something light and upbeat, but will settle for a human-interest item. It will appear on Monday, the day the trial begins, so the judge and the prosecutor will be displeased. However, that's less distasteful than the alternative, which is having my editor displeased.

And so I drive to the house on Proud Street. It's an old two-story that's already showing signs of neglect. There's a sinister aura that comes over a house after a tragedy has occurred within its walls. Of course, that may be more in the mind than in the eyes of the beholder.

Proud Street no longer lives up to its name. In the boom years following the Second World War it was overtaken by commercialism. First a large shopping center was built nearby and then came spot zoning. One by one, fine old homes were chopped up to create as many apartments as their absentee owners could squeeze in. Walls of thin plywood turned spacious rooms into cramped cells. Repairs were made only in dire emergencies and with each turnover in tenants the neighborhood decreased in desirability. Eventually the city fathers began to wonder what had brought on urban blight.

The Endicott house stands near the middle of a block. The lots are small and the houses big. A few are well cared for, but most look like refugees from an Army street-fighting course.

Marie Endicott was shot to death in an upstairs bedroom of the Endicott house on a Friday evening in March. On Monday her husband, Ken, goes on trial for first-degree murder.

Marie, who worked in a bank, had filed for a divorce, so they were living apart. At her request, Ken returned to repair the automatic washer. Their two daughters, ten and twelve, had left to spend the weekend with their grandmother before their father arrived.

The daughters will be the focal point of my column. A moment of anger and one life is ended, others torn apart. The sort of thing once referred to as a sob-sister piece by newsmen. Not my favorite way of filling space, yet I know it will be well received. I may not like it, but selling newspapers is my job.

Marie Endicott's body was discovered on the morning after her death by her boss, Palmer Tryon. She normally didn't work on Saturday but she had agreed to help him with a project. When she failed to show up or answer her phone, Tryon drove to the house, entered, and found the body.

The gun belonged to Ken Endicott. It was kept in the drawer of a nightstand just inside their bedroom door. The drawer was partially open.

The gun, wiped free of fingerprints, was on the floor near the table about ten feet from the body.

A neighbor, Luella Peck, told the police she saw the defendant leave the house shortly before she and her husband went out to a movie. The pathologist fixed the time of death as 8:30 p.m., give or take an hour. The Pecks had left for the movie at eight o'clock.

Ken Endicott claimed that after repairing the washer he drove to his rooming house and didn't leave again until the police arrived at noon the next day. He denied killing Marie but no one believed him.

The trial begins routinely on Monday. Driscoll's first story is nothing but a rehash of the shooting and the start of jury selection. The copy he files just before the noon deadline Tuesday says little other than that the jury was seated late in the morning. Jake Richards, the *News-Banner* city editor, shakes his head and says, "Pretty dull stuff, Grady."

30

"Damn it, Jake, I just report the news, I don't make it happen," Driscoll replies in an aggrieved tone. It's a declaration he makes at least once a week. I smile, and he catches it.

"What's so funny, big-shot?" he snarls. Driscoll is aware that Monday's "Around Town with Hal Blinn" was a success and that he furnished most of the material. I hand him a note I'd made on a humorous story. He reads it and is mollified.

The drought of material has ended for me. I've gathered enough to last me the rest of the week. After a bowl of chili at Horner's Tavern I accompany Driscoll to the courthouse to hear the opening testimony. That's one advantage of writing a daily column – you're free to wander about at will.

The first witness is Palmer Tryon. The prosecutor, Jeff Mothersbaugh, intends to impress the jury with a dramatic opening. After the preliminaries he asks, "Why was Mrs. Endicott going to work that Saturday?"

"I was in charge of a promotional campaign. There was a lot to do before Monday morning and she agreed to help."

"But she didn't arrive?"

Tryon shakes his head in reply. Judge Otis Main purses his lips. "Answer the question," he says testily. "The recorder doesn't pick up head shaking. " I make a note of it.

"No," Tryon murmurs, embarrassed.

"So what did you do?"

"I called my – I called her house."

"And?"

"There was no answer. I tried several more times and then decided to go over."

"Did you suspect anything was wrong?"

Tryon chews his lower lip. "Well, I don't know. It wasn't like her not to show up without calling."

"So you went to her house. Go on."

"I knocked, but there was no answer. The door was unlocked so I went inside and called her name."

"Continue. Tell the jury what you did."

"I walked through the house calling her name and then I went upstairs."

"And what did you find?"

"Her bedroom door was open and I saw – I looked in and saw her body."

"You say 'body.' Did you know she was dead?"

"There was blood. I – I didn't know, but I thought she was."

"Tell the jury exactly what you saw."

"She was lying on her side. She only had on her" – Tryon clears his throat self-consciously – "her bra and underpants. Then I saw the gun."

"Where was it?"

"On the floor just inside the door."

After more routine questions it is Murray Townsend's turn. He's chief public defender and, while soft-spoken and mild-mannered, he has a way of making witnesses squirm. Tryon does when he asks, "Why did you choose Mrs. Endicott to help you?"

"Well, she had helped me before."

"On Saturday mornings?"

Tryon nods, remembers in time, and says, "Yes."

"Would you and she be alone in the bank?"

"Uh – usually."

"Did she get paid overtime?"

"Well, no," Tryon said reluctantly. "The bank doesn't make provision for that but – well – I'd see she was compensated in other ways." There is snickering and Tryon blushes. "I mean, I would see that she got time off to make up for it."

Townsend smiles knowingly. "Did anyone else ever help you on Saturday mornings?"

"Uh – no."

"How did you know where Mrs. Endicott's bedroom was located?"

Mothersbaugh is out of his chair like a shot. "Your Honor, that question is out of order!"

Judge Main scowls at him. "He said her bedroom door was open." He turns to Tryon and adds, "Answer the question."

"I didn't know where it was. I just looked in the room and saw her."

Townsend's knowing smile reappears as he scans the jurors' faces. He looks back at Tryon and says, "When you testified that you called Mrs. Endicott you started by saying, 1 called my—' You called your *what?"*

Tryon is flustered, doesn't know how to answer. "You called your what?" repeats Townsend.

Tryon inhales deeply, then blurts, "My wife."

"You called your wife?"

"Yes."

"Before you called Marie Endicott?"

"Yes. No – afterward."

"Which was it?"

"Afterward."

"Why did you call your wife?"

"I wanted her to go over there. We live just on the other side of the shopping center."

"But she didn't go?"

"No."

"Why not?"

"I guess she was busy."

"Did she know Marie Endicott?"

"Yes."

"Did she like her?"

Tryon flushes again and Mothersbaugh objects. The objection is sustained.

"So you went yourself?"

"Yes."

"And your wife knew you were going?"

"Your Honor –" Mothersbaugh begins, but slumps back in his chair when the judge glares at him.

"Yes, she knew I was going," Tryon says.

"Then if someone told her they saw you entering Marie Endicott's house she wouldn't have thought anything of—"

Mothersbaugh is out of his chair, shouting. "Your Honor, I object to this entire line of questioning! It's—"

"Sustained."

Townsend smiles at the jurors, gives a little shrug, and goes back to his chair. Tryon hurries from the courtroom, mopping his brow.

Driscoll and I look at each other. Townsend's only prayer is to establish doubt. In effect he has been saying to the jurors: "See, the great State of Indiana may not be telling all."

The next witness is Luella Peck, the neighbor. She's a wizened scarecrow of a woman. Mothersbaugh is handling it well; he has Marie Endicott dead and now the Peck woman's testimony places Mrs. Endicott's estranged husband at the scene. The pathologist will make his visit fall into the time period of the murder. Mothersbaugh will have everything neatly tied together while the jurors are still attentive. Later he will bore them with monotonous police testimony.

Luella Peck rises to leave as Mothersbaugh turns away. She is only half out of the witness chair when Murray Townsend says, "Just a minute, if you don't mind." She remains poised, giving him a nasty look, then sinks back down. He advances with an expression of innocence that means trouble for her. At the very least he'll want to give the jurors the impression she keeps a battery of telescopes trained on the houses of her neighbors.

Already Luella Peck despises him and he hasn't even asked his first question. When he says, "How can you be sure Mr. Endicott left his house precisely at eight o'clock?" she replies vehemently, "It wasn't his house any more!" and looks around the courtroom for approval. After savoring her triumph she goes on. "I already told you, my husband and I left right after he did so we could catch the eight-twenty feature at the Tivoli."

"Was he in a hurry?" Townsend asks. "Did he run out of the house?"

"Of course not. That would have looked suspicious."

Townsend smiles wryly at the jurors, raising his eyebrows. Luella Peck is leaving little doubt that she is out to get his client, and Townsend is delighted. "Did he look around furtively or anything like that?" he presses on.

Luella Peck snorts loudly. "No, for heaven's sake! That would have been a dead giveaway."

Townsend smiles again and Mothersbaugh shifts uncomfortably. He is itching to ask the judge to order her merely to answer the questions, but is hesitant to do so with his own witness.

"So he just walked casually to his car?"

"Yes."

"Was he carrying anything?"

"No."

"He had nothing at all in his hands?"

Luella Peck sits quietly for a moment, frowning. At last she concedes, "Well, not the first time."

"The *first* time?" Townsend's eyebrows shoot up again, but I can see he's not surprised. I look at Mothersbaugh. He is.

34

Without waiting to be asked, Luella Peck says, "He went back inside for a minute. When he came out again he had a little black box."

Mothersbaugh whispers to Greg Staley, the police detective seated with him at the table. Staley shakes his head and shrugs.

Townsend gives Luella Peck an exaggerated look of disapproval. "You didn't mention previously that Mr. Endicott went back inside."

She draws herself up. "I forgot. It wasn't important."

Townsend says, "What did he do when he came out the second time?"

"Got in his car and drove away."

"How long was he inside the second time?"

"I said a minute. Well, maybe two or three."

"Then he drove away with the little black box?"

"Yes."

Townsend smiles ingratiatingly, thanks her, and sits down. He has managed to inject a little mystery into the proceedings. Mothersbaugh asks her about the black box on redirect, but only makes it more intriguing.

The final witness of the afternoon is Fred Shuman. He testifies that Marie Endicott was to meet him at a tavern on the evening of her death but didn't show up and that he drove by her house at ten o'clock, but there were no lights so he kept going. On cross-examination he says it would have been their second date.

After leaving the courtroom I walk down the corridor to where Driscoll has cornered Murray Townsend. As I approach, Driscoll is asking, "So what was the little black box?"

"Will you keep it under your hat?"

Driscoll says, "The box or your answer?"

Townsend shakes his head, grimacing. "O.K., but it's off the record. It was a pocket transistor radio. He didn't have one in his room and he asked Marie for this one. A man wouldn't murder his wife and then go back into the house for something like that, would he? Or go back in for it and just shoot her in passing?"

I feel sorry for him. An attorney is in trouble when an assumption like that is a key point of his defense.

Driscoll and I stroll back to Horner's, which good fortune has placed on a corner midway between the courthouse and the *News-*

Banner office. We ease quietly past the stool where Jake Richards is sitting and go on to the back room.

Gloria Thompson, who covers the school beat, sits alone at a table, so we join her. Gloria is cute in a hard-boiled way. Driscoll tells her about the trial. When he finishes she grins and says, "The husband didn't do it."

Driscoll frowns at her. "Why do you say that?" he asks.

"Because a woman who kicks her husband out and files for divorce wouldn't parade around in front of him in her underwear."

We wait for more, but nothing comes. Finally Driscoll and I laugh. He says, "That's ridiculous. In the first place, she wasn't parading around. She was in her bedroom getting ready to go out for the evening."

"With another man, right?" Gloria retorts. "All the more reason. Under the circumstances an estranged husband is the last person in the world she'd let see her that way."

I laugh again and say, "Gloria, you've never been married, how would you know?"

"I'm a woman."

Driscoll picks up his beer irritatedly and walks out front. I wink at Gloria, give her arm a little squeeze, and follow him.

He has edged up to the bar next to Jake, but Jake pretends he doesn't know he's there. After a few seconds Driscoll taps his shoulder and says, "Jake, would a woman separated from her husband walk around in front of him in her underwear?"

Jake turns a little and fixes his watery grey eyes on Driscoll. His upper lip curls. A moment goes by. Then he says, "Grady, you're really getting weird."

Driscoll whirls around and stalks out the door. I return to the back room and try to convince Gloria that we could drink less expensively at my apartment. She doesn't agree.

When Driscoll leaves for the courthouse on Wednesday morning, I tag along. We run into Murray Townsend in the corridor and Driscoll repeats Gloria's theory, expecting him to laugh. Instead he looks thoughtful and says, "It's not a bad point. I may use it in my closing argument."

Driscoll peers at him, wondering if he is kidding. When he realizes Townsend is serious he turns to me and says, "Great, isn't it? Between that and the little black box, Endicott has

36

nothing to worry about."

At that moment Ken Endicott walks by, escorted on one side by a deputy and on the other by a dyed redhead clinging to his arm. The three of us watch until they enter the courtroom, then Driscoll and I look at Townsend. He's scowling. "Who's the woman?" I ask.

"Damn it, I told her to stay away from him," Townsend says, more to himself than us. "That looks bad to the jurors: They'll think he had another one all lined up."

"Who is she?" I repeat.

"Juanita Colson. An old girl friend who sees herself as the new girl friend. I'm beginning to think Endicott does too, since she's the only one who offered him a shoulder to cry on when Marie filed for divorce."

"Were they dating?"

"They had dinner once or twice. Nothing serious – at least on Endicott's part."

We follow them into the courtroom, but the testimony is boring and I soon leave.. Late in the afternoon I run into Driscoll in the back room at Homer's. "How did it go today?" I ask.

He shrugs his shoulders and doesn't answer for a minute. Then he says, "I've been thinking." I make a smart remark but he ignores it and says, "Suppose Endicott didn't do it?"

"Then who did?"

"Palmer Tryon, maybe. It doesn't take a dirty mind to figure he was thinking about more than business with Marie. Or how about Fred Shuman, the new boy friend?"

I shake my head. "It wasn't a passionate attack, so I'd strike Shuman. And why would Tryon kill her?"

"I don't know. O.K., how about a woman?"

"Who, Luella Peck?" I laugh.

"How about the Colson woman? Or Tryon's wife, Ilka. Why wouldn't she go over to the Endicott house? Did you notice that Tryon wasn't going to say anything about calling her?"

"He probably didn't see any importance to it."

"There's Martha Kanaday, the grandmother."

"Now you're being ridiculous! Another thing – who would have known the gun was kept in the bedside table other than Endicott?"

Driscoll has no answer, so he doesn't say anything more for a few minutes. Then he looks at his watch, finishes the beer in his glass, and gets up. "I've got to meet Greg Staley. He's taking me out to the Endicott house."

"For what?"

"I just want to see the inside – add a little color to my coverage."

That isn't the reason and I know it. Driscoll is playing detective again. He once uncovered information that was instrumental in solving a case and now he sees himself as another Sherlock Holmes. More often than not he's 180 degrees out of phase with reality. Still, I'm curious and say, "I'll go along" although I know Driscoll isn't keen on having company. We work for the same paper, but he looks on me as a competitor, which in a sense is true.

Greg Staley is the closest thing Driscoll has to a friend in the police department. We drive the half-mile to Proud Street in his unmarked car. The house has been sealed since shortly after the murder and as we enter the side door we're hit by a stench that makes me wonder why I left the comfort of Horner's. I breathe through my mouth and walk up three steps to the kitchen.

The odor comes from spoiled food in the refrigerator. It has been unplugged and left standing open. Other than that, the kitchen looks much as it did the night of the murder. Dirty dishes remain on three sides of the table. More are in the sink. Two lunch boxes are on the counter and a note sticks out from under one. I pick it up and read: "Mom, I have to have a dollar Monday for a notebook. Don't forget. Janie."

My column hits home with a vengeance, right in the pit of my stomach. The big things are what people see in a murder; the little ones pass unnoticed. But those who do notice are marked by what they see, the pitiful reminders of how it once was but will never be again. An uncleared supper table, moldering food, a note that went unheeded, lunch boxes that won't be packed for another routine day because, for that routine, time has run out.

When Driscoll and Staley go upstairs, I follow along. The bedroom hasn't changed much either. The gun and the body are gone but a dark stain on the beige carpet shows where the one had been. Here too the little things make the deepest impression – a container of blue eye shadow standing open on a vanity, beside it an uncapped bottle of nail polish, now hardened. Across a corner of the bed is a pale-blue dress on which dust has settled.

Driscoll is busy with his detection, bustling about, pulling out drawers, and opening closets. Staley watches condescendingly. I look too as Driscoll explores the drawer of the bedside table. It contains nothing but an electric razor without a cord, a small flashlight, and a wristwatch with only half a strap.

He goes on to the other rooms but I settle for watching him from the hallway until he lifts the lid on a wicker clothes hamper in the bathroom. I walk up beside him and see it's empty.

Staley and I trail behind when Driscoll heads for the basement. Several patterned dresses and pastel blouses hang from a clothesline. The washer is empty but a dozen pairs of girls' knee socks are in the dryer. Driscoll closes the lid on the washer and pushes the start button. It rumbles and water begins surging in.

"Why the devil did you do that?" Staley growls.

"Just curious," Driscoll answers. "I want to go back upstairs for a minute." Staley looks pointedly at his watch, but we follow behind again.

Driscoll goes first to the girls' room, opens drawers, and reaffirms that they are empty. He hurries on to Marie's bedroom, does the same, and verifies that the dresser contains only clean things. I save him the trouble of opening the closet door again. There are five white blouses on hangers. Driscoll gives me a knowing look.

On the way back downtown, Staley says, "I see what you were driving at back there but it doesn't mean a thing. Maybe she did some of the wash the night before and then the machine broke down so she called Endicott and he fixed it."

Driscoll shakes his head. "Then why no dirty clothes in the hamper! Are you trying to tell me three people didn't take off any dirty clothes in twenty-four hours?"

"Maybe the grandmother washed them when she picked up the girls clothes."

Driscoll snorts disbelievingly. "Sure, then hung up her daughter's blouses in the room where she was murdered and walked out with the girls' socks still in the dryer. Fat chance."

Staley doesn't answer. A minute later he drops us off at Horner's. Driscoll goes straight to the phone and calls Martha Kanaday, the grandmother. When he comes back to the table where I'm sitting he has a smug look on his face. "She didn't do any washing – never even went down into the basement."

"So what?"

"So Marie Endicott was washing clothes after her husband left."

It does seem reasonable, I admit to myself. I'm weary of the subject, though, and leave after one beer.

I learn from Driscoll's Thursday story that the State has rested its case. In the evening he tells me Endicott will take the stand on Friday morning and the jury should begin its deliberation by mid-afternoon. He slams his fist down on one of Horner's round tables and says, "Damn it, Hal, I don't think he did it."

I've had a good dinner and several beers so my mood is mellower than the night before. He wants to talk, so I say, "Run down the other possibilities again."

He ticks them off on his fingers. "Scratch Martha Kanaday and Luella Peck. That leaves Juanita Colson; Fred Shuman, Palmer Tryon, and Ilka Tryon."

"Or a party or parties unknown. It could have been a burglar."

"No, it couldn't. It was someone she knew. You know why? Because Marie Endicott got up from the vanity, but didn't bother to reach for the dress to hold in front of her."

There is logic in what he says. "Of course," I say, "it could have been an unknown party to us but someone she knew. Anyway, cross Fred Shuman and Juanita Colson off your list.

Driscoll scowls. "I agree on Shuman, he doesn't fit. But why the girl friend?"

"Because Marie was doing exactly what Juanita wanted – getting a divorce. Why kill her?"

He sees my point, but grudgingly. "That only leaves Palmer and Ilka Tryon," he says, and then goes into a funk. After a couple of minutes his face lights up. "I think it was Ilka."

"Why, for God's sake? You've never even seen the woman, have you?"

He shakes his head but hurries on. "Suppose she suspected something was going on between Marie Endicott and her husband. She found out they were planning another of their Saturday-morning get-togethers, so she goes over and confronts Marie. Or

40

say she and Palmer fight about it, he goes out, she assumes he went to see Marie, and goes there herself. She walks in, figuring to catch them in the act, but he isn't there and Marie gets mad or maybe laughs at her so Ilka blows her stack."

"'And then what?' I ask him. 'Does she say, 'I want to shoot you – where do you keep your gun?'"

Driscoll's face falls. "Yeah, how would she know where the gun was?" He brightens suddenly and says, "Maybe Marie got it out while they were arguing and Ilka took it away from her."

I shake my head. "There was no sign of a struggle, and the shot was fired from a distance."

He sits disconsolately for a minute, then mumbles, "I still bet she did it."

Ken Endicott's testimony is something I don't want to miss, so I arrive at the courtroom early Friday morning. Endicott hasn't been getting enough nourishment and his sandy hair looks dull and sparse. His brown eyes have a harried look, but for a man standing close to a life sentence he could look worse. Murray Townsend leads him through the night of the murder. Endicott says fixing the washer turned out to be an easy job.

"What did you do when it was working again?" asks Townsend.

"Marie put in a load of things, then she went upstairs. I watched it through the cycle to make sure it worked O.K. Then I left."

"You went out to your car?"

"Yes."

"And then what did you do?"

"I remembered something and went back inside."

"What was it you remembered?"

Not even the sound of breathing disturbs the silence. This is the moment everyone has been waiting for.

"I remembered my transistor radio. I didn't have one in my room and I knew this one wasn't being used."

"Did you get it?"

"Marie got it for me."

"From where?"

"The drawer of the night stand beside the bed."

"Did you go upstairs with her?"

"No, I told her where it was and she brought it down to me."

41

"Then what did you do?"

"I left. I bought a battery for it and went back to my room."

Anticlimactic sighs and a few whispers rise from the spectators. They're disappointed, but when I look at Driscoll I see he's excited. When I leave a few minutes later, he gets up and follows me out.

"That's it!" he exclaims. "It was Ilka, all right. Marie was in a hurry when she got the radio and didn't bother to close the drawer all the way. While they were arguing Ilka looked down, saw the gun, and picked it up. That completes the picture."

"It completes nothing, Grady," I warn him. "Talk that way to other people and you'll end up in court yourself."

I avoid Horner's at lunchtime because I don't want to get in an argument with him. He finds me eating a breaded tenderloin at the Backstage Bar. "I'm going out to her house," he says. "I'm going to confront her with it." Of course I know what he's talking about but I pretend I don't, or that I'm not interested.

When he sees I'm not going to say anything he gets up again and starts for the door. I throw my sandwich down on the plate and call, "You can't do that, Grady!" He doesn't acknowledge me so I go after him.

He won't be swayed. I can't credit him with possessing common sense but he does have the courage of his convictions. I decide I'd better go with him and hope I can find a way to keep him out of jail.

My first look at Ilka Tryon comes when she opens her front door. Her appearance shocks me. She is far too thin, so her waxy skin clings to the bones of her face. Round dark eyes emphasize her death's-head look. Still, in a mysterious, exotic way, she's attractive.

As we enter the living room I notice a vodka bottle and a half-empty glass beside it. Has guilt made her a midday drinker, I wonder, and can see that Driscoll is wondering the same thing.

On the drive to the Tryon house I had tried to temper his determination with caution and believed I had succeeded. When he sees she has been drinking, my work comes unglued. He charges ahead, surprising even me with his bluntness when he says, "Mrs. Tryon, I know what happened in the house on Proud Street the night Marie Endicott died."

While his words stun me, Ilka Tryon's reaction leaves me transfixed. She springs at Driscoll like a tigress protecting her

42

lair. Taking an ex-Marine off his feet isn't easy, especially for a woman spotting him close to a hundred pounds, but she does it. They hit the floor with her on top.

I stand there a moment, unable to react, watching Driscoll trying to grab her clawing fingers. Finally I move, but before I reach them Driscoll launches a solid right that connects with her jaw. She jerks back, then slumps over on her right side, out cold. It has all happened too fast for me. Driscoll sits up, breathing heavily. His face is a mess. He stares at the unconscious woman. "You see?" he says. "I was right."

I walk to the phone and dial the police. Luckily Greg Staley has stopped at headquarters after lunch. "Driscoll just kayoed Mrs. Tryon," I tell him.

A long pause, then a disbelieving, "He *what?*"

"You heard me – he decked Mrs. Tryon. Don't waste time, get out here before she comes to." I give him the address on Dicks Street.

"I shouldn't have done it," Ilka tells Staley. "But he looked so helpless standing there, and when he begged me, well—"

"What are you –" Driscoll manages before Staley tells him to shut up.

"I followed him," she goes on. "I had known for some time that something was going on between them. Of course, Palmer didn't know that. When I overheard him on the telephone, pleading with her – well, I knew he was upset, so when he went out I followed him. I'd just walked up on the porch when I heard the shot. I knew what I should do, but—"

She looks at each of us again, still hoping we'll understand. Then, more forcefully, she says, "The one thing I wouldn't do was go back there the next morning and pretend I found the body."

Two other detectives and a policewoman have arrived. They leave Ilka Tryon with the policewoman and head for the bank. Driscoll and I are close behind.

Palmer Tryon crumples as soon as he sees them. Staley reads him his rights, but Tryon insists on telling the story. He had wanted to break it off, but Marie demanded that he live up to their agreement and file for a divorce; otherwise she'd tell everything. Not only to Ilka but at the bank. They aren't too happy about things like that at banks.

He had planned to plead with her again on Saturday morning, but before she left the bank on Friday she told him she wouldn't be there. He was desperate so he called her that evening, didn't get anywhere, and went to her house. He begged, but Marie laughed. He saw the gun and – well; everyone knew the rest.

Jake Richards frowns as he hears the story. He looks at the clock and says, "Damn it, Grady, why did you do it on *Morning Sun* time? Now they'll have the first story."

"So what?" Driscoll laughs. "They may have the first, but I'll have the best."

Jake scowls at him. "You will? Grady, you're not writing any first-person story."

I haven't said a word, but Jake glares at me and growls, "Neither are you!"

So Gloria Thompson writes it It's across the top of page one on Saturday with her byline. I feel sorry for Driscoll. His biggest story, and he doesn't even get co-billing. Of course, Driscoll will be the hero of my Monday column, but it's not the same.

The whole sordid business has left me depressed. I try to busy myself with other things but my mind keeps going back to it. Finally I call Driscoll and offer to buy him a drink.

We meet at the Backstage Bar. I expect him to be in a foul mood, but he isn't. His cheerfulness irritates me, so after a few minutes of it I say, "You didn't get much satisfaction out of this Endicott business, did you?"

"Not much satisfaction?" he says. "Did you see those lunch boxes in the kitchen, and the note? Those little girls lost their mother, but at least they've got their father back."

He's right, of course. I buy him another drink. A little later Greg Staley comes in and buys us both one. He stares at Driscoll. "I just can't figure it, Grady," he says. "How'd you know it was Palmer Tryon?"

Driscoll tosses down his drink, then shrugs. "I thought it was pretty obvious right from the start."

CLASS REUNION

The rain beats against the pavement, creating a shifting pattern of white circles on grey asphalt. A real Hoosier gully-washer. I decide against making a dash to the parking lot across the street and go back inside the hotel. A right turn at the lobby takes me to the lounge.

The crowd is elbow to elbow, every table occupied to capacity, standing room only at the bar, the small dance-floor bulging. A combo, straining to be heard above the buzzing voices and raucous laughter, plays "Frenesi." The old Artie Shaw arrangement scaled down for piano, sax, trumpet, and drums.

I edge my way to the bar. A man standing with one side pressed to it pushes back against the fellow at his left. He gains three inches, allowing me six. I squeeze an arm and shoulder into the thin slice of space, nod my thanks, and ask, "What's the occasion?"

"Class reunion," he replies. "There was a cocktail party in the ballroom earlier, then everybody came in here on account of the rain." He sips his drink. "This is a preliminary – the big affair's tomorrow night."

"What class?" I ask, not really caring.

"Midland Central, 1940"

I catch the bartender's eye. When a cognac is placed in front of me I warm it with my hands, then swallow, savoring the sudden heat in my throat and the slight tremor along my spine. I signal for another, then turn to the dancers and the people cluttered around the small tables.

All are middle-aged couples – the jitterbug generation – but it isn't "Jukebox Saturday Night" any more, no one is mopping up soda-pop rickies. Now the liquid refreshment is supplied by Jack Daniels and John Jameson.

My eyes settle on one couple. They remain close to the edge of the floor, engrossed in an exhibition of virility. It comes across that they've prepared for this at Arthur Murray's. They're dressed for the part, he in a checked sport coat of pale green, white pants, and white shoes, she in a flimsy dress that billows out every time she pirouettes.

They move much faster than the other couples, perhaps to conceal the fact that they can't keep time. He remains in a little crouch, not facing his partner, his feet gliding quickly over the polished wood. There is much dipping and bending and every so often she kicks a foot out behind her, holding it poised there for a second. Some people may be impressed but it seems to me that rather than having found the secret of eternal youth they are merely calling attention to the ravages of time.

I recognize them. The man is Arvil Ritchey, a Midland investment broker who's running for Congress, and the woman is his wife. Perhaps the show is designed to gain votes in next week's primary.

Now that my eyes have grown accustomed to the subdued light I see other familiar faces. Jack Gerhart, Ritchey's partner; Mack Douglas, an overweight county commissioner; Jim Rakish, a downtown businessman; Harley Lane, the postmaster; a few others I can't attach names to.

I turn to the bar again. Someone has moved and I have enough room to face it. After a few minutes I hear someone say the rain has stopped and realize the crowd is thinning out.

Suddenly there is a commotion in the lobby. Loud talk and then a man yelling for the police and another for an ambulance. I gulp the rest of the drink, walk to the lobby, see nothing but confused faces, continue past them, and step out into the night air, cool now after the storm.

Women are gathered in small groups on the sidewalk, jabbering excitedly. Across the street a number of men stand near an alley that runs beside the parking lot. I cross and work my way to the front, then kneel beside a man lying on the wet ground at the edge of the parking lot. I recognize him from the crowd at the hotel.

He's dead, struck down from behind by a weapon that must have been cushioned so that it crushed the skull rather than splitting it. His pockets are turned out and one side of his jacket is thrown back. A wallet lies close to the body and papers are strewn about.

I look up and ask if anyone knows who he is. Several start to reply, but hesitate when a police car pulls into the mouth of the alley, red light flashing on top. A lone officer approaches and kneels facing me, then rises, returns quickly to the car, and radios for assistance.

Apparently it's the work of a mugger with too heavy a hand. A story for Steve Granger, the *News-Banner* police reporter; column material for me, a short lead-off item for "Around Town with Hal Blinn." A reunion with friends from long ago, death creeping up from behind, an ignominious end of life on a rain-splattered parking lot. Melodramatic, but melodrama seldom hurts a newspaper's circulation figures.

As it turns out, I write the murder story rather than Granger. Only a skeleton crew staffs the *News-Banner* on Saturday. After a breakfast of biscuits and sausage gravy at the Bull's-Eye, I drop by to check the mail and find myself alone in the newsroom when the phone rings.

Granger's on the line. "Can you bail me out, Hal?" he asks. "I let the murder rewrite go till I'd checked on new developments, but now I'm tied up on something else. The clip's on my desk."

"What's come up?"

"Fatal hit-and-run at Washington and Vine. Jim Rakish, who owns the office-supply place on Jackson, was killed."

The news shocks me, as the violent death of someone you know always does. Rakish, a big taciturn man who kept to himself, was only a nodding acquaintance, but still I'm stunned. I remember him sitting quietly at the table in the lounge the night before. I want to question Granger but he's in a hurry so I let him go after asking if there's anything new on the murder.

"Yeah, they picked up Tobe Gilson just around the corner right after it happened."

"Who's Tobe Gilson?"

"A probationer. Knocked over a convenience food store last year. First offense, so he pleaded guilty and got probation."

The *Morning Sun* clip on Granger's desk is little more than an obit, and a scanty one at that. The murder victim was Wendell Spurner, a resident of Davenport, Iowa, back in Midland for the reunion. An accountant, unmarried, survived only by a sister whose address is in Shedtown, a neighborhood in southwest Midland with a fitting name.

I walk two blocks to the jail and ask to see Tobe Gilson. The sheriff, as usual, is obliging to the press. Gilson is outraged by his arrest. His black skin glistens with perspiration and his eyes flash belligerently.

"Man," he asks, "would I be stupid enough to bash some guy alongside the head and then stand waiting on the corner?"

"What *were* you doing there?"

"The wife's shopping at Clay's and I get sick of waiting around so I step out for some air and a smoke. I walk down to the corner and the next thing I know they grab me. But they don't have nothing – they're just blowing wind."

After reading the arrest sheet I'm inclined to agree. But he's black, handy, and has a record. A common enough occurrence.

My story is short, only seven graphs. It's puzzling that the *Sun* reporter didn't pick up on the arrest, but it gives me a fresh lead. When it's finished I unlock the library, pull the file on Jim Rakish, and leave it on Granger's desk. The few clips inside are business-related. Then I walk the block to Horner's Tavern.

Grady Driscoll, the *News-Banner* court reporter, is alone in the back room playing pinball. I tell him he may have a murder arraignment to cover, repeat Gilson's denial, and inform him of Rakish's death. When I add that I had seen both victims at the hotel he looks up from his game, frowning, and says, "Quite a coincidence."

A little later Steve Granger comes in. The paper is out and his story's on page one.

Rakish was walking to work when struck down a block from his home, one of the houses in a historical district being restored to its former elegance. Only his wife survives.

"This witness you wrote about," I say to Granger. "Didn't she see anything more than that it was a blue or black pickup truck?"

He shakes his head. "She was bent over picking up her paper on the porch half a block away. She couldn't see the driver but says he took off burning rubber before he hit him."

I raise my eyebrows. *"Before* he hit him?"

"That's what she says. The truck was parked a few doors down the street, took off fast, and kept going a block after hitting Rakish, then turned right on Main."

Driscoll has been listening. He walks over and sits down, a thoughtful look on his face. "Maybe it *wasn't* an accident," he says, "For one thing, I don't believe in coincidences."

Granger stares at him, puzzled, so I tell him about seeing both Rakish and Spurner at the hotel. It doesn't really interest him and he leaves after a quick bowl of chili and a beer.

Driscoll remains at the table, deep in thought. After a few minutes he says, "Let's drive out and see where Rakish was hit. Maybe talk to that witness."

I have nothing else planned so I get up and lead him around the corner to my car. Under the circumstances, Granger can't complain about us crossing his beat.

The witness tells us nothing new but points out the spot where the pickup truck was parked. I pull the car ahead until we are at the same point. From it we have a glimpse of Washington Street between the houses.

Driscoll, beginning to get excited, says, "The driver could have seen Rakish approaching. It was no accident, Hal – it was an ambush."

His impetuosity never fails to put me off. "We can't be sure, Grady," I say testily.

He snorts and says, "Let's go see Rakish's wife."

Interviewing a woman who has just lost her husband has never been my idea of a fun way to spend a Saturday afternoon. Driscoll appears unaffected, however, and to my surprise Irene Rakish is quite composed. She is alone, which is also surprising, because in Midland people gather around the bereaved like cats around a wingless bird. Of course, Rakish was a loner and his wife may have been the same way.

She pours coffee from a pot and hands steaming mugs to each of us, giving me the uneasy feeling we're making a social call. When Driscoll asks, "Did your husband always walk to work?" she

49

nods, and after a short pause says, "Unless the weather was real bad."

"Did he know—" Driscoll begins, but then looks at me, unable to recall the murder victim's name. "Wendell Spurner," I tell him.

Again she nods and again hesitates in responding. "They were in the same class at school."

"Good friends?" asks Driscoll.

This time she shakes her head and after the usual delay says, "They weren't close. Jim was never one to make friends easily."

"Did you know them in school?" I ask.

"I was two classes behind, but Jim and I dated so I knew who his classmates were."

"Did they talk last night at the cocktail party?"

"They said hello, that was all. But Jim said Wendell had stopped by the store yesterday afternoon."

Driscoll leans forward. "Did he say why?"

She shakes her head.

"Strange that he'd do that if they weren't friends," I say.

She shrugs, apparently tiring of the conversation. Perhaps her composure is a mask. After a little while she says, "Maybe it had something to do with their military service. They enlisted together."

Driscoll stiffens, frowning. "You mean they served in the war together?"

"Not really. They were with each other a few days at Fort Ben, but then they were assigned to separate units. I don't think they ever saw each other again until yesterday."

"How did they happen to enlist at the same time?" I ask.

She makes a clucking sound, then says, "Don't ask me, they just did. August 24, 1942. It surprised everybody."

Her most of all, I can see. Even after all these years and with her husband dead it still annoys her. Driscoll and I repeat our condolences and leave.

"Another coincidence"," he says when we're outside. "This case has too many to suit me."

"It isn't a case, Grady," I remind him. "It's two cases – and at this point there's nothing to connect them."

He glares at me. "The trouble with you, Blinn, is you're a frustrated lawyer. You spout the same stuff I listen to all week in court. You wouldn't believe you had a nose unless you had fingers to feel it with."

As usual when Driscoll gets mad, I laugh. It only makes him angrier. To placate him I say, "It does seem strange, not seeing each other all those years and then both dying violently within twelve hours."

As we drive west on Main Driscoll says, "Stop at Rakish's store."

I tell him it's closed on Saturday afternoon. Nevertheless I go a block south to Jackson and pull into the lot beside Midland Office Supply. Driscoll bangs loudly on the locked door and a man walks toward us from a back room, scowling and pointing at his watch. He calls, "We're closed," but then recognizes us, takes a ring of keys from his pocket, and opens up. He is George Covart, Rakish's partner.

"Won't take a minute, George," I assure him. "Were you here yesterday when Wendell Spurner stopped in to see Jim?"

He was, he says, though he didn't know who Spurner was at the time. The two of them had talked for an hour in the rear office.

"Did you hear anything they said?" asks Driscoll.

"Only when Spurner was leaving. Jim said, 'Are you going there now?' and when Spurner said he was, Jim told him, 'Let me know how he reacts.'"

"He didn't say who he was going to see?" I ask.

Covart shakes his head and we learn nothing more from him.

Driscoll says, "Something was going on, all right. Something involving both of them."

This time I agree without hesitation. "Let's look at the microfilm files for August of '42 in the library. Whatever it was might date back to their enlistment. Maybe we can pick up a lead."

Driscoll looks skeptical but follows along to the library a block away.

He leaves after an hour, convinced we're wasting time. We've covered only the first ten issues of the *News-Banner* for the month and have found nothing that might tie in with the case. It was an exciting time for war news however – the invasion of Guadalcanal, the commando raid on Dieppe, the battle outside Stalingrad. I keep turning the crank and the days slip by. Nothing

51

pertinent appears on the screen but I spend a lot of time reading war stories.

Finally, in the issue of August 22, a Saturday, I find something that draws my attention. That would have been two days before Spurner and Rakish enlisted. As I read the story I feel more and more certain it's what I am looking for.

The body of a nineteen-year-old girl, Marcia Hesston, had been found that morning in a thicket along the Burlington road southeast of town. Cause of death was a blow on the back of her head. Some of her clothing had been torn and police theorized she died trying to fight off an attacker. The murder had occurred elsewhere and the body had been dumped from a car.

The story had been written by Jake Richards, now the city editor of the *News-Banner,* but a young reporter at the time. I make a few notes during a second reading, then quickly scan the pages for the rest of the month. No arrest had been made to that point.

As I start down the outside steps it occurs to me that I've overlooked a possible source of information. I do an about-face, go back inside, and climb the stairs to the stacks where old city directories are stored.

There isn't a 1942 directory so I flip pages of the '41 directory to Sixteenth Street, where Marcia Hesston had lived. My heart skips a beat as I read the entry and I turn quickly to the alphabetical listing and confirm what I've found: Marcia Hesston's next-door neighbor had been Jim Rakish. Further checking reveals that Spurner's sister still lives in the old family home only a few blocks away.

Driscoll isn't at Horner's and there's no answer when I call his apartment. It's getting late so I gulp a sandwich, return to my rooms at the old hotel, change clothes, and then walk to the Midlander where the reunion should be getting under way.

The early arrivals are having a drink in the lounge before going to the ballroom on the mezzanine. The man who made room for me the night before stands in the same spot at the bar but this time without being crowded. I begin talking about the two deaths.

The man, who tells me his name is Harry Speck, knew both victims, but only casually. He's unable to recall who might have been their intimates forty years earlier. "Ask Arvil Ritchey," he suggests. "He was class president. He knew everybody."

It doesn't surprise me. Ritchey's the kind that always has to be at the center of things. Running for Congress is an extension of running for class president He feels a need to reaffirm his popularity. He inherited the brokerage business in which he's now a partner and .grew up believing that money and power are God-given rights to a special few.

He's hovering around the ballroom entrance when I reach the mezzanine, greeting each arrival as if it's a private party at his expense. For a moment I watch from a distance, repulsed by his veneer of charm, thinking that without the head start afforded him by family money he would be considered a bumpkin.

When I mention Spurner and Rakish it unsettles him, almost as if he'd hoped the violent deaths of two class members could be ignored for the sake of a good time. He takes my arm and leads me to a quiet corner away from the others. In the kind of near-whisper usually reserved for mortuaries he says, "Yes, of course I knew them. A terrible thing, just terrible. What is it you want to know?"

"Who were their friends? Who did they run around with?"

He cradles his jaw in one hand, trying to look contemplative. Eventually he says "I really can't tell you. They weren't – well –"

"They weren't part of our crowd," purrs a female voice behind me. I turn as Eloise Ritchey glides up to join her husband. "We had different interests, so naturally Arv didn't know them well."

Naturally. Kids from the west side had little to do with kids from Shedtown.

"How about Marcia Hesston?" I ask. "Did either of you know her?"

Eloise recoils as if I had uttered a vulgarity in church. Arvil too looks shocked. "Only by name," Eloise says. "And reputation, of course. There again—"

The thought goes unfinished, but her meaning is clear. If a Shedtown boy had little chance of breaking into the country-club set, a Shedtown girl had none at all.

Jack Gerhart, Ritchey's partner, joins us. Sensing the tension, he talks casually for a moment, but between comments on the gathering crowd he asks several carefully camouflaged questions to find out why the Ritcheys are keyed up.

Gerhart is the partner with brains. The one smart move Ritchey ever made was recognizing the fact that his money and Gerhart's head would make a winning combination. As a result their investment firm has prospered and expanded.

When he discovers the subject of our conversation Gerhart says, "Jim and Wendell were smart kids in school, but real loners. It wouldn't be true to say they went from rags to riches, but they certainly rose well above the point where they started."

"Did you know them well?"

Gerhart shakes his head. "No. I don't believe anyone really did."

I circulate a while, talking to others, but learn nothing. When the line begins forming at the buffet table, I leave and head up High Street toward Horner's. When passing the old school I think that, for all anyone remembers about them, Rakish and Spurner must have walked its halls in a vacuum.

Driscoll is still nowhere in sight but, surprisingly, Jake Richards is. He's an afternoon drinker and retires early, even on weekends. Finding him at Horner's is a stroke of luck.

The stools on each side of him are taken so I stand at his elbow and say, "I was reading one of your old stories today, Jake. Remember the Marcia Hesston murder?"

He turns, scowling at me for having the temerity to question his power of recall. "Of course I remember," he growls. "But damn it, that was forty years ago, how did you come to be reading about it?"

"Just doing a little background work on the murder last night and the Rakish hit-and-run."

"Why. Do you think they're connected?"

"Could be. Was anyone ever arrested for the Hesston girl's murder?"

"No, the police never had a real lead. About all they knew was that someone picked her up in a car the night before. They figured she was killed in the car, but probably unintentionally. Whoever she was with tried to get her clothes off and she was fighting him; they found traces of skin under her fingernails. Apparently she was pushed pretty hard and her head hit something sharp – a door handle maybe. It wasn't a hard blow, but she connected just right and it killed her. Myself, I always thought there may have been something the matter with her before it happened."

"Nobody knew who she had a date with?"

"No. She lived alone with her mother and the mother worked second shift. She said Marcia didn't have a date lined up when she saw her that morning. The girl worked days in a restaurant downtown, so somebody must have asked her out there. Either that or called later."

"Was she a hustler?"

Jake glares. "Who, Marcia Hesston? God, no. She was a real beauty, but quiet. Sang in the church choir, didn't go out much. A real nice girl."

As I walk back to my hotel the air is raw and the wind that never seems to quit blowing across the Indiana plains in May makes it more so. It clears my head but doesn't sort the pieces and make a picture emerge.

Driscoll walks in while I'm reading the Sunday paper in the lobby. He's close-mouthed about where he spent Saturday night but wants to know what progress I've made. The story of the long-ago murder interests him. When I tell him Rakish lived next door to the victim he gets excited.

"That's it, Hal!" he exclaims. "That's the key!"

"And what door does it open, Grady?" Before he can answer I get up and lead the way to the coffee shop. I order a hard roll with butter and coffee. Driscoll, not wanting to disturb the ideas flying around in his head, murmurs, "The same," forgetting that he hates hard rolls.

When the waitress leaves he presents his theory. It was Spurner who picked up the girl. Rakish went along and when the girl died they panicked and enlisted to avoid questioning.

When he finishes, I chuckle. "O.K., smart guy," he flares. "What's wrong with the idea?"

"It's crazy. If it happened that way, why were they killed?"

"Revenge."

"Someone knew they were guilty but waited thirty-eight years to do something about it? Ridiculous."

"So what's your solution, big shot?"

"I don't have one, but let's say Rakish saw who picked her up and he—"

"—left town because he was scared? I don't buy it, Hal. And where does Spurner fit in?"

I shrug off the question. "We're not getting anywhere. Let's talk to Spurner's sister. Maybe she can tell us something."

We drive the two miles to Shedtown in Driscoll's old VW. The Spurner house is a cracker box, but aluminum siding helps and the small yard is neat.

Gertrude Spurner, a thin, hard-eyed, no-nonsense sort of woman, invites us in after I explain why we've come. She welcomes the idea that her brother's death wasn't a routine mugging.

When we're seated in the cramped living room I ask, "Was Wendell's enlistment a spur-of-the-moment decision?"

"Yes, but it was no big surprise, because he was about to be drafted. He did make up his mind all of a sudden though – told us about it on Saturday night and left on Monday."

"Can you remember that weekend?" asks Driscoll. "Was there anything special about it?"

She chews her lower lip a moment, then says, "No, nothing special. On Friday night Wendell drove down to a dance hall in New Castle like he always did. Gas was rationed back then, but he always saved enough for Friday night."

"Why New Castle?" I ask.

"Wendell never felt welcome here in town at the kind of places he liked to go. Big bands and dancing – that's what he liked."

Driscoll, looking puzzled, says, "Didn't feel welcome?"

She gives him a speculative look. "How long you been around Midland, Mister? Wendell was a Shedtown kid, remember."

"Anything unusual happen that Friday?" I ask.

"Not that I know of."

"How about Saturday? Can you remember what Wendell did?"

For a moment she rubs a finger across her lips, then says, "He was gone most of the afternoon, I remember, because he got home about suppertime and told us he'd decided to join up."

"Any idea where he was?"

She shakes her head. "Wendell never was one to say much. I remember he got a phone call, right after lunch. He didn't get many and I was waiting for one, that's how I remember. He went out right after that."

56

"But you don't know who called?"

"No."

"What about the day before yesterday, Friday? Did he say anything about going to see someone?"

"No. But, like I said, he kept things to himself."

"Had he changed much from when he was a kid?" asks Driscoll.

"Not much. More prosperous, I guess. Oh, and he got religion a few years back. Very serious about it, but he didn't wear it on his sleeve like some people."

When we're back in Driscoll's VW he asks, "Where do we stand now?"

"I don't know. Let's stop and get coffee."

I head for a phone booth when we're inside one of those antiseptic places they call family restaurants, then join Driscoll at a table. "Who'd you call?" he asks.

"Irene Rakish. She said the first Jim knew about Spurner's death was when they heard it on the radio just before he left the house yesterday morning."

"What's that got to do with anything?"

"I think if he'd known it Friday night he'd have gone to the police."

"About what?"

"About whatever happened in August of '42. I think he saw who picked up Marcia Hesston, then Spurner saw them at the dance hall in New Castle. The call Spurner got the next day was from the killer."

"I don't get it."

"Only two people, Rakish and Spurner, knew who was with Marcia Hesston. They were paid off to forget what they saw and it was conditional on their getting out of town – enlisting, in other words – so they wouldn't be around to be questioned."

Driscoll mulls it over. "Not bad. It could have been that way, but it would have taken somebody with real money. Then, after all this time, they go back for more, so the killer gets rid of them for good."

"I don't think so. Only Spurner went to see him, whoever he is, and I don't think he was after money. I think he threatened to tell what happened."

"Why, after all this time?"

"I don't know."

Driscoll sighs and slumps down in his seat. My answer doesn't satisfy him. He wants it all wrapped up in a neat package right now. After a little he says, "So who's the killer?"

"No idea," I tell him, but one is beginning to take shape in my mind.

It's a morose group I find slouched around a table at the Backstage Bar, trying to dissolve their Monday-morning blues in cups of black coffee. Driscoll moans that the trial he must cover will be long and dull. Granger complains that all criminals are stupid and therefore writing about their activities is a job for a moron. Gloria Thompson contends that dealing with school administrators during the final weeks of the term will result in her taking a one-way ride to the state hospital in Richmond.

When they finish and start reluctantly on their rounds, I walk as far as Walnut with Gloria, then south to the offices of Ritchey, Gerhart & Company on the ground floor of a building that's been given a face lift. The arched-brick entry is imposing and the interior elegantly appointed, for the purpose, I'm sure, of letting clients know that here is a rock-solid firm worthy of taking whatever resources they have and multiplying them many times over. To me it looks like a Parisian cathouse.

Jack Gerhart's at his desk in the second of two glass-enclosed offices. He motions me in before the receptionist can begin her questioning. I've known him for years as a result of covering civic affairs. He's regarded as a pillar of the community, active in all causes considered worthy and likely to result in having your name or photo in the paper.

Gerhart asks if I'd like coffee but I decline and settle in a chair across from him. He seems unusually cordial and for a moment I wonder if he's foolish enough to think I've come to invest the fortune I've accumulated in the newspaper business. Then I remember that tomorrow is primary day and his partner is running for Congress.

The wall behind him – the only one not of glass – is covered with photos of horses. Gerhart breeds them on a farm west of town and is a leader of Midland's horsey set. I open the conversation, having decided earlier to use the I-already-know-the-answer approach.

"Were you in on the meeting Ritchey had with Wendell Spurner on Friday afternoon?"

The strategy pays off; he assumes I know much more than I do. His jaw muscles tighten and his pale blue eyes are icy but he says, "No, they talked privately in Arvil's office."

"So you didn't talk to him or hear what was said?"

"I said hello, but I don't make a habit of eavesdropping on private conversations, if that's what you mean."

I assure him it isn't but note that his office and Ritchey's are separated only by panels of glass that don't extend to the ceiling. We talk for a few moments about business and the election, then I leave and walk two doors south to the vacant storeroom serving as Ritchey's campaign headquarters.

The candidate is in conference with several advisors and Eloise Ritchey is giving instructions to a group of women at a bank of telephones. She turns and leads me to a corner near the display window where we can talk privately. I ask, "Did Wendell Spurner stop here on Friday when he visited your husband's office?"

For a moment she studies me from narrowed eyes, then says, "What is it you want, Mr. Blinn? What are you driving at?"

"Just piecing together Spurner's movements."

"Then you think there was more to his death than just a mugging?" Her features are taut and spots of color have appeared on her cheekbones. A hard, ambitious woman, I think, but I smile a little and say, "I don't know at this point. Was he here?"

"No, he wasn't, and I hope you won't bother Arvil with this just before the primary."

I tell her this is all I wanted to know, leave, and walk north to Jackson and two blocks east to City Hall. In the detectives' room off a narrow hallway in the west end of the building I find Greg Staley, Driscoll's friend on the department and the easiest of Midland's detectives to deal with. We go around the corner to a coffee shop and spend an hour discussing the case.

Driscoll is at his desk when I return to the office. After his story is filed we walk to the Backstage for lunch and along the way I tell him what I've been doing. He listens without interruption, which is unusual, but after we're seated and have ordered he says, "It was Ritchey then?"

I grin and say, "Grady, have you ever seen what you thought was a conclusion without leaping at it?"

"It's obvious, isn't it? So when are we meeting Staley?"

"At one-thirty. You want to go along?"

The look he gives me speaks for itself.

The Ritcheys and Jack Gerhart are together in the back room at campaign headquarters when Staley, Driscoll, and I walk in. The color leaves Ritchey's face when he sees Staley, but there's no reaction from the others.

Staley, still skeptical about my conclusions, has told us he's tagging along for the exercise so I say, "Ritchey, we'd like to talk to you in private."

Ritchey's mouth opens, but it's Eloise who speaks. "Anything you want to say to my husband can be said in front of Jack and me."

Officious women infuriate Driscoll. His faces flushes and he blurts, "We've got it figured out, Ritchey – everything. You killed Marcia Hesston when you were a kid and then paid off Rakish and Spurner to keep them quiet."

Ritchey's mouth stays open, but still no sound comes out. Eloise jumps up and screeches; "You nosy idiots! Arvil never killed anyone! He—"

"Wait, honey," Ritchey says, finally finding his tongue. "They know about it. I can see that. I don't know how, after all this time, but they do."

Eloise turns on him. "Don't say anything more! What can they know?"

Ritchey reaches out and takes her hand. "They know, all right." Then, looking at Staley, he says, "It was an accident, believe me. I panicked, did a foolish thing in trying to cover it up. Then, when I told Dad, instead of marching me down to the police station he panicked too. Thinking of the family name and all.

"Jim had seen me pick up Marcia and we ran into Wendell at a dance hall in New Castle. I had driven there because I didn't want anyone in Midland to see us together." He pauses, darting a look at his wife, then continues, "Dad gave Jim and Wendell a small fortune to keep quiet about seeing me with Marcia. He made them agree to enlist so they couldn't be questioned."

Driscoll looks at me gloatingly. "See? It was just the way we figured." Turning to Ritchey he says, "Then when they came back for more you killed *them* too."

"No—" Ritchey begins.

Eloise, face livid and eyes flashing, steps in front of him and says, "You people really *are* fools. Arv could no more deliberately kill someone than – than —"

As she runs out of steam, Driscoll says, "Come on, lady, it's obvious. Spurner hit him up again so—"

"Hold it, Grady," I interject. "Spurner didn't ask for money on Friday, did he, Ritchey?"

"No."

"What he did was say he'd tell what happened in '42 unless you withdrew from the congressional race. Right?"

Ritchey nods and Driscoll asks, "Why?"

"Because the cover-up preyed on his mind all these years," I say. "He lived with it because he'd given his word, but he'd gotten religion and when he came back to Midland and learned Ritchey was running for Congress he decided that changed the situation. Knowing what Ritchey had done, Spurner couldn't accept the idea of him in Congress, so he threatened to expose him unless he withdrew from the race."

"It all comes out the same in the end," Driscoll says.

Staley glares at me, thinking I've misled him. "What are you saying, Blinn?"

"I'm saying Ritchey was responsible for the girl's death, but he didn't kill Spurner and Rakish."

"Then who did?"

I nod toward Jack Gerhart.

"Now just a minute," Gerhart says, bristling. "Don't drag me into this."

"You did that yourself," I say to him. "You overheard what was said on Friday and you knew Ritchey wouldn't withdraw. For one thing, Eloise wouldn't let him. Maybe Ritchey thought Spurner was bluffing too, but you didn't. Not that you cared about the race, but you cared about the business. How many clients would you have left after the story came out?"

Gerhart's attempt to laugh is a failure. "Ridiculous," he says. "You can't prove any of this."

"I think we can," I tell him. Then, to Staley, "Take a look in the barn at his horse farm and I'll bet you'll find a pickup with a battered front end. He killed Rakish too because he was afraid he'd tell the story when he found out what happened to Spurner."

Without warning, Gerhart lunges at me, but Staley intercepts him. Eloise has slumped down in a chair, suddenly an old woman. Driscoll stands scowling at me, confused by the turn of events.

He's still cool when I see him later at Horner's. In less than an hour he disposes of the better part of a bottle of Bushmill's. His pride is hurt. He fancies himself as the sleuth on the *News-Banner* staff.

Tobe Gilson has been released from jail, his cell taken by Gerhart. Staley found the pickup truck in the barn and Gerhart's been charged with Rakish's murder. Another likely will be filed for the killing of Spurner.

Ritchey has withdrawn from the race but remains free, at least temporarily. The prosecutor has doubts about bringing him to trial at this late date. There are no witnesses to call other than those of us who heard his confession, and after talking to his lawyer Ritchey doesn't plan to plead guilty and may deny ever having said anything. Still, with the story coming out, he's finished in this town.

I sympathize with Driscoll and say, "Remember, Grady, I had more time to work on it than you did. The advantage was all mine."

He nods and seems to brighten a little. "Well," he says, "a lot of people will be reading your column tomorrow. Jake says he's going to run it on page one."

I shrug and order another round. It doesn't matter to me where Jake runs it – my paycheck will still be the same. No overtime, he'd told me, despite the weekend work.

MEANINGLESS MURDER

The Oar House, named after a couple of canoe paddles that hang over the entrance, is about what I expect. A long room with a bar on one side and booths on the other. Dim lights, the jukebox playing country: a mournful admission that now and then there's a fool such as I. Half my beer is still inside the Falstaff bottle and already it's played three times, courtesy of a man at the end of the bar who keeps feeding in coins and pressing the same buttons.

I study him surreptitiously. He wears the haunted look that spells woman trouble as clearly as if it were stamped on his forehead. It's a familiar story, I'm sure. One that's been repeated a million times, but that doesn't ease his pain. Another man, maybe, or perhaps he tried a little tomcatting himself and got caught. Whatever, to him the story is brand new and the wound is raw.

Another man, headed for the restroom, says to him, "Hi, Earl," and he nods in return. Our eyes meet and I look away. He's the trouble some people go looking for, but I'm not one of them. The hair style, the lean look of the hills, something in his bearing, all tell me he is from the small Tennessee town that sends half its native sons to Midland in search of the big bucks in the factories. I'm in long-knife territory and that's not my sport.

The Oar House is a favorite south side hangout of the Tennesseeans. Live music on Friday and Saturday, fights any night of the week.

I decide, to finish my beer, then take my drinking habit uptown where I feel more comfortable. The place is slowly filling up with men and women who will never be at home on the plains of Central Indiana, will never stop yearning for the rocky hills, piney forests, rushing streams. Good men, hard workers, but with a different set of values from mine, a pride so easily affronted that even their casual friendliness warns others that a wrong word, a wrong look at their woman, means trouble.

As I take a final swallow of beer I sense a new tension in the man called Earl. His eyes are riveted on the latest arrivals, a man and woman laughing intimately together as they walk arm in arm to a booth. The woman casts a sidelong glance at Earl, enjoying her triumph and his torment. His eyes don't waver from her but there is a subtle change in them, one she either doesn't see or doesn't heed.

I slide the empty bottle to the inside of the bar, the universal signal for another. I tell myself this is what a newspaperman is paid to do. Study human nature, human responses, the interaction of personalities and events that in themselves create new events. Where else does the material come from, the grist for the insatiable appetite of a daily column? But somewhere in my head a voice is saying, "It isn't 'Around Town with Hal Blinn' you're thinking about, you're just nosy."

The new arrivals share one side of a booth. Heads together, still laughing quietly as they order drinks, exchanging banter with the waitress, ignoring the man alone at the bar. They're aware of him, though. He's being teased, baited, and even that fool in the song would recognize their performance for what it is.

Several moments pass. The jukebox winds down, the tension in Earl doesn't. He gets up suddenly, walks to the booth and for a few seconds stands looking down at its occupants. The explosion I am braced for doesn't come. Instead Earl sits down across from them and talks quietly to the woman, ignoring the other man.

The woman seems amused by what is happening, savoring her power over him. They are too far away for me to hear what is being said but I pick up scattered words – divorce, kids, sick baby, need you, never again.

The explosion finally occurs, but not in the way I anticipated. The woman picks up her drink, and throws it in Earl's face. A hush falls over the room, all eyes are on the one booth.

Earl doesn't react, just sits unmoving as the liquid drips from his face to his shirt. The woman laughs again, but it is shrill and hollow and her facial muscles have tightened. The other man also is motionless, wearing a stunned expression. Then, when Earl does nothing, his smile spreads slowly.

The seconds pass interminably. Finally Earl gets up without a word, walks to a side door and on outside. The tension drains away and I realize another song is playing on the jukebox, something about going ninety miles an hour down a dead-end street. I leave a nearly full bottle and head uptown.

The story in the *Morning Sun* is a bare-bones account, written at deadline with little time to gather facts. A woman stabbed to death in the parking lot at the Oar House. A police search for her husband, James Earl Hartley, who had been arguing with her in the tavern and had followed her outside. So Earl had gone back.

I push the paper aside, no longer interested in the other news. I want more information so I gulp my coffee, go back upstairs to my rooms for a few minutes, then walk the two blocks from the old hotel to the *News-Banner.*

Steve Granger, who covers the police beat, is already out on his rounds so I go to the city desk and ask Jake Richards if there's anything new on the murder.

"Granger's out checking," he says without looking up.

"Have they arrested the husband?"

He looks up now, reaching for one of the two cigarettes burning in his ashtray. "I said Granger's out checking. Go bug somebody else, Hal – somebody who doesn't have work to do."

"I saw the woman and her husband at the Oar House a little while before it happened. She threw—"

"But you left before the murder?"

"Right, but . . . You're not interested in my story, are you, Jake?"

"I will be when you have one."

Old grouch, I think to myself, and decide to hit the street. At eight in the morning that means the Backstage Bar where the beat reporters will be drinking black coffee, comparing stories on the night before, complaining about Jake, their jobs, their pay.

Grady Driscoll and Gloria Thompson sit morosely at a table with five dirty cups. I tell my story but they are unmoved. A court bailiff joins us so I tell it again. Driscoll squirms impatiently and begins talking about the trial he'll be covering when court convenes. Gloria leaves to cover some function at the college just as Granger walks in.

65

"Have they caught Hartley?" I ask.

"Picked him up at a bar over on Madison an hour after it happened."

"Has he admitted doing it?"

"Not yet, but he will. There were thirty witnesses."

"In the parking lot at midnight?"

He sighs resignedly. "Of course not, but they saw them arguing inside and saw him follow her out and his knife was in the body. Why are you interested, anyway?"

I repeat my story. Driscoll leaves as I begin and when I'm finished Granger shrugs and follows him.

Late in the afternoon I find the three of them again at a table in the back room of Horner's Tavern. Jake is with them, his eyes red and glassy from the beer he's been drinking for two hours. Jack Homer brings a fresh round and sits down so I tell him my story after learning from Granger that Hartley still hasn't confessed.

Driscoll sighs when I finish. "You know, Hal, this isn't a classic mystery. It's not even very interesting. Everybody knows the who, what, where, when, and how, so suppose you quit talking and start writing – tell the readers *why*. That's a columnist's job, isn't it?"

While I'm framing a sharp retort, Jake sits nodding his head. When my mouth opens he holds up his hand and says, "He's right, Hal. You're getting to be one of those newsmen who know everything that's going on, but talking about it with your cronies satisfies you. You never get around to writing it. If a reporter knows more than the readers, nine times out of ten he isn't doing his job."

The annoying thing is I know he's right. Nobody's going to get me to admit it, though, so I get up and leave, walk two blocks to the jail, then wonder what I'm doing in the place. Had Hartley confessed, they might let me talk to him. Since he hasn't, my chances are slim.

The outer office is crowded. I ask a county policeman the reason and he says the people are Hartley's friends and relatives. He points out Hartley's sister and a minister – a man who looks like he might grab you by the arm and say, "Brother, are you saved?"

They haven't a prayer of seeing Hartley and I have only one, a press-conscious sheriff. When the chance comes, I take Joe McAuliffe aside and state my case. He slips a finger inside his collar and moves his head around. "Jeez, Hal, I don't know . . . let me see what I can do."

66

He walks away, then returns a few minutes later with Greg Staley, a city detective who knows me. I tell him why I want to see Hartley and he surprises me by saying, "Sure, why not? You can have five minutes, but only because I figure you have enough sense not to blow the case some way."

McAuliffe escorts me to an interrogation room, making sure I'm aware of the big favor he's doing me. A few minutes later he hustles Hartley in the door. He's surprisingly well groomed but looks haggard, more like forty than twenty-seven.

He recognizes me. "You were in the Oar House last night, right?"

"You have a good memory."

"I knew who you were, I've seen your picture in the paper. What do you want?"

"They tell me you deny killing your wife."

"I loved her. Why would I kill her?"

"If you didn't, any idea who did?"

"Why do you want to know?"

The way he's countering questions, he should have been a politician or a salesman rather than a factory worker. An intelligent man with the distrust of strangers common among hill people.

"It's my job," I tell him. "What happened when you left the tavern?"

"I was trying to make Flo see some sense but she wasn't interested so I gave it up and drove over to Fat Frank's for another drink. That's where they picked me up."

"Where was she when you left?"

"By her car, rummaging through her purse for her keys." When my five minutes are up I still have no idea what's going on inside Hartley's head. I have material for a column, but not the one Jake and Driscoll were talking about. To know why Florence Hartley died, I'll have to talk to more people, piece it together myself. I decide to start with his sister.

The house on South Elm is old and large, uncared for, past its prime. A boy about four answers my knock, a girl a year younger peers at me over his shoulder. Wanda Hartley follows them from the kitchen, wiping her hands on a towel. I explain my business and she sizes me up warily, then gives a little shrug and invites me inside.

I guess her age at thirty-five. Tall, but twenty pounds overweight. No makeup, hair pulled back in a severe style. Clean, but beyond that unconcerned about her appearance.

She orders the children upstairs and they obey without argument. When we are settled on old overstuffed chairs she cautiously answers a few preliminary questions. She has lived with her brother since shortly after the boy was born, has always cared for the two youngsters and a year-old baby girl who has been sick since birth. Before that she had her own place, worked in a factory since coming to Midland from Tennessee twelve years ago. She was laid off and moved in with Earl and Florence, became a full-time nanny because Florence kept on the go, never had time for the children.

I try to butter her up through the children, compliment her on their behavior and neat appearance, but she isn't having any of it. Her suspicious attitude is inbred, can't be overcome, so I have nothing to lose by being blunt.

"Florence wasn't a good wife or mother, was she?"

Her lips compress, she starts to say something but stops. Then: "It's wrong to speak ill of the dead."

"But Earl tried to make her take more interest in the kids?"

"Of course. My brother's a fine man, a good father."

"But without you, things never would have gotten on here?"

"I've done my best."

The conversation sounds like a lawyer examining a witness, but a judge wouldn't allow my leading questions. Without them, though, I'd learn nothing.

"Earl claims he didn't kill Florence. Any idea who might have?"

She grunts, then says, "Half the men south of the tracks. And their wives."

I grin, although she hasn't meant to be funny. "Anyone specific?"

"I've kept my nose out of their business." She pauses, thinking, deciding whether to say more. "Bradley Scruggs, he's the latest."

That would be the boyfriend. A good candidate, unless he was still in the tavern when it happened. And, remembering Wanda's words, Bradley's wife.

"How about Earl? Maybe he just had more than he could take."

She looks away, hesitates a second or two. "No. My brother's a gentle man, a God-fearing man."

"Why'd he carry a knife?"

"Because every man and boy down home carries a knife. He never used it, never even marked anybody."

"Marked anybody?"

"Put his mark on them – cut just deep enough to leave a scar but not do any real damage. You've seen a man point to another and say, 'That's my mark,' haven't you?"

I shake my head. "How can they be sure they won't cut too deep?"

She looks around for something, settles on a knitting needle and picks it up. "By holding their thumb right near the tip of the blade like this."

Just fun and games, a little sport of an evening. We talk another few minutes, then I leave without having learned anything specific other than the name of the boyfriend. I've picked up a lot, though, have a better feel of things in general about a way of life I want no part of.

Bradley Scruggs's house on Twelfth Street is only a few blocks from Hartley's. Scruggs and his wife are finishing supper when I arrive. I suggest talking to him alone, but Audrey Scruggs has other ideas. "It's about that woman, isn't it?" she says, and there is no doubt what woman she means. Her husband has a hangdog look, not at all the gay romancer of the previous night.

"Were you at the Oar House when Florence Hartley was murdered?" I ask him.

"No, I left a couple hours before."

"How long had you been dating Florence?"

"Never dated her," he mumbles. "Just ran into her now and then and had a drink or two."

"Yeah," Audrey says scornfully. "He just ran into her every day the past six months."

"Now that ain't true, honey," he whines.

"Don't 'honey' me," she answers, giving him a scathing look. Then, to me, "Ask the great lover about the packed suitcase in the back of his closet."

"Now, honey, I told you I figured on having to make a business trip, then forgot to unpack when it was called off."

Talking as if he's somewhere else she says, "Factories send shop workers on business trips all the time, don't they, mister?"

"I meant for the lodge," he says. Enough of this, I decide, and leave.

The Reverend Harlan Fleece is alone in the small house next to his frame church not far from the Oar House. He talks as I expect: Midland is good, his "children" are good despite occasional backsliding by a few, and, although he doesn't come out and say so, he is good. Only I am suspect.

He's fat and fortyish, his clothes are rumpled and not too clean. Still, he has a certain charm, a magnetism that undoubtedly serves him well with some people. He describes Florence Hartley as a good Christian woman, a fine wife and mother. The lie of his words shows on my face so he adds, "Misguided at times, perhaps. Misguided."

"Who was doing the guiding, you?"

His cheeks and fat jowls flush a little. "I tried to be her spiritual guide, of course. Her spiritual guide, nothing more, although I'm sure some people . . . "

"Some people what?"

"Some people may say differently, those who jump to the wrong conclusions and read evil intent into perfectly normal. . . " Again he fades out. The conversation isn't to his liking.

I take a guess and say, "You mean the talk about Florence coming here alone a lot?"

"Exactly. It was all perfectly natural. She was in the choir and we often got together to plan the musical programs."

"But Earl didn't like it?"

"On the contrary, he approved wholeheartedly. He was glad to see her taking an interest in the church."

"Until recently, you mean?"

"And then it was only malicious gossip that, that . . . "

"Suppose Florence decided to tell all?"

"Why would she . . . I mean what would she have told?"

He suddenly realizes I've been guessing, just priming the pump, and I can see there will be nothing more forthcoming.

It's after nine when I walk into Horner's and only Driscoll is in the back room. "Hear the news?" he asks, and when I shake my head, "You know the new outdoor recreation area back of the jail? Well, they let Hartley out for a little fresh air, left him alone a minute, and he decided to exercise by climbing the fence."

"He escaped? He's free?"

"As a bird."

The news disturbs me and, for some reason, does what all the talk failed to do – makes me think Hartley may be innocent.

Catching him the second time proves more difficult than the first. By the second morning after his escape everyone is convinced he has managed to make his way back to the hills around Flintville. I'm relieved because I had feared he might be set on taking his own revenge.

I try to interest myself in other matters but my mind doesn't cooperate. Even my favorite lunch, a bowl of Jack Horner's hot chili with a tall beer to put out the fire, fails to distract me from the plan I've been kicking around, one that doesn't really make good sense. Despite that, I decide to go ahead with it as I drain the last of the beer.

Deadline has passed and Jake is leaning back with a cup of coffee and a cigarette as I walk into the newsroom. I tell him, "Jake, I want to go to Tennessee."

"They say it's nice in June. A little fishing, a hike in the Smokies, browsing around Gatlinburg, the Grand Old Opry."

"You know what I'm talking about, Jake. I want to go to Flintville and try to find Earl Hartley."

He chuckles derisively. "They wouldn't even talk to you down there, you wouldn't get to first base. Of course you might manage to get yourself shot."

"I think I'd have a chance. Even if I didn't, it'd make a good column or two."

"Forget it, Hal. Advertising's down, the budget's tight, the company isn't okaying trips to Indianapolis to cover the legislature, let alone wild goose chases in Tennessee."

As usual he's right, and I'd figured on a turndown. "Okay, I'll go on my own. Starting tomorrow I'm on vacation."

Jake sighs, shaking his head. "It's your money, Hal."

He's also right about people in Flintville not talking to me, or any nosy stranger. If Hartley's hiding up in the hills they'll know it, but an outsider isn't going to find him. The sheriff down there might, if it was important enough, but then again he might not.

I go back to Horner's and think about it over coffee. John Morgan comes to mind, a tough Flintville native who served five years hard time at Pendleton. He heads up a program for ex-cons and I've given it some exposure when no one else was interested.

Morgan's at home when I phone so I drive out. When I leave half an hour later I've got a head full of information, a few old sticks, and his spare knife. I'm pleased with the information but not thrilled about the knife.

At the hotel I toss a few things in a suitcase and hurry downstairs, figuring the long June days will enable me to make Flintville by dark. As I start out the revolving door, Driscoll starts in from the opposite side. I keep going and so does he, in a circle back to the sidewalk.

"Hold it, Hal," he calls. "I'm going along."

"No, you're not, Grady," I say over my shoulder, still walking toward the car. "Everything's planned and you don't fit in." I should have expected it. Everywhere I go, Driscoll tags along or turns up. Either he thinks I'm incapable of handling a situation alone or is afraid of missing something, I'm not sure which.

He hurries to overtake me, the spare tire around his waist jiggling. "We'll go by my place. It'll only take a minute to get what I need."

I stop and face him. "You're not going, Grady. How do you even know about it?"

"Jake told me." He tugs on my arm and says, "C'mon, if you quit wasting time we can make it by dark."

Driscoll chatters on about nothing for a while, then falls silent until we are south of Indianapolis on I-65. As we near the Franklin exit he asks, "What are you trying to accomplish, Hal?"

"I'm not sure. I want to talk to Hartley again."

"Still looking for the 'why'?"

"I guess. There's more to the story than that, though, but I'm not sure what it is."

"You're not crazy enough to think he didn't do it?"

I look at him and grin. He snorts and turns to stare at the passing cornfields.

When we leave the interstate at Glasgow we still have a hundred miles to travel on a state highway that twists and turns through the hills of Kentucky, then Tennessee. That's when I lay down the ground rules for Driscoll, tell him he is to go his own way while we are in Flintville but isn't to pump the residents for information. I have little hope that he'll pay any attention.

The headlights have been on for half an hour when we reach Flintville, but there is enough daylight to see it's about what I expected of a town of two thousand tucked away in the hills. At that it's the biggest town for miles around so the business district covers several blocks. Most of the buildings date back sixty or eighty years and few are higher than two stories. An ancient courthouse towers over everything. Aside from a few young toughs milling around in front of the theater, the streets are nearly deserted.

Finding Flintville's only hotel is no problem. It's an old three-story building with a roof supported by wooden pillars extending over the sidewalk. Wooden benches line the wall under the overhang. A few loungers eye us without comment.

Several more occupy chairs in the small lobby, interested in us but not showing it. The man at the desk is lean and surly, but he erases my fear of having to share a bed with Driscoll by saying .a room with twins is available. He also tells us a restaurant two blocks away is still open so we freshen up and head for it.

Driscoll starts for a booth but I take a stool at the counter. He backtracks and joins me, grumbling.

The lone waitress leaves the only other customer and stands in front of us. Life hasn't been easy for her and it shows. She's curious, though, and after turning in our orders comes back and says, "You fellas from outta town?"

I nod and say, "From Midland, Indiana."

Her scrawny, lined face brightens. "I've got friends up in Midland. You know my brother, Kenny James?"

I shake my head. "You know Earl Hartley?"

A guarded look comes over her. "You guys ain't cops, are you? You don't look like cops."

"No, we're not cops. I know Earl and need to talk to him. Who're his friends?"

"Don't ask me. Didn't ever know him much, he was young when he took off north." She starts away, then stops. A scornful look, a sniffing, nose-in-the-air look, replaces the one of distrust. "I knowed his sister, though – Miss High and Mighty."

"Wanda? You didn't like Wanda?"

73

"Nobody liked Wanda. Nobody liked her uppity ways. Always acting like she was better'n everybody. The whole town was laughing, believe me, when she went and got herself pregnant."

"Wanda? I didn't know she has a child."

"She don't, it died aborning. Then Wanda hightailed it outta town."

When she walks away, Driscoll asks what the talk was all about. I tell him about Wanda and that it really wasn't about much of anything.

After eating, we go to a bar down the street, have a couple of drinks, but don't talk to anyone. We have been sized up by the few regulars on hand but none makes an overture. Not even the bartender, who talks about the weather and then leaves us alone. Driscoll can't understand why I don't corner somebody and ask questions.

"I've been coached," I finally tell him. "Just drink and be quiet." He sulks until we go back to the hotel.

When we have finished breakfast at the same restaurant, I send Driscoll off on his own after warning him to stay out of trouble, then walk back to the hotel. Half a dozen men already are lounging on the benches, several of them whittling. I lean against one of the pillars by the curb, my back to them. After a few minutes I take John Morgan's knife and one of the sticks he has given me from my pocket, open the blade, and take a few swipes at the stick, feeling foolish and self conscious.

Half an hour passes and I am ready to give up, convinced the ploy recommended by Morgan is far too obvious. Only his warning that any direct approach will meet with a rebuff keeps me at it. The sun, already high in the sky, is warm and I am considering moving to a shady spot when a slim, hard-eyed fellow of about thirty eases up beside me and says, "Take a look at yer knife?"

I nod and hand it to him. He examines it closely, turning it over again and again, studying every detail. To me it looks pretty much like any other knife. Finally he hands it back, nodding, too, apparently in approval. "Knowed a fella once had one like it," he says.

"Got yours?" I ask, trying to sound casual, knowing darn well he'd go out without his pants before his knife.

He takes it out and hands it to me. I follow his example, wondering what it is I'm supposed to be looking at. After enough turns and re-examinations, I nod sagely and give it back. A moment or two pass in silence, then I look up at the cloudless sky and say, "Nice day."

He looks up, too, and says, "Yeah." More time passes with each of us glancing up at the sky every so often. I close the knife and put it away, check the sky one more time, and say, "Lookin' for Earl Hartley. Know him?"

"Might."

"Talked to him the other day. Like to talk to him again."

"Friend?"

"He knows me. Like for somebody to tell him Hal Blinn wants to talk to him."

"That you?"

Conserving words obviously is a virtue in Flintville so I nod. "Be around later?" he asks, and I nod again, then he walks away.

I sit on a bench till noon, whittling a little now and then, but no one else approaches. I wonder what Driscoll's been up to and expect to find him at the restaurant, but don't. The waitress from the night before serves me a hamburger without being too friendly, then I go back to the hotel and lean against the pillar again.

An hour goes by and I'm getting bored and restless. A foolish waste of time, I think, and consider forgetting the whole thing.

When a battered pickup truck stops in front of me, it takes me a few seconds to recognize the man behind the wheel as the one I talked to earlier. "Take a ride?" he asks. I nod and climb in beside him.

He drives out of town on the highway, then follows side roads on a twisting route deep into the hills. After half an hour and about six miles, he stops in a clearing surrounded by tall pines and we get out. Neither of us has spoken and it continues that way.

More waiting, more standing around. For Earl Hartley, I assume, but don't ask. My hard-eyed driver leans against a fender, takes out his knife, and begins notching a stick. I remember times when I've felt more at ease.

The sound of an engine in the distance breaks the silence, grows steadily louder until another pickup appears and pulls into the clearing. The lanky, dark-haired driver gets out and takes the same position as my own against a fender. Earl Hartley climbs from the passenger's side, walks toward me, and stops six feet away. I feel safe enough but this isn't a gathering I'd care to stumble on by accident.

I nod and say, "Earl."

"Hear you wanna talk more, Blinn."

Again I nod, beginning to feel natural doing it.

"What about?"

"I saw Wanda and Bradley Scruggs. Talked to the minister, too – Harlan Fleece."

Hartley snorts and the three men exchange sneering grins. I'm not sure which name was responsible.

"Who killed her, Earl?"

He shakes his head and looks away.

"Why'd you run off? You can't hide up here forever."

He turns back, shrugs his shoulders, then says, "You got influence, Blinn?"

"Not much. Why?"

"I don't want the kids with Wanda any more."

The statement catches me off guard. After a long pause I ask, "Why?"

Hartley shakes his head again. "Can you fix it?"

"Maybe. I can talk to people . . . it'd mean the Children's Home."

He nods this time. "Lemme know tomorrow."

He turns and starts for his truck but stops when I say, "Then what, Earl?"

"Then maybe I'll go back." He goes on to the truck, the interview is over.

Only when we are on our way back to town do I realize he has answered all my questions. I should have figured it out for myself. If you accept the fact that Earl didn't kill Florence, that leaves only one person who would have had access to his knife. It also explains why he didn't take his own revenge as I thought he might.

I'm missing one piece of information, though. I still can't write a column explaining why.

I dial three numbers before tracking down Greg Staley. After hearing my story he warns me I'm flirting with a charge of harboring a fugitive. I laugh at that, and think I even hear a chuckle from him. He tells me he'll see what he can do, lays down a couple of conditions, and promises to call back by early the next afternoon.

He asks why, of course. I'm not lying when I answer, "Hartley didn't say."

I find Driscoll in the lobby. He is close-mouthed about where he's been all day and I don't press him, I tell him what's been going on, leaving out only my own conclusions.

The evening begins like the previous one – supper at the same restaurant, a walk down the street to the same bar. This time, to our surprise, it's crowded. Every table is occupied, no one is talking, all eyes are on us. We find stools at one end of the bar and order beer.

When the bartender sets them in front of us he quietly says, "Drink your drinks, don't say anything to anybody, then walk out the door."

"What's going on?" Driscoll asks softly.

"It's 'stomp night.' Every other night of the week we're open late but tonight we'll be closed by nine-thirty, the sheriff'll see to that. They're waiting to pick out somebody to stomp and up till now you're the best candidates."

The beer doesn't taste as good as I thought it would. I'm trying to decide whether it would be smarter to make a dash for it or walk out casually when the door opens and a little guy wearing a big cowboy hat walks in. Somebody says, "Well, hiyuh, Tex," and everybody laughs. Without exchanging a word, Driscoll and I get up and slip out quietly.

The call from Staley comes just after lunch. "It wasn't easy," he says. "The welfare director and Judge Main cooperated, though, after I explained the situation. 'A children in need of services' petition was filed, the judge heard it immediately, and the kids have been picked up and are at the home. Now try to hold up your end of the bargain."

The pickup appears on schedule and we repeat the trip of the day before. This time Hartley is waiting. He stares, arms folded, until I say, "It's been handled."

His reply is the usual nod.

"I want you to go back with me, Earl."

He grins. "Figured on doin' that."

We arrive in Midland a little after midnight – the *Morning Sun's* deadline. I had called ahead and Staley is waiting in a parking lot at the edge of town. We follow them to the jail, then I drop Driscoll at his apartment.

A dim light burns somewhere inside the house but when I knock there is no response. I turn the knob and the door opens. Wanda Hartley sits alone in a dark corner, staring from dull, rounded eyes.

Seconds tick away on a mantel clock. "I thought you might come," she finally says.

I pull a chair around and sit facing her from a few feet away. "You know, then?"

"I had a feeling you'd figure it out. I heard about you talking to people." After a pause she continues, louder, "She was going to run off with that no-good Scruggs. I heard them talking on the phone, I knew what they were up to. I couldn't let her take the children away from me like that."

"But why hang it on Earl?"

"I didn't really mean to. But you know, *he* would have taken them away, too. He'd been talking about it, about taking the children and going back to Flintville."

"You could have gone along. He'd have needed someone to take care of them."

"Never!" she says angrily, eyes flashing. "I'd never go back to that place. All those women with their little minds and their evil tongues that never stop wagging as long as there's somebody to hurt. In those little towns they never let you forget."

She's probably right. But I don't think Earl would have gone back, either. He would have stayed in Midland and could have gotten custody of the kids. He wouldn't have needed to, though – I'd bet my last dollar that Florence had no intention of taking them along. If she even intended to go, which is doubtful. Everything that's happened has been for nothing. A meaningless murder.

"We have to set things straight, Wanda. I'll go with you. You won't have trouble, they'll treat you okay."

She nods dispiritedly, not caring any more. "I know. Earl has to get out so he can take the children out of that place." The tears finally come. She covers her face with both hands and sobs quietly, her body shaking spasmodically. "God, when I think of them being there, being in a place like that . . . "

It's eight in the morning when I finish my column, one that's twice the length of the usual twenty inches. In addition, Steve Granger has written the story of Wanda's arrest and the events in Tennessee from information I've supplied. I am bone weary but rather than head for the hotel and bed, I pour a cup of coffee and wait for Jake's reaction.

There is none. When I know he has finished reading and released the column to the composing room, I walk over and say, "Okay, Jake?"

He waves impatiently with one hand and says, "Fine, fine."

"I was tired. Do you think I touched all the bases?"

"I said it was fine, Hal. Go to bed."

I turn and have taken a few steps, figuring that 'fine' is as far as Jake intends to go with compliments, when he says, "Hal."

I stop and look back. He continues, "I didn't turn you in for vacation. You've been on payroll status."

"What about expenses?"

"Hal, why do you always have to press your luck?" he says, scowling. Then, after I've taken a few more steps, "Turn in a voucher and I'll see what I can do."

I don't see Driscoll until late afternoon. He's alone at a table in the back room of Horner's and motions toward a chair. "You did a good job, Hal," he says.

I sigh with relief. I didn't know how he'd take all this, wondered if he'd be mad because I hadn't told him my conclusions, let him be in on the finish.

I order a Bushmills for each of us and when they arrive he takes a long drink, then wipes his mouth with the back of his hand. "Yes, you did a good job. Of course you wouldn't have done a damn thing if I hadn't pushed you into it."

Same old Driscoll I think, chuckling. And he's probably right, too.

MISSING MELINDA

Something is bothering Driscoll. It amuses me for a moment or two, watching him gnaw his lower lip while his brows arch, then curl in a frown, then arch again. He is so transparent and so unaware of it. No wonder he always loses at poker but can never understand why.

We sit at a round table in the back room of Horner's Tavern, alone with the soothing sound of Tommy Dorsey's "Marie." It occurs to me that on a July evening forty years after the era of the big bands, the jukebox at Horner's may be the only one offering its music exclusively. Criticize it within Jack Horner's hearing and you will find yourself out on the street.

Eventually I grow tired of Driscoll's facial gyrations and say, "What is it this time, Grady, a jealous husband or another bill collector?"

My third-beer humor annoys him. He turns his round Irish face toward me and opens his mouth, then snaps it shut again in the way a frog might catch a fly. I grin and that adds to his annoyance.

"Have to make a joke of everything, don't you?" he says. "Trouble with you, Blinn, you get your kicks out of other people's problems, then can't wait to use them in that column of yours so everybody in town can have a good laugh."

I go on grinning, aware that both of us know "Around Town with Hal Blinn" has never been that kind of column. Even if I wanted it that way, a writer using such an approach wouldn't last a month in an Indiana town of eighty thousand. A Hoosier enjoys gossip as much

81

as the next person, but not when it hits too close to home and appears in print. Passing it from mouth to mouth is something else again.

As usual, Driscoll's anger cools as quickly as it heated. He brushes a hand over the few sandy hairs remaining on top of his head and says, "Dammit, Hal, I don't know what to do about this."

"About what?" I ask, surprised to hear him admit he doesn't know how to cope with a situation. Even when he doesn't, Driscoll has never been one to own up to the fact.

"That's just it, Hal," he replies, sighing. "I promised not to talk about it." He waits for me to say something. I don't, so he sighs again, then lowering his voice says, "Do you swear to keep it to yourself if I tell you?"

"That's exactly what you did, isn't it?"

"This is different," he tells me, but doesn't explain the difference. He has aroused my curiosity, though, so I nod and say, "Okay."

He looks over both shoulders, sees no one, then in a solemn tone says, "Melinda Clay is missing."

I wait for more but nothing comes. Perplexed, I say, "So?"

"So?" he repeats exasperatedly. "You know who Melinda Clay is, don't you?"

"Of course I know who she is. How could anybody live in this town and not know? But how does it concern you if the whole Clay tribe is missing?"

"Have you forgotten I'm covering for Granger while he's on vacation?"

I have forgotten, but even after being reminded the connection still escapes me. Steve Granger covers the police beat for the *News-Banner* and Driscoll is filling in for him along with covering the courts, his usual job. I fail to see how it affects him if a young member of Midland's leading family turns up missing. I ask him again.

"They're trying to keep it hushed up. Staley's working on it and only he and the chief are supposed to know about it outside the family. I found out, though, and asked Staley a couple of questions and he had a fit. Said he'd be back riding a squad car if I didn't promise to keep quiet."

Greg Staley, a Midland detective, is Driscoll's buddy and the best contact any of us has in the police department when we need a little off-the-record cooperation. Alienating him would cause problems, obviously. I say, "So you promised and now you're out on a limb?"

He nods dispiritedly. I appreciate his predicament. A reporter, particularly on the police beat, runs into situations that require sitting on a story, but that usually means being aware of something that will happen in the future, then waiting for it to break. This is different. Driscoll is dealing with something that has already happened and if it's to be kept out of the paper the decision lies with an editor, not him. By telling me he has put me in the same awkward position.

If I am in trouble of someone else's making I want to know why, so I insist on hearing the story. At first each fact must be pried from Driscoll but as he goes on he warms to the task and for a while I am overwhelmed by the amount of detailed information he has uncovered. Eventually, though, he admits Staley briefed him after extracting his promise to keep it to himself.

Melinda Clay, an attractive, unmarried woman of twenty-two, left the headquarters of Clay Brothers International shortly after four o'clock the previous afternoon. Those who saw her later told Staley she appeared tense, perhaps angry, after a short visit to the fourth-floor office of her uncle, Martin Clay, president of Midland's largest industry.

When questioned by Staley, a company guard named James Short said he watched Melinda cross the street at the rear of the six-year-old Bedford limestone building on the city's east side. She pulled from the parking lot in her new LeBaron two-door, black with tan vinyl top, at a speed Short described as "too fast" and drove north to Indiana 32, then west toward downtown.

When Melinda failed to appear for dinner, served promptly at seven as usual, her mother asked the family's lone male servant if she had called. Charles Morton – butler, waiter, and chauffeur – replied that she had not. Lenore Clay ate alone without further comment. She then had coffee and a glass of sherry on a screened rear porch facing the river and shielded from the noise of light traffic on nearby Burlington Pike by the three story, eighteen-room house built in 1907 by her late husband's grandfather.

At nine o'clock, when Melinda had neither arrived home nor telephoned, Lenore called the house of her brother-in-law a hundred yards north on Wapahani Drive, a cul-de-sac leading only to the four mansions built by the original Clay brothers near the turn of the century. She was told Martin had gone to Indianapolis and wasn't expected home until the early hours of the morning. Lenore watched television until eleven and then went to bed, although she had grown increasingly apprehensive because Melinda had always informed her of any change of plans.

In the morning she found Melinda still had not come home and again called Martin's residence. By then she was close to hysteria so Martin walked the short distance to her house. At his insistence they did some checking on their own and it was early afternoon before the police were notified.

"Why," I ask Driscoll, "didn't he call the police right away?"

"You know how the Clays are, always trying to set an example for the rest of the town. I guess in Martin Clay's mind having something happen as commonplace as a girl running off didn't go along with the family image. He wanted to keep the police out of it altogether, but Lenore wouldn't go for the idea. Clay wanted Joe Harvey, the head of plant security, to handle it."

"Is that what Staley thinks, that she just ran off somewhere?"

"That's what I think. Probably at a motel in Indianapolis with some guy."

"Jumping to conclusions again, aren't you, Grady?"

"Come on, Hal, just because she's a Clay doesn't mean the girl's an angel. If it was anybody else the police wouldn't even bother to check it out this soon."

On that he's right. Rank does have its privileges. Or, looking at it from Martin Clay's point of view at the moment, its disadvantages.

After mulling the situation over in my mind I say, "If the *Sun* has the story in the morning you're off the hook. If not, you've got to tell Jake what's going on."

The thought of trying to explain what he's done to city editor Jake Richards makes Driscoll's face sag until he's all jowls. Jake won't appreciate being put in the position of either letting a reporter make deals he must abide by or countermanding the decision with the result that every cop in town will think the *News-Banner* can't be relied upon. Jake will take the problem to Hayden Clarke, the editor. Because it involves the Clays, Clarke probably will go along with the deal. But Jake will be hot about it, figuring Driscoll took too much upon himself and in effect by-passed the chain of command.

Although neither of us says so, I think that for once both Driscoll and I hope *The Morning Sun* finds out what's going on and beats us to the story.

It doesn't happen, though, and I know it even before I drop a quarter in the paper dispenser at my hotel. It isn't across the top of page one on the display copy and that's where it would be if they knew. Unless, of course, the *Sun* has made a deal, too.

The coffee shop is just opening and the waitress is shocked to see me coming down at six in the morning, an hour when I sometimes am getting in but never preparing to go out. I skim over the *Sun* while my coffee cools, confident I won't find the story buried somewhere inside. I'm right.

The morning air is damp and a blustery wind makes me wish I had worn something heavier for the two-block walk to the *News-Banner*. I warm up fast, though, thinking of the approaching scene with Jake. I intend to be there to protect my interests.

Jake eyes me suspiciously as soon as I walk in. He knows something is up; I would never arrive so early otherwise. I pretend not to notice and busy myself elsewhere.

I buttonhole Driscoll the second he arrives and say, "Let's get it over with."

He sighs heavily, as is his custom when unhappy, but goes to Jake's cluttered desk and says, "We have to talk to you. Alone."

Jake turns to me with a triumphant look that conveys more than an "I knew it" or an "I told you so" ever could. He gets up without a word and leads us down the hall to a small conference room. How, I wonder, can an underweight, slightly stooped, sixty-two-year-old body look so formidable? It wouldn't, I suppose, to anyone who didn't know Jake.

He listens to Driscoll's story without interruption, choosing to present a mistreated, hangdog attitude rather than letting his irritation show. Of course he knows that's harder to cope with than anger. When the story ends, Jake stands up and says, "I'll talk to Clarke when he gets in and see what he wants to do."

I breathe easier, thinking we have escaped his wrath, but when his hand is on the doorknob he turns to me and his watery gray eyes are flinty as he says, "Just where do you fit into this?"

"Grady told me about it last night."

Jake looks around at Driscoll.

"I thought you agreed not to tell anybody?"

"I did, but—" The rest of whatever he intended to say is lost in a loud snort from Jake and the sound of the door slamming behind him.

It is evening before I see Driscoll again, this time in the bar at my hotel. He's in a foul mood and decides to vent his anger by criticizing the surroundings. "How can you live in a fleabag like this?" he asks, certain the question will get a rise out of me.

He's right, it does. The Delaware may reek of faded glory, may have reached its prime when Coolidge was in the White House, but a fleabag it is not. Perhaps a beautiful debutante now matured to a gracious dowager, a treasure worthy of love and appreciation. I start to tell him as much but stop after a few words, convinced it is a waste on anyone so crass. Instead I ask, "Have you talked to Staley?"

"Nothing new," he says irritatedly. "No word on the girl, no trace of her car. Would you believe they still haven't put out a bulletin on either one because Martin Clay hasn't given his okay? All Staley's been able to do is talk to the family, a few friends, and a couple of people at the company."

"Doesn't sound like they're too anxious to find her."

"Martin Clay isn't. Well, maybe he is, but he wants it done without publicity."

"I should think it would be past the point where he has any say in the matter."

"So does Staley, and that's what he's telling the chief right now. He's insisting on having a free hand."

"You know, Grady, one way or another the story's got to break tomorrow."

"I know," he agrees without enthusiasm. "So does Staley and he's telling the chief that, too. If he doesn't get the go-ahead, though, and we run the story anyway, I'm still going to be in his doghouse."

Even knowing the power of the Clay family in Midland, it amazes me that it extends this far. When Driscoll leaves again in search of Staley, I review what I know of the Clays and, their rise to omnipotence. The four Clay brothers had a small factory in the South before being lured to Central Indiana in the 1890's by free-flowing natural gas wells that everyone assumed were bottomless, and an abundance of unskilled labor.

Also a cash settlement for relocating in Midland, one of many towns in the area vigorously recruiting industry.

Each brother possessed a separate skill. Howard was an engineer, an innovator, a master craftsman. Rayburn was a bookkeeper and a canny businessman. Lyle, the youngest and the extrovert of the family, could sell almost anything to anyone. Clifford, the soft-spoken eldest brother, inspired trust so people were willing to follow and eager to please. As plant superintendent he had few peers and together the Clays made a formidable team.

At the beginning they manufactured a variety of goods ranging from buggy whips to baby carriages. However, within a few years of their arrival in Midland the area became a hotbed of the emerging automobile industry. Sensing a weak point, Howard designed and perfected a simplified, nearly trouble-free transmission. Soon the other products were forgotten and as competition grew heated in the infant industry, Clay transmissions were featured in fifty models of automobiles.

Midland had a number of successful businessmen and industrialists but by the beginning of the First World War the Clays had moved to the forefront, had become the torch-bearers in every community activity, business and otherwise. They lived by a stern moral code they expected others to follow.

Few did, of course, though many pretended to.

There were children and the sons entered the business, as did the men the daughters married. The firm expanded into other fields but control remained with the family over the years. The temptation to sell stock, to go public, arose many times but was successfully resisted. It became a heated issue when Loyal Clay died in 1977, leaving his two sons as the only blood descendants of the founders in the company, excepting the wives of several executives. Battle lines were drawn, with Martin favoring going public, Orval opposing the idea.

Orval, Melinda's father, prevailed, but when he died unexpectedly six months ago it appeared that the sale of stock in Clay Brothers International was only a matter of time. In thinking it over, though, I realize I have heard nothing on the subject in months.

My contemplation, aided by the martinis placed in front of me at regular intervals, is interrupted by the return of a now-beaming Driscoll. The chief has given Staley a free hand, a bulletin on the car, and the girl has gone out, the secrecy is ended. The frosting on Driscoll's cake is that only an hour remains until *The Morning Sun* deadline and his opponent on the police beat is a rookie who is miles away at the scene of an accident. Under any conditions Driscoll will have the best story and with any luck it will also be the first.

"How do you intend to play it?" I ask.

"Big," he says, chuckling.

"Seriously, Grady. It's still going to be touchy, you know."

Nothing will bring him down off his high. "Look," he says, "it's public knowledge now. If nothing's turned up by morning I'm going to talk to Martin Clay, then Melinda's mother. Maybe they can steer me onto something."

"Handle it wrong and Martin Clay'll steer you on a one-way ride out of town."

He thinks I'm amusing. "Look, Hal, why don't you come along in the morning and do a quick column on the human interest angle while it's fresh?"

"Forget it, Grady. You nearly got me in a mess with Jake and you're not about to get me in one with the Clays."

"No guts, huh? Going to kowtow to the big shots. Afraid of losing your plush job so instead of doing it right you'll sit back and hack out more of that ice cream-social stuff."

I whirl on him, although after four martinis it isn't much of a whirl. "I never wrote about an ice cream social in my life," I tell him. "Okay, I'll go along. And let me tell you, Grady, I'll pack more news into a twenty-inch column than you'll have in a story three times that long."

He slides off his stool, laughing, and leaves a half-full glass of beer behind. Obviously he's serious about this so I decide against one final martini and climb the stairs to my third-floor rooms.

The Morning Sun hasn't a word on Melinda Clay and I feel a little sorry for the new kid on the police beat. Someone will further his education when he reports for work after the *News-Banner* is already on the street. We ride to the headquarters of Clay Brothers International in Driscoll's battered VW beetle, much to my discomfort. "Do you ever clean this thing?' I mutter, trying to touch as little of it as possible with my newest suit, one barely a year old. He ignores me, of course.

Even though Driscoll has called ahead and arranged to see Martin Clay, actually getting inside his office on the top floor is a little like reaching an inner chamber at Fort Knox. Along the way everything is glitter and glare but the president's office itself is all rich mahogany, soft lights, and ankle-deep burgundy carpet.

The man fits the surroundings. At fifty, Martin Clay is trim. Golf course and athletic club trim. A pencil-line mustache above a mouth that seldom smiles and dark hair streaked with silver give him an aura of success and authority. While the face is familiar, it's the first time I've actually seen it. I guess we don't frequent the same establishments.

In a chair at the side of Clay's desk sits a burly, florid-faced man I recognize as Joe Harvey, chief of security for the operation. A former Chicago policeman, Harvey looks like he'd be more at home behind the collection desk at a loan company.

Clay stands up and extends a hand, though not a warm one, but Harvey remains seated, content to raise a few fingers and say, "Hiyuh, boys." One cold fish, I think to myself, and one bully.

What follows is more of a military briefing than an interview. Clay repeats what we already know, in terse, clipped sentences, obviously looking on it as an onerous chore but one best dispensed with as quickly as possible. When he concludes with, "Any questions?" I almost expect him to tell us to synchronize our watches.

Driscoll sits nodding his head for a moment, then hits a nerve by asking, "Why did Melinda come here to see you Monday afternoon?"

Clay's already thin lips all but vanish. After a few seconds of uncomfortable silence he says, "I don't see that that has any bearing on the matter."

"But why did she?" repeats Driscoll. I silently applaud his persistence.

Clay glances at Joe Harvey, who is conveniently examining a fingernail, then turns back to Driscoll and says, "All right, there's no reason not to tell you, but it isn't for publication." Driscoll opens his mouth to tell him otherwise but is too late as Clay continues, "Since her father's death, Melinda thinks she should assume an active role in the company and we discussed the matter again."

"You don't agree?"

"Clay women have remained outside the business from the beginning and I see no reason to change policy now."

"That's kind of out of touch with the times, isn't it?"

The urge to toss Driscoll out on his ear is written all over Martin Clay's face. He musters his restraint, looks pointedly at his watch and says, "If there are no further questions—"

"So Melinda left mad?"

"We weren't in total agreement." As he says it, Clay stands up so Driscoll and I do the same, thank him, and head for the door. My hand is on the knob when Clay says, "Do you intend to talk to my sister-in-law?"

"Right," Driscoll replies.

"Please keep in mind that she's a very distraught woman. I'd prefer that you not disturb her but if you do, be discreet about it."

Joe Harvey, still in his chair, looks at us, his pig-like eyes zeroing in on Driscoll. "Yeah, fellas," he says, "don't come down with the heavy hand."

I open the door and Driscoll follows me out without comment. He's seething, though.

When we're back in the car I say, "Are you going to use that bit about Melinda and her uncle disagreeing?"

Driscoll shifts into second and the VW lurches forward violently. "You'd better believe I'm going to use it!"

I admire his nerve but wonder if he realizes that in Midland, tangling with Martin Clay is as risky as playing with a nest of rattlers. As we travel southeast on Burlington toward the complex of Clay mansions, I decide that he does. I ask myself if I would be equally bold in the same position. As I am not, the answer eludes me.

The red brick Georgian occupied by Lenore Clay is the only one of the huge houses built by the brothers that has ever appealed to me. The others seem oppressive, more like feudal castles than a warm place to go home to at night. Even the grounds are a little too neatly manicured for my taste, although the spacious rear lawns sloping down to the trees lining the river bank are an impressive sight. While they present a far different picture than the rustic scenes of James Whitcomb Riley, somehow on this sunny July morning they make me think of Riley's Indiana.

We are escorted into what I suppose is a drawing room by a man I assume is Morton, the butler. I'm not sure what I expected Lenore Clay to look like, someone more matronly, I guess, but finding her a slim, attractive woman, in her early forties catches me off guard. Her dark brown hair is beautifully coiffed, her tailored suit not something taken from a rack in a Midland department store. Only the vacant look of her hazel eyes and the faint redness of their rims betray the fear she has worked so hard to conceal. For the first time it hits me that when talking of Melinda Clay we are not referring to a cardboard figure but to someone real, someone loved.

I know it has nothing to do with Joe Harvey's warning, but Driscoll questions Lenore gently. He even manages to ask for a photo of the missing girl with tact. When the preliminaries are out of the way he says, "Melinda has never gone off somewhere for a few days without telling you?"

"Never."

"Weren't there times when she was away at school in the East when she was out of touch?"

"Not really. Even then if she was going somewhere for a weekend or just out of town for an evening she'd let me know. We've always been very close, always enjoyed sharing, things. That's why now..."

For a moment I fear she's going to break down but Driscoll skillfully steers her onto another subject by asking, "Does Melinda date regularly, does she have any steady boyfriends?"

"She goes out, of course, but aside from Michael she hasn't seen anyone regularly since that young man last winter, that Joel Black. She met him at one of those protest meetings she's always going to and they went out together for a while. It wasn't a serious relationship and I don't believe she's seen him for months now."

"Protest meetings?"

91

"About nuclear energy, that sort of thing."

"Does this Joel Black live in town?"

"He's doing post-graduate work at the university. I believe Melinda said he has an apartment on West Adams."

"Who's Michael?" I ask, joining in for the first time.

"Michael Clay, Lila's son."

I try to sort out the Clays in my mind. Lila, I recall, is Martin's wife. "Her cousin?" I ask, realizing too late that my surprise shows.

"Not really. Michael is Lila's son, Martin's stepson. His father was killed in an accident before Michael was born and he was just over a year old when Lila and Martin married. Of course everyone thinks of Melinda and Michael as cousins but they aren't."

"And they date?" asks Driscoll.

"Yes, they've been going out frequently the past few months. They grew up almost like brother and sister but I've noticed a subtle change in their relationship recently, although Melinda just laughs when I mention it."

"Michael lives at home?"

"Yes. Since graduating he's been taking his training with the company. All the Clay men do that, you know, start at the bottom and learn every facet of the business."

Driscoll looks at his watch, tells her we must leave, and we do. He hasn't much time to write his story and breaks every traffic law on the way downtown. I stare down at the photo of Melinda he has given me to hold. A pretty girl with the brown hair and hazel eyes of her mother, the easy smile of self-assurance. After a few moments I shake my head and turn toward Driscoll.

"Staley's not going to find her," I say to him. "Not alive, I mean."

He looks at me and nods.

Driscoll's story is low key, less sensational than I expected, but all the facts are there. The only genuine surmising is in my column, a hastily written piece that doesn't turn out the way I intended and leaves me dissatisfied. Jake was at his best, taking copy from both of us right up to the last minute, correlating it so the tail end of my column didn't turn up in Driscoll's story or sidebar, and projecting that aura of haste tempered by coolness that maintains a steady flow and brings out the best in everyone.

The Clays are Midland's aristocracy so people are stunned by the news. For several hours of the afternoon there is a feeling that we have moved back fifty years to the time when newsboys shouted headlines from every downtown corner. The *News-Banner* dispensers are emptied as fast as harried circulation department employees can refill them and outlets around town keep the phones tied up with pleas for more papers. Little else is discussed in the stores, restaurants, and taverns or at the courthouse and city hall. Only down the corridor in the newsroom of *The Morning Sun* is there a stony silence.

Driscoll is exhilarated. He is determined to maintain his edge on the *Sun* staff and continues hot on the trail. In mid-afternoon we knock on the door of Joel Black's apartment and find him home. He admits us reluctantly and I give him a quick appraisal. An average young man but highly strung and with the look of someone always championing a cause, probably a lost one. Driscoll's quick questions make him squirm.

"Look," he says, "I told the police everything I know. Of course I don't really know anything."

"We're just trying to fill in a few gaps," I tell him, trying to sound reassuring. "How long has it been since you've seen Melinda?"

"I'm not sure. A couple of months, maybe longer."

"Why did you break up?" asks Driscoll.

"Break up?" Black echoes. "Look, you've got it wrong. We went out a few times but not on dates. We'd go someplace and talk, that's all."

"About what?"

"Different things. We met at a meeting on nuclear power – the dangers of it – I mean, so we talked about that a lot. Melinda was interested but she wasn't really dedicated. She wasn't serious."

"How about you?"

"About the danger? Yes, I'm very—"

"About Melinda."

Black flushes a little. "Like I said, you've got it wrong. I liked her, sure. I mean I could have liked her a lot, but she wasn't interested that way. Not in me as a person, I mean."

"But you tried to get her interested?" Driscoll presses.

"No. Just once I put my arm around her in the car and she tensed up so I backed off. That's all, honest."

Driscoll's line of questioning has run its course so I say, "Did Melinda talk much about herself? What she enjoyed and what she didn't?"

Black shakes his head slowly.

"How about places? Did she ever mention a favorite city or resort?"

"I don't think so; I don't think she ever got that personal." His face brightens suddenly and he adds, "She did say her family has a place up on Lake Wawasee and she likes to spend time there in the summer."

We learn nothing more from Black.

When we are back at the paper, Driscoll phones Staley and finds he knows about the summer home and it has already been checked out by the Kosciusko County police.

We return, this time in my car, to the office of Clay Brothers International, where Driscoll hopes to see Melinda's cousin, Michael. Or the man everyone thinks of as Melinda's cousin. It's only four o'clock but we find he has left for the day.

On the way out we see a company guard and Driscoll asks if he is James Short, the man who watched Melinda leave forty-eight hours earlier. He is, and he tells us much the same story Driscoll heard from Staley.

"You think she seemed agitated when she left?" I ask him.

Short, one of those men who must work at being muscular half his waking hours and enjoys parading around with a gun, badge, and uniform, leers at me and winks. "You know how those rich broads are, pouty about everything that doesn't suit them. Yeah, she was teed off about something, but she acted that way every time I tried to talk to her. Just a little better than the rest of us, know what I mean?"

In his case I knew. We are interrupted by a similar type who walks up buttoning the coat of his uniform. Short scowls at him, then at the clock on the wall. "Late again," he says. "That's the third time in a row."

"Sorry," the other man replies but it doesn't seem to bother him.

After the changing of the guard, Driscoll makes a phone call from a booth in the lobby, then tells me we are going back to the complex of Clay mansions to see Michael. I begin to wonder if he'll run out of steam in time for me to enjoy the evening.

The massive stone residence of Martin, Lila, and Michael Clay looks as if it leaped out of the pages of a Gothic novel. That's in the late afternoon sunshine, so I try to visualize how it would be at dusk with a fog rising from the river.

Michael waits at the door for us. An almost too-perfect scion of the moneyed class with the unreal handsomeness of a Brooks Brothers model. But there is a tightness about his mouth, a distressed look in his eyes. He stands at least six-four and beside him Driscoll seems squat, tubby, and rumpled. It's almost a social commentary, an illustration of the haves and have-nots, the beautiful and the unsightly, the immaculate and the unkempt.

Along with being too pretty, Michael is too cooperative. In the movies and on TV people are usually nasty to reporters. That seldom is true, but they are a little wary, a little restrained. Michael acts like we are knights who rode up on white chargers. I get the impression he has us confused with the police, thinks we somehow will bring Melinda back to him, but he should be too smart for that.

He starts with the day she was born and tells us more than we want to know, yet tells us nothing. He has turned her to cardboard again but we can't get him stopped long enough to ask a question or two. The truth suddenly dawns on me – he doesn't really know Melinda. The more he talks, the less real she becomes.

At last he pauses for air and Driscoll says, "How long have you been dating her?"

Michael doesn't play coy. "Since late February," he replies. "Of course we've gone places together since we were kids, but that isn't what you mean."

Driscoll nods. "So you just suddenly fell in love?"

That one throws Michael for a loss.. He considers it for a minute, then says, "No, it developed gradually after she came home from college a year ago. Little by little I came to see her differently from before. I'm not sure I recognized what was happening, though, until after the first of the year when she started dating another man and I realized it bothered me."

"Joel Black?"

"Yes." Michael pauses, then chuckles softly. "So I began monopolizing her time."

"Apparently she didn't mind."

Michael gives him a perplexed look, as though the idea had never occurred to him.

"Did you set a date?" Driscoll asks.

Michael shakes his head. "No, but we had an understanding. I told her how I felt but we hadn't made an announcement or anything like that." He chuckles again and says, "Melinda thought I was kidding at first. We've always kidded around a lot."

He doesn't strike me as much of a kidder. I clear my throat and say, "Tell me, did Melinda feel the same way about you?"

His eyes widen in surprise. It's another idea that never occurred to him. He says, "Of course," then thinks it over a little more. "Of course you'd have to know Melinda. She isn't the type to get mushy, anything like that. But there are ways to express love without putting it into words."

"You mean—" Driscoll begins, but Michael raises a hand to stop him. "Oh, no, don't get me wrong," he says, "I wouldn't think of a thing like that with Melinda. Not now, I mean ... you know I'm having a hard time getting across what I mean. People can just share a feeling. You understand, don't you?"

I nod my head, not sure if I do or not. An urge to leave hits me so I look at Driscoll and can see he feels the same way. So apparently Michael is right. Getting away from him and out the door takes another five minutes. His parting words are, "You'll keep me posted, won't you?" and again I wonder if he has us confused with someone else.

As we approach the car, a maroon Mercedes pulls up close behind and a petite woman slides quickly from under the wheel. If Michael exuded an air of money, she exudes one of unbounded wealth. She is deeply tanned and her pale blonde hair didn't come from a bottle, or if it did, someone who knew his job was responsible. Her light summer dress probably cost more than my wardrobe. But her eyes have the warmth of a leopard's and they are fixed on us in a way a headwaiter might view a cockroach on the banquet table.

Lila Clay, I assume. I nod, smile, and say, "Good evening."

"Can I help you with something?" she says, not bothering to smile back.

"We're from the *News-Banner*. We've been talking to Michael Clay."

"I'm Mrs. Clay. Why were you talking to Michael?"

Driscoll doesn't like the inquisition. "About his girlfriend disappearing," he says as bluntly as possible.

She turns on him with fangs showing. "I beg your pardon! Are you speaking of his cousin Melinda?"

"Yes m'am," I say, hoping to avoid open warfare. "But we were led to understand there was more to the relationship than that."

She isn't mollified. If anything, she's angrier. "You'd better understand the truth and understand it well," she says in something close to a snarl, looking at each of us in turn. "Print anything that even hints at something other than their family relationship in that paper of yours and it will cost the owners more than both your salaries if you're there a hundred years."

Her approach is definitely not the one to take with Driscoll. "Now just a second, lady," he says heatedly. "Michael. himself told us—"

"Damn what Michael told you! He tries to tell people what he thinks they want to hear. Now mark what I've said about anything you print."

"What's the fuss, lady?" Driscoll counters. "They aren't even really—"

"That's enough! Don't say any more. Now I want—"

"Mrs. Clay, we're sorry if there's been a misunderstanding," I interject. "Have you any thoughts on where Melinda might be?"

"None, and I don't care to discuss it further. Now if you gentlemen" – she comes down heavy on the word – "will excuse me. And keep what I said well in mind." She turns abruptly and strides toward the house.

"Wow," says Driscoll when she is out of hearing. "Some dame." There is the hint of something approaching admiration in his voice.

I shake my head and open the car door. "And you certainly handled her with your usual diplomacy."

The back room at Horner's is crowded but I am content to sit alone at a table, wanting people around but not wanting to be involved with them. Reviewing the day's events, trying to tie all the interviews neatly together so a picture emerges, proves fruitless. A thought that won't quite come together nags at me, makes me feel I should see something. I don't, but the more I try to bring it into focus the foggier it becomes.

My tormented reverie is shattered by the arrival of a breathless Driscoll. He has forgotten the reporters' old axiom: No matter how big the hurry, always walk the last block so you have enough breath to talk and ask questions. Just enough air remains in his lungs for him to gasp, "They've found the car."

"Where?"

"Midland Mall."

"My God, you mean the police have been looking for twenty-four hours and it's been practically under their noses?"

He pants for a moment, then says, "It was backed into a space near the rear entrance by the theaters. Cars were all around it so you couldn't see the license plate."

"What about last night and early this morning? Cars weren't around it then."

"They were until two a.m. – there was a late show. After that the midnight shift was kept hopping. They didn't get back there again."

I shake my head, thinking it's a pretty flimsy excuse. Shoddy police work. I would bet most of the patrol cars managed to get back to the all-night restaurants a couple of times.

Driscoll has recovered enough to down half a mug of beer at one gulp. He wears a foam mustache as he says, "They've towed it to the police garage and they'll give it a good going over, but there's no sign of violence. Looks like Melinda just parked it and walked away. It's still possible she met somebody there and they went off together for a few days."

"No, it isn't, Grady. That wouldn't fit her pattern. It would be contrary to everything she's ever done. For that matter, there's nothing to prove she parked it there herself, is there?"

"Not yet. Staley has a crew checking out the mall." Driscoll finishes his beer, then gives me a frosty look. "So what do you think happened, smart guy?"

I shrug one shoulder and think about it. "Maybe she met someone, all right, but it wasn't a rendezvous. She may have left with whoever it was, but either she didn't want to or planned to come back in a short time. But hell, Grady, I don't know."

"Then don't be so quick to discount any possibility," he says smugly.

It is late morning when I put the finishing touches on a column for Monday, make a copy, and send it to Jake. When he sees I have finished, Driscoll walks over and says, "I just called Lenore Clay. She gave me the names of Melinda's only close friends in Midland. Two friends and one cousin. Let's grab a bite to eat, then talk to them."

The idea doesn't excite me. Friday afternoon is the time to get serious about starting the weekend revelry, not for worrying about the things that have worried you all week. Nevertheless, after a sandwich at the Backstage Bar I find myself in Driscoll's blue VW again, heading back to Wapahani Drive. He has called ahead so the cousin, Ellen Stevens, is expecting us. She is three years younger than Melinda and lives with her parents in a grim stone product of an architect's nightmare. Reproducing the battlements, the arches, the towers, would cost millions today if anyone was foolish enough to want to.

Ellen is plain and twenty pounds overweight but the Clay bank account probably makes her a beauty in the eyes of ambitious young swains. She's thoughtful, though, and steers us away from the old fortress to a screened summerhouse down at the river bank. A chipmunk, disturbed by our arrival, sits upright on a log and chips at us from deep in his throat. Man and the trouble that follows him seem a world away in this pristine setting.

Driscoll leads the girl through a series of boring questions she couldn't possibly answer unless it were she who engineered Melinda's disappearance. Finally, when I am near the point of dozing off, he says, "What about Melinda and Michael? Were they really serious about each other?"

"Michael may have been," she replies. "Melinda certainly wasn't." All things considered, I suppose it's natural that both are using the past tense.

"You're sure about that?" I ask. "Melinda's mother seems to think otherwise."

She smiles at me, the all-knowing smile of youth. "Aunt Lenore is naive in some ways."

You could have fooled me, I think to myself, but then realize she's referring to the eternal generation gap that prevents a parent from truly understanding a child. And vice versa, of course.

"Well, Michael seems to think otherwise, too," I say a little lamely.

"Michael is out of it," she answers airily. "He decides how things should be, or how he wants them to be, and then that's the way they are. It's funny in a way because up till now it's always worked out for him. He hasn't exactly had obstacles thrown in his path, you know."

A perceptive girl I think, then tell her, "I understand what you mean. His mother would have seen to that."

Ellen sniffs and says, "Aunt Lila still makes him wear, rubbers on a rainy day. She absolutely hovers over him." She giggles and adds, "I'll bet she tucks him in at night."

"She's an overbearing bitch," says Driscoll, and gets up to leave.

"Right on, brother," agrees Ellen, still giggling.

When we are heading toward the northwest part of town where Driscoll has set up a meeting with one of the friends, I groan a little and say, "Grady, why are we wasting what could be an enjoyable afternoon this way?"

He doesn't bother to reply, concentrating instead on guiding the stubby little car to Kenwood, a neighborhood more accustomed to Cadillacs, Continentals, and mammoth station wagons driven by tanned women who all bear a remarkable resemblance to each other. The houses are stately, the streets shaded and winding, and soon Driscoll is lost. After wandering aimlessly a few minutes and passing the same intersection three times from different directions, he finally finds the street he is looking for and pulls into a drive leading to a brick colonial nearly hidden among tall oaks and syca- mores.

Aside from being a few years younger, Lori Johnson is a carbon copy of the women in the station wagons. She is working her way up to their level. Or down, depending upon the point of view. She leads us to a spacious, high-ceilinged living room that doesn't need the air-conditioning that has cooled it to an uncomfortable level. Although the girl is pointedly cordial, something in her manner makes me feel she is well suited to the temperature.

Driscoll begins by asking if she thinks it possible that Melinda has gone off somewhere with a man without bothering to tell anyone. Lori isn't a giggler. She studies him coolly, head to toe and back again, then says, "Obviously you don't know Melinda or you wouldn't waste time on such a question."

Her snippy reply makes Driscoll flush a little. It shouldn't. If Lori Johnson were as smart as she thinks she is, she'd know we have to ask such questions. But no one ever claimed intelligence necessarily goes with money and big houses and fancy cars.

"So what do you think?" I ask her.

She gives me, a similar appraisal, then shrugs. "How should I know? Somebody's murdered her, I suppose."

Her answer probably shouldn't surprise me, but it does. "Why do you say that?" I ask.

"What else could have happened to her?"

"Suppose you're right, any idea who might have done it?"

"Probably one of those sex killers. There are a lot of them around, you know."

I know, but I'm not sure she does. Not many circulate in her crowd. Or drag people kicking and screaming from a crowded mall. "I was thinking more of people who knew her. Any thoughts along that line?"

She shrugs again. "Michael, I guess. Or an older man – I don't know who he was – who was pestering us while Melinda and Tricia Peters and I were having dinner two weeks ago at The Embers. A salesman type, half drunk I think. Tricia and I ignored him but Melinda made the mistake of leading him on, kidding around with him. She enjoyed doing silly things like that."

I'm not sure which of her ideas to pursue first, finally settle on the best and say, "You're sure you don't know who he was?"

"No. I had never seen him before, and haven't since. The manager escorted him away when he saw what was happening."

"Did Melinda mention him later? Did he even know who she was?"

"She didn't mention him. I don't know if he knew who she was but they weren't acquainted and she didn't tell him her name. Even Melinda wouldn't have done that."

Driscoll, unable to contain himself any longer, leans forward and asks, "Why do you think Michael Clay might have killed her?"

The look she gives him indicates she thinks it's another foolish question. "Maybe he finally woke up to the truth. Michael can be such an ass at times, you know. I'm not sure he could have taken it."

"Being rejected, you mean?" I ask.

Her smile reeks of superiority. "For newspapermen, some of your questions are almost infantile." She pauses a moment, then adds, "I suppose I should tell the police about the man at The Embers, don't you?"

"Definitely," I tell her, with a few thoughts about infantile questions.

The Embers is only a few blocks south so we stop on our way downtown. The manager is there, remembers the incident, but doesn't know who the man was and attaches little importance to what happened. "The ladies were at a table near the bar and he had one drink too many and tried to get friendly, that's all. Things like that happen but they don't mean anything."

Maybe, but I'd still like to know who he was. I've had enough for one day, though, and when we are in the car again, I tell Driscoll, "That's it for me. If you're going to see this Tricia Peters, drop me off first."

"We can't," he replies, "she's up at the lakes." He's silent a moment, then says, "Tomorrow's Saturday. Maybe we should drive up."

I snort for an answer. When we get back to the office I don't go inside, just walk down Jackson to the Delaware. But Driscoll is hard to shake and when I go back downstairs after freshening up he's sprawled in a lobby chair.

"Grady," I say, "I'm going in to the dining room to have a martini. Then I'm going to treat myself to a well-done filet. Then a cognac, or maybe two. I'm not even going to think about Melinda Clay."

He follows along anyway. When he's comfortable in a chair at my favorite table he says, "I think we should summarize what we know. Let's hash it out and maybe we'll see something we've overlooked."

"There's nothing to summarize, Grady. Just a hodgepodge of commonplace things in the lives of some very rich and very dull people. If we're going to talk, let's talk baseball."

"The Cubs are looking better."

"The Cubs are in fifth place."

102

"But they're looking better."

"Than what?"

"Than ...Dammit, there's something about this case that bugs me but I can't put my finger on it. You know, Hal..." So we hash it out over martinis. Nothing is accomplished and I insist on calling a halt when the salads arrive.

After my cognac and Driscoll's Irish Mist we head for Horner's, three blocks away. It's the tail end of one of those lingering Indiana twilights that create a glow of contented ambience, a feeling that all is right with the world. For the first time in days I'm mellow and my mind is at rest. Nothing, I'm determined, is going to interfere with my plans for a relaxed, pleasant evening. I think about calling Gloria and . . .Then I see the two huskies in three-piece suits climb out of the car parked across from Horner's and start toward us. Unless they've been at the courthouse, which closed hours ago, strangers dressed that way never show up at Horner's.

"Trouble, Grady," I murmur. "Get inside fast."

Instead he stops and turns to face the pair. Foolishly, I do the same even though they don't look any friendlier at close range.

"Driscoll? Blinn?" one of them asks, knowing beforehand that we are. "Joe Harvey isn't happy with you boys."

"We're not too tickled with him, either," I say, then wish I had bitten my cognac-loosened tongue.

"It's no joking matter," the spokesman says. "Joe tried to find you all afternoon but you were never around. He says he warned you to go easy on bothering the Clays, but you didn't get the message so he wants to make himself perfectly clear. Stay away from them from now on. The Clays aren't used to being laid on by nosy newsies so Joe says no more of it. If you want to talk to any of them again you'll have to clear it first with Joe and he doesn't think that's going to happen. Got that, do you?'

The color has spread from Driscoll's collar until even his scalp is red. He makes a guttural sound; then says, "Tell Joe to go—"

"Hold it, Grady," I tell him, laying a hand on his arm as the second of Harvey's strong-arm boys moves a step closer. I look at the spokesman and say, "We'll pass the word to our editors and see what they think about it."

"Do whatever you want," he replies, grinning but not nicely, "except talk to any of the Clays without clearing it with Joe." He turns and walks toward their car, motioning his stooge to follow.

Even after gulping two shots of Bushmills, Driscoll still quivers with rage. "I just can't believe it," he keeps repeating. "I just can't believe a company like Clay Brothers would send out a goon squad to threaten newsmen."

"Believe it, Grady," I tell him. Yet I agree. Until I learn otherwise, nothing will convince me Martin Clay was behind Harvey's crude approach. He's too smart for such tactics. So I have no problem believing it happened, but a big one understanding why.

Rather than making it more comprehensible, a night's sleep makes it less so. It dawns on me suddenly that if I had the explanation I'd probably have the answer to everything. While I'm figuring out the best way of getting it, the desk clerk enters the dining room to tell me I'm wanted on the phone. I push aside my third cup of coffee, irritated by the interruption.

It's Driscoll, of course. He answers my sharp "Yes?" with a cheery "Good morning, buddy. Grab your swim trunks, we're going to the lakes."

"No, we're not, Grady."

"Yes, we are. I've got a feeling about it."

"So have I and it's very negative."

"I'll pick you up at the entrance on Mulberry in half an hour."

"Grady, I'm not riding that far in your VW so—"

"Fine, you drive. I'll be waiting."

"Grady—" but a click and the dial tone tell me I've been flimflammed. Calling back won't help, he won't answer. I consider letting him stand there on the sidewalk, but then I'd have to spend the day either hiding from him or listening to him harp at me. I kick the leg of the nearest chair, then head upstairs for a jacket and my car keys.

When you say "the lakes" in Midland you mean Tippecanoe, Little Tippy, Barbee, Webster, or, if you can afford it, Wawasee. All are clustered around two little towns ninety miles north, towns like any other little towns around any other lakes. The Clay brothers built summer homes for their families on Wawasee, so going to the lakes became fashionable and has remained so. From April through October the highways are crowded Friday evenings with Midlanders heading north. On Sunday nights they reverse direction. I like to go up myself. About once every ten years to make sure everything's the way I remember it.

When we find the place we're looking for on the west bank of Wawasee, it's a rambling white brick Norman enclosed by a wrought iron fence. Owning it might change my attitude about weekends at the lakes and Tricia Peters' dad would probably let me have it for a few hundred thousand. But then I'd have to buy a cabin cruiser, get a suntan, wear one of those white caps with a black bill and gold piping. Too many complications.

We are there all of two seconds when I realize I will have to do the talking. One glimpse of Tricia and beads of sweat pop out on Driscoll's forehead and upper lip. She has one of those frizzy hairdos, brown eyes the size of quarters, a figure that would send Bo Derek in search of the nearest bar, and a bikini that could be rolled up and not make a bulge in a tight pocket.

It turns out she's easy to talk to, though, but we keep hearing the same old things. Even another giggle when I ask about Melinda and Michael. Then she says, "I ran into them one night at a place in Indianapolis and it was so funny." After another giggle she turns serious. "Actually, it was pathetic, Michael was so attentive and Melinda was so bored with it all. But you know Michael… or do you?"

"We've met him."

"Then you know how seriously he takes himself. Melinda says that's because of the way his mother has always doted on him. He's all right, I like him and all that, but he's always preening and posturing. He's so busy with himself I don't think he understands what's going on around him. He's aware, but unless something's right on the surface he doesn't get the drift."

"Like Melinda not caring for him?"

"Oh, she cared for him, but not in the way he thought."

"How would Michael have reacted if he found out the truth?"

Tricia shakes her frizzles. "I'm not sure. It would have taken him a long time to comprehend, if he ever could."

"What about the man who was annoying Melinda at The Embers a couple of weeks ago?"

"Oh, that wasn't anything. Lori got all uptight, but she's always doing that."

"You don't have any idea who he was?"

105

"No, but I saw him again just last night."

My heart thumps a couple of times. I look at Driscoll and he's reacted the same way. "Where did you see him?" I ask.

"At Henry the Eighth's in North Webster. We were having dinner and I noticed him in the bar."

"Did he approach you?"

"I don't think he even saw me. He was with people. His family, I think."

"Do you go there often?"

"No, it was the first time in two or three years."

"Describe him, will you?"

"Oh, I suppose he's about fifty. Dark hair but gray around the sides. That's about all I remember except he was wearing a funny outfit. Real wild pants with beer cans printed on them and one of those flowery Hawaiian shirts."

"How big a man is he?"

"About the size of Mr. Flynn there,"

"That's Mr. Driscoll. I'm Blinn." So we want to find a short, overweight man in beer-can pants and a flowery shirt. Even at the lakes that shouldn't be hard.

For some illogical reason, castles and palaces are fashionable along North Webster's one commercial street. One is Henry the Eighth's, and like the others it sits incongruously among souvenir shops, barbecue vendors, amusement rides, and a miniature golf course.

The decor is Old English and the bartender is suspicious. He knows whom we are inquiring about but is tight-lipped until Driscoll slips him five dollars. Information comes cheap at the lakes, probably because there is little demand for it. He tells us we're looking for a Denzel Withers, an office supplies salesman from South Bend. He has a cottage on Tippecanoe. The bartender gives us directions and says Withers has been a regular visitor for a dozen years.

He's still wearing the beer-can pants. No one could look less like a man who goes around molesting young women. That doesn't mean much in itself but after talking to him for a couple of minutes I'm ready to cross Withers off the list. He remembers the incident at The Embers and is red-faced while we discuss it. He says he didn't know who Melinda Clay was and seems genuinely shocked to hear she's disappeared. He was in Chicago all day Monday, stayed the night there, and gives us the names of half a dozen people who will verify it.

An hour after saying goodbye to Tricia we're heading south on Indiana 13 toward Midland. I review the morning and decide we've accomplished something in a negative sort of way. When he spots a Jim Dandy in Wabash, Driscoll insists on stopping for a wet tenderloin and strawberry shortcake, which delays us half an hour.

We are five miles north of Marion when we hear the bulletin on a Midland radio station. A woman's body has been found partially submerged in the Mississinewa River about ten miles from Midland.

"That's it," Driscoll says.

I nod, calculating that we are less than forty miles away but will need an hour to get there because of having to drive through Marion. I speed up a little and we ride in silence until we are on a county road that more or less parallels the Mississinewa. Mostly less because it's a river that has a hard time deciding which direction it wants to flow. Luck is with us, though; a county police car is parked at an intersection and Driscoll knows the man standing beside it. He's diverting all but local traffic from the spot where the body was found a few hundred yards away.

Despite him, a crowd has managed to gather. The police have set up a restraining line but we are waved on through. I find a place to park among a couple of dozen cars, most having Midland, state, or county police markings. A dark green one bears the state conservation department emblem. We walk along a freshly made path to the river, being warned twice to stick to it because the underbrush is being combed. We find Staley with a group near the water, but he's deep in conversation.

Joe McAuliffe, the sheriff, sees us and walks over. "The body's been taken away boys," he says, then points to a place to the left of the group and adds, "It was caught on those rocks."

"Melinda Clay?" I ask.

McAuliffe nods his head.

"How was she killed?"

"They're going to do an autopsy, but she was hit on the left side of the head with the proverbial blunt instrument. No other visible wounds, but don't quote me on this. You know how things show up at an autopsy."

"How long had she been dead?" Driscoll asks.

"Don't quote me again, but probably since Monday. It's been pretty warm this week and the body was badly decomposed."

"Who found her?" I ask.

"A fisherman. That guy over there in the striped shirt. She was pretty much out of the water except for her legs and it gave him quite a turn. Tossed his cookies."

"Was she killed here?"

"C'mon, fellas, we're working on that stuff right now. Be patient a while." McAuliffe wipes his face with a handkerchief, struggling in his mind whether to give in to his desire for publicity or to keep quiet in fear of saying something that will be contradicted later and make him look foolish. The Clay family involvement doesn't make his decision easier. After a minute or so he starts walking, motioning in a conspiratorial manner for us to follow. He stops after we go about twenty feet and restrains us with his arm.

"See that?" he says. "That kind of trail leading up to the road? The body was dragged along there. There's bits of clothing caught on briars along the way and a shoe up near the road."

Driscoll bends over and peers at a particle of cloth impaled on a thorn, then straightens up and says, "So she was probably killed somewhere else and the body dumped here."

"That's the way I figure it, too," McAuliffe says. He takes another pass at his ruddy face with the handkerchief, obviously hoping everyone will see it that way. He's stuck with the body, but wants the murder to have taken place in somebody else's jurisdiction.

"Do the pieces of cloth seem to match the clothes she was wearing?" I ask.

"Most do, definitely," McAuliffe answers. "Of course the boys are gathering everything up and it'll be checked out at the state police lab. But you can see with the naked eye that most of it came from the dress she was wearing."

"Any tire marks up by the road?" Driscoll asks.

McAuliffe shakes his head. "Too dry lately."

"I wonder how much Melinda weighed?" I say to no one in particular.

"One-oh-five, according to the description," McAuliffe replies. "No more than that for sure."

A crew of county policemen has been working carefully toward us, placing scraps of cloth in plastic bags. One has been photographing every step. We get out of the way and walk to where the group near the river is breaking up. Staley talks to us a few minutes but doesn't tell us anything we haven't already heard from McAuliffe. He refuses to speculate so we leave after Driscoll tells him about locating the man from The Embers.

It's after four when we get back to town and I'd pass up the nectar of the gods in favor of a cold beer. When we are settled at a table in Horner's back room, Driscoll sighs lamentably. "Saturday afternoon," he says. "The Sun'll have two editions out before our next one. Some luck. What do you think about all of it, Hal?"

The jukebox is playing "Marie" again so I say, "I think this is where I came in." He has no idea what I'm talking about so I tell him, "I want to know why Joe Harvey sent his boys to lean on us. The heavy-handed stuff doesn't make sense." I nod toward the jukebox. "It doesn't ring true any more than it would if Dorsey hit a clinker in his opening solo."

Driscoll straightens up in his chair, interested again. "You're right," he says. "Let's find Martin Clay and ask him about it."

"But what about Joe Harvey's warning?" I say, and we look at each other and laugh.

Martin Clay makes no pretense of being pleased to see us but he is more subdued, less the commanding figure. The events of the week have shaken him and it shows in his face and his voice. He is alone in his library, where we have been led by an elderly housekeeper. She looks as if she has been part of the household since the time when Rayburn Clay himself sat in the worn leather chair near the fireplace and read in the soft glow of the Tiffany lamps that still light the room.

We have agreed that I will lead the conversation. I express our condolences, which Martin dismisses with a curt wave of his hand, but before I can get to the purpose of our visit a door closes in the distance and after a few seconds Lila walks into the room. Her features constrict in hostility when she sees us. Her lips part as if she intends to speak, but close again after she darts a look at her husband. After acknowledging her, I turn back to Martin and say, "Mr. Clay, we appreciate the turmoil your family has been experiencing but were surprised you'd have Joe Harvey warn us off like he did, try to intimidate us into staying away from you and the rest of the family."

He stares at me uncomprehendingly. "What are you talking about?"

"About two of Harvey's goons threatening us last night," Driscoll tells him.

For a moment he looks even more bewildered, then his face hardens and he's the tough executive again. He lifts the receiver of a phone on his desk as he says, "I still don't know what you're talking about but I'll find out in a hurry."

Lila takes a step toward him, her bronzed features yellowish now. "Wait, Martin," she says softly, and then more determinedly, "I had Joe tell them to stay away from the family."

He lowers the phone to its cradle, lets his hand rest on it as he studies her the way a scientist might study an unfamiliar organism under his microscope. A few tense seconds go by, then he shakes his head disbelievingly and says, "You did that, Lila? Why, for God's sake?"

"They were bothering everyone, upsetting people and making nuisances of themselves." Her confidence returns with a vengeance as she gains momentum. "I caught them nosing around here the other day, prying into our affairs and threatening to print malicious lies and gossip. They had Michael so confused he didn't know what he was saying and they used the same tactics with Ellen. They wouldn't even let poor Lenore alone. I decided someone had to look after the interests of the family and told Harvey to do his job and keep them away from us."

"His job ...?" Martin repeats, but doesn't know what to say after that.

The time to get out has arrived, I decide, and say, "We were just curious. No need to trouble you further."

Neither of them responds, or even seems aware of our leaving. It would be interesting to linger in the hallway, hear what Martin says when the explosion comes, but it wouldn't be wise so we keep going. When we are in the car again, Driscoll launches a diatribe but I can see he is a little amused by finding Lila was responsible for Harvey's actions. When his chatter becomes tiring I say, "Any idea where we might find Staley?"

"How about the police station?" he replies sarcastically. It was a foolish question but it served its purpose and he is quiet the rest of the way.

We find Staley behind a mound of papers on his desk. His face, thin under any conditions, is drawn with fatigue and he welcomes the suggestion of a sandwich and cup of coffee. We walk a block to the Delaware and enter the deserted dining room. When we have ordered I ask whether the autopsy has been performed.

Staley nods and says, "If she hadn't been a Clay they wouldn't have done it until Monday. I haven't got the complete report but we were right, cause of death was the blow to the left side of her head. There were other scratches and cuts but all came after death from being dragged through the underbrush."

"Why do you suppose the killer dumped her there?" Driscoll asks him.

"Probably thinking the current would wash the body downstream and we'd never know where it entered the water. The river's low, though, so it only went a few feet and then caught on the rocks."

"The killer must know the area to have picked such an isolated spot," says Driscoll.

"Not necessarily. He could have just driven around the back roads looking for a place and you can see the river from the road along there."

"Any ideas about the weapon?" I ask.

"A bottle in a paper bag," Staley replies. "A fairly large bottle. Traces of the bag and fragments of glass were still in the wound and the liquid stained her dress. They're checking everything at the state police lab and with a little luck we'll know what was in the bottle and which store the bag came from. Or narrow it down to a few, at least, assuming it came from the mall."

"Checking the stores out there hasn't paid off yet?"

"No. Melinda was known in a number of them, but no one saw her Monday and none of her charge cards were used. It's only a guess, but I don't think she ever went inside. Another guess is that she was killed with a wine bottle, and if that proves out it will narrow it down to one drugstore in the mall. Assuming again that it came from there."

Driscoll shoots a knowing look my way. "So you think she met somebody there, right?"

Staley bites into his sandwich and shrugs. "Probably, but it would have been an accidental meeting in my opinion and would have occurred in the parking lot. Of course it could have been prearranged or she could have been forced into a car, but that's unlikely. I think she ran into someone she knew, got into the other person's car, there was an argument and she was killed."

"A spur-of-the-moment murder," I say.

"Right. And that's going on the assumption it took place between the time she left her uncle's office and the time she was due home for supper."

Driscoll, looking owlish, says, "Somebody might have followed her there."

"I've thought of that," Staley replies. "At this point I'm not ruling out any possibility completely."

"Any theories on who killed her?" I ask.

"Not yet, except I think it was someone she knew and thought she had no reason to fear. Right now we're trying to piece the facts and the suppositions together. Maybe after we get the lab reports..."

"I have a theory," I say.

Driscoll turns to me, his mouth opening in surprise, then twisting in a sneer. Staley just stares across the table, waiting for me to go on. I clear my throat a little self-consciously and say, "It's only a hunch, understand, without anything solid to back it up."

At first Driscoll can't decide whether to take me seriously, but as I go on he begins to get a little excited. Staley listens impassively. I conclude by telling him, "Remember, it's based on a different approach from the one you have to follow and hinges on things that were said when you weren't around to hear them."

He sits quietly a few moments, running it back and forth in his mind. Finally he shrugs and says, "Even if you're right, there's nothing I can do about it at this point."

"Yes, there is," I tell him. "Lay it on the line, including what you think the lab reports will show, and I'll bet you get a confession. I think I'm right, Greg."

"Yeah, and if I follow your advice and you're wrong, by the time the Clays finish with me I wouldn't be able to get a job as town marshal in Oakville. I'll sleep on it, but don't count on anything."

When Staley goes back to the station, Driscoll sits nodding his head a while. When he tires of it he says, "You know, it's funny, you coming out with what you did because it's what I've been thinking, too. I didn't say anything because I didn't want Staley thinking I was trying to tell him how to do his job. That was a nice touch, throwing in that about his not being around to hear the things we did."

You never really know what's going on in another person's mind. Maybe Driscoll really had been thinking along the same line.

Sunday has always been a day I could do without. I hate the deserted downtown streets and the feeling that everything is in limbo. More often than not, I don't wander beyond the lobby of the Delaware, where people are coming and going or busy at their jobs. Life goes on in the hotel and I am content to sit back and watch it or ignore it as I choose. Sometimes I read, or even doze, and if the waiter isn't in sight when my glass is empty I ring the little bell on the nearest table. Late in the day, when they have grown bored with whatever they were doing, Driscoll or Granger or Gloria Thompson often drop by and even Jake Richards has been known to walk in purposefully, motion for me to follow, and head for a stool at the bar.

So it comes as no surprise to see Driscoll and Staley entering the revolving door from Jackson Street. I tear a corner from a page of *The Sunday Sun* and slip it between two of those in the book I have been reading. Staley settles in a chair at a right angle to the couch where I'm sitting and Driscoll takes the one beside him. I nod toward the bell but both shake their heads.

"I'm holding a briefing with the Clays at Martin's house," Staley says to me. "It'll be off the record unless I say otherwise, but you're welcome to come along."

"A briefing?" I say, raising an eyebrow. "I didn't know it was police procedure to hold briefings with the victim's family."

"I'm learning lots of new routines on this case."

"Do you mean a briefing or will it be a confrontation?"

"A briefing, at least at the beginning. If it turns into anything more it'll happen of its own volition. Frankly, I don't think it will."

"Then why are you letting us tag along?"

Staley grins just a little. "That's the same question the chief would ask if he knew. I've been thinking about what you said, though, and figure having you there just might jar something loose. But you're to keep your mouths shut unless I give the okay, understood?" I nod and he turns to Driscoll and repeats, "Understood?"

We go in an unmarked police car recognizable on sight to every petty thief, hustler, and con artist in Midland. Painting it in red and white checks wouldn't make it any more so. At such times I focus on the block ahead, watching certain figures fade into doorways and mouths of alleys or turn to stare at a display window suddenly alive with interesting objects.

When we arrive the elderly housekeeper escorts us to a living room where Martin stands posed before a massive stone fireplace. Without a fire it has a menacing look, like some giant mouth ready to devour anyone who ventures too close. Lila and Michael are waiting, too, as is Ellen Stevens and several family members I don't recognize. In a dark corner off to one side of the fireplace sits Joe Harvey. Only Melinda's mother is missing. Ellen waves a hand and smiles tentatively at Driscoll and me, but the others acknowledge our unexpected presence with stony glares.

Michael appears to have spent a sleepless night. His features are wan and tight, his eyes vacant. Lila makes no pretense of being anything but bored and impatient. Martin is an enigma. His manner, his expression, could reflect impatience, too, but more likely it is indignation that the well-ordered routine of the Clays has been shattered by events that to him seem inconceivable. I have the impression he would like to have someone to blame for all this, preferably someone who could be given the sack. Two of the other men, obviously husbands of Clay women, glance at Martin every so often in a way that indicates they are relishing his discomfort.

Staley chooses a chair that has him facing the family, gathered now near the fireplace in a loose semicircle. Driscoll and I take others at his left and slightly behind him. A hush falls over the room and all eyes are fixed on Staley, who clears his throat uncomfortably and begins. He leads them step by step through what has happened, what is still in the process of being checked out, and finally what

114

he believes happened at the mall and his opinion that the lab reports will enable him to find the killer.

A few seconds of silence follow, then Martin says, "But what about suspects and motive? Haven't you made any progress in those areas, don't you have any theories?"

"We feel certain she was killed by someone she knew," Staley replies. "Probably someone she knew quite well and felt she had no reason to fear."

Michael shifts position, grows more attentive. "Why?" he asks.

"Because she apparently got into the killer's car willingly. It's unlikely force was used. She would have been on the passenger's side and wasn't expecting violence, was caught completely off guard. And we don't believe the murder was premeditated. More likely there was a quarrel, a sudden burst of anger, and the blow was struck with the only weapon handy. It adds up to someone Melinda knew quite well and felt safe with."

"But what possible motive could anyone have?" Martin asks testily. "Especially someone who knew her well. It doesn't make sense to me."

"When does murder make sense?" Staley answers. "You're familiar with the usual motives – greed, jealousy, passion, pride, revenge, and so on. Fitting them to this case, greed could be related to business, passion and jealousy to unrequited love, pride to the family name and reputation—"

He is interrupted by one of the men I don't know saying, "Are you implying that a member of the family killed Melinda?"

"I'm not—" but again he is interrupted, this time by Martin's indignant, "By business, I suppose you mean the difference of opinion Melinda and I had about her playing an active role in company management?"

Staley shifts uncomfortably, feeling he is under attack. But it is only the beginning. Lila, her face ashen despite its suntan, rises suddenly and leans toward him, almost tottering. In a near-whisper from deep in her throat she says, "You're accusing Michael, aren't you?"

"Mother—" her son begins, but she cuts him off with a wave of her hand and continues, "You're looking for a scapegoat, someone to arrest just to make yourself look good."

Staley is taken aback. Under other conditions he might be angry, but these are people of power and influence who could hurt him badly. It has gotten out of hand and he doesn't know how to regain control.

The thought flashes through my mind that I should say something in his support, but Driscoll is quicker to respond. He is on his feet, saying in a surprisingly calm yet steely voice, "You're wrong, Mrs. Clay. It's you we think killed Melinda."

They stand facing each other, Driscoll and Lila Clay, while the rest of us sit in stunned silence. The seconds tick away on a Seth Thomas upright. Finally Lila looks to her left at her husband and son, then to her right at the others. Her rage has been triggered and there is an animal wildness in her eyes. She is more than just haughty, proud, and possessive, she is sick of mind.

"Is that what you think?" she says to Driscoll in the same throaty whisper. She glances left and right again and repeats, "Is that what all of you think?"

She is frightening in her fury and no one responds, no one offers the reassuring word that might calm her. Even Driscoll, now that his flare of temper has cooled, is awed by her and remains silent. For a brief moment we are powerless and she is in command. Fortunately she didn't come armed.

It is Lila herself who breaks the spell with a hysterical laugh that in itself is frightening; a sound of madness from deep within some chamber best left unopened. She has begun to tremble and her voice trembles, too, as she says, "Of course I killed her. I did it for you, Michael. I did it for all of you."

The words provide a release and suddenly her rage evaporates. She slumps back down in her chair, still trembling, still ashen, but no longer menacing. Nothing now but a sick, frightened woman, completely alone, even in the midst of those most dear to her. An outcast who has burned her bridges and not so sick that she is unaware of it.

Michael is the first to speak. "You, Mother? You killed Melinda?"

She turns to him, eyes pleading. "You understand, don't you? You could see what she was doing. Chasing you the way she was. So shamelessly. She wasn't thinking about the family, about how it would look to have cousins marry. Can't you imagine what people would have thought, how they would have laughed behind our backs? And it wasn't because she cared about you, you know that. She was just using you. Using you to gain more power in the company. Just ask your father, he'll tell you."

Martin Clay has risen from his chair and stands staring down at her uncomprehendingly. He slowly shakes his head and says, "My God, Lila."

Staley, who either has forgotten such things as the rights of the accused or no longer cares, leans toward her and asks, "Did it happen at the mall, Mrs. Clay?"

For a moment she continues looking at Michael, then turns to Staley and says, "Yes. It was just as you said. I was leaving and saw her get out of her car. I thought it would be a good time to talk to her in private. She went with me to the car, but she wouldn't listen to what I was telling her." She pauses and turns to Michael again. "Melinda laughed at me. She didn't care about you, she thought it was funny."

Her head bows, the fight drained from her. The words are barely audible as she says, "I really don't know what happened then. Something just seemed to pop in my head when she laughed. I don't remember hitting her. The brandy from the bottle was running down my arm and she was dead, that's all. I didn't know what to do so I pushed her down on the floor where no one could see and drove around out in the country, trying to think. Then I saw the river and..."

Staley and Driscoll remain with Lila, Martin, and Michael, but the others drift away, chattering among themselves like a flock of busy sparrows. I go outside, too, filling a pipe and wanting a drink badly.

Ellen Stevens leaves her parents and walks back to where I'm standing. "Was all that true, Mr. Blinn?" she asks. "Did Aunt Lila really believe that about Melinda?"

"Apparently so," I reply, thinking how stilted, how conventional it must sound to her.

"But Mr. Blinn, didn't she know? I thought everybody knew. Melinda didn't keep it a secret."

I stare at her, puzzled. "Keep what a secret?"

Now she is puzzled and returns my stare. "You mean you don't know? Didn't you understand what I was saying? Melinda was a lesbian. She didn't plan to marry anyone, ever. I thought everyone knew but Michael, and I couldn't understand why he didn't."

And that, I realize, is the missing piece. The one thing I couldn't put my finger on even though I was aware of knowing something that wouldn't come into focus.

I look down at Ellen, shaking my head. "You and Lori and Tricia knew. Probably her close friends at school, too. But no one else did, Ellen, none of the older generation. Certainly her mother didn't and I think it would be best not to say anything now, don't you?"

"But if Aunt Lila had known..."

"You're right, of course, but it's too late to think about that now."

She turns and starts toward home again, walking slowly and murmuring, "If I had just said something, Melinda would—"

"Ellen," I call after her and she looks back. "Don't saddle yourself with that."

She stares at me vacantly a moment, then goes on her way.

Driscoll has joined me at the bar in the Delaware and he's unhappy. "The timing was all wrong," he complains. "The *Sun* had the story today about finding the body and in the morning they'll have the one about the arrest."

"Yours will be better," I say consolingly. "Firsthand information is always better."

I have decided to keep what Ellen told me from him, however. Nothing would be gained by mentioning it even though it isn't something he'd use in his story.

Driscoll doesn't want to be comforted. "She'll never stand trial," he says. "I won't even have that to write later."

I can't suppress a chuckle.

"Grady, it's too bad events like this can't be arranged to fit your schedule."

He opens his mouth to retort but instead nods his head, and grins a little.

It is close to midnight when Staley joins us. We take our drinks to a corner table and sit in silence for a few moments. When Staley's glass is empty he sets it down and says, "I'm not taking anything away from you. guys, but we'd have put it together ourselves in a day or two."

"We know that," I tell him. "Our encounters with Lila gave us an edge, plus that dumb trick with Joe Harvey. Like you, we figured

118

it was someone Melinda knew and it had to be someone too small to carry a hundred-pound body from the road to the river instead of dragging it. But it was what we heard about Lila and what we saw of her ourselves that gave me – "I glance at Driscoll "– that gave us a head start."

"You know," says Driscoll, "the whole thing was so stupid when you think about it."

I grin wryly. "More than you realize, friend, more than you realize."

KICKBACK

For weeks now August has been behaving as expected. By mid morning, shimmering heat waves make it appear the flatlands of Central Indiana are submerged in some nebulous substance, close enough to reach out and touch but shying just a little farther away if you try.

Those not fortunate enough to spend their nights in air-conditioned bedrooms toss fitfully between sweat-soaked sheets. Each succeeding day finds tempers growing a little shorter. When keeping cool becomes a luxury, domestic killings and murder among acquaintances flare in neighborhoods unaccustomed to luxury. There the heat truly is murderous.

So I decide to finish my drink and leave quickly when an argument erupts at the next table in the back room of Horner's Tavern. Two men and a lady friend have been consuming pitchers of beer in rapid succession, laughing in boisterous camaraderie. But suddenly one of the men has grown surly and makes threatening noises. The other draws back from him, saying, "Hey, I thought we were friends."

The angry one bangs his mug down on the table. "That was two pitchers ago."

Stifling a chuckle, I take my empty glass and walk out front, find an empty stool at the bar and climb aboard. Too late I discover it is next to one occupied by Clint Mawby. He makes me aware of my mistake with his usual sarcasm. "What an unexpected pleasure," he says. "Joined by a fellow denizen of the fourth estate, that noted purveyor of daily inspiration in 'Around Town with Hal Blinn.'

Tell me, Hal, how often do you get around any part of town beyond staggering distance of your squalid pad in the Delaware Hotel?"

I ignore the question and mumble an unenthusiastic, "Hello, Clint." Unless I make a fast escape, I'm in for another of his harangues. They grow more biting with every swallow of Cutty Sark.

Mawby is a one-man newspaper, publisher of a vitriolic tabloid that once a week attacks every custom, institution, and person of prominence in Midland. Political affiliation offers no protection from his vindictiveness, and he respects no sacred cows. Quite often I agree with what he writes, but I would never admit as much to him.

As might be expected, the daily press ranks near the top of Mawby's hate list. He singles me out as a particularly bad example because I don't load my column with the same inflammatory material that dominates his paper, The Lens. There are times when I do, but not too often and always subtly. A few days of his sledgehammer approach and I'd be down filing an unemployment claim. Of course, he thinks I'm gutless.

He switches to a friendlier tack. It's so unlike him that I grow wary when he says, "I enjoyed your piece on the mayor's padding his staff, taking care of his old buddies. Been spending much time at City Hall lately?"

"No."

"Thought I saw you going in the controller's office the other day."

"I haven't been inside the building in a month or the controller's office in a year." After I've said it he seems relieved, so I decide he's onto something. He must have feared I might be chasing the same story. The News-Banner has a city hall reporter to take care of such things, but he isn't a digger.

We trade banalities awhile in unfamiliar cordiality, then I grow weary of it and tell him I'm ready to turn in. He finishes his drink. "I'll walk out with you. Time to get back to work."

Even at ten the night air is lifeless, superheated. We exchange goodnights, and while I wait on the corner for the light to turn green, he walks west on Main toward his office, in what once was a drive-in restaurant. He hasn't gone more than fifty feet when a sharp report makes me flinch, then turn when I hear a cry of pain. Mawby is slumping to the ground, but my head pivots again as tires squeal and a car speeds away from the curb across the street. I see only the rear, but it's enough to tell it's a late-model Buick sedan.

The driver is alone. The lights aren't on so I can't read the license plate.

I yank open the door of Horner's and yell for someone to call the police and an ambulance. When I get to Mawby, he is writhing on the sidewalk, clutching his left shoulder and moaning softly. The front of his shirt is soaked with blood, so I can't pinpoint the wound. I try to reassure him, tell him help is coming, and at that instant a siren blares as a county ambulance leaves its garage three blocks away. The crowd from Horner's has emptied out onto the sidewalk and gathered round us. A police car glides to a stop, silent but with lights flashing.

Mawby raises his head a few inches, stares at me from panicky eyes, takes hold of my arm with wet fingers, and squeezes hard. "My story," he says in a croaky whisper. "I've got to write my story. Durkee's kickbacks and—" Then he realizes what he's saying and who's listening. No one else can hear and I move aside for two paramedics, who tend him with speedy proficiency.

When I straighten up, someone hands me a towel to wipe my arm. People ask questions but I ignore them, trying to think about Mawby's words. There is no time, though. As the ambulance pulls away, I am hustled into the back seat of the police car. I tell what I know to a man in uniform, then repeat it to two detectives, but I leave out what Mawby said. There hasn't been time to think it through, and the short ride to the police station doesn't provide any. When I leave an hour later, after signing a written statement, I'm still the only one who knows.

The station in City Hall is across the street and less than a block from the Delaware, where I have a drink to settle me down. Then I climb the stairs to my third floor rooms to try to make some sense of the whirlwind events. Of course, "Durkee's kickbacks" are at the center of my thoughts.

Walt Durkee is the city engineer. The job entails a multitude of responsibilities, and some aren't clear to me. Maintenance of streets and city property is the big thing. Along with the city attorney and the controller, the engineer sits on the Board of Public Works and Safety. It runs in my mind that Durkee also has something to do with the Board of Sanitary Commissioners, which reminds me of a favorite saying of city editor Jake Richards: "If you're wanting corruption, get into sewers. You can flush away the evidence, or bury it."

Durkee is a gangly man, about six four, one of those people who seem all arms and legs and whose clothes hang like gunny sacks. He's more of a politician than an engineer and has fed at the public trough for at least half his fifty years. Like most of that breed, he's friendly enough, works one side of the political street vigorously-but keeps as many doors open as possible on the other, and does about six bits' worth of work for every dollar in his paycheck. He has always impressed me as okay as long as you keep in mind the kind of person you're dealing with.

Back trailing Mawby shouldn't be hard, but I'm confused about ethics. Do his words constitute a legitimate lead, or would following up on them be taking advantage of a man when he's down? It would be easy if he dies, but I push aside that line of thinking. There also is the question of whether the police should be told. Probably, and positively if they prove to be his final words. But I'm back to that again so I decide to sleep on it.

The phone jars me awake at six. Steve Granger, the police reporter for the News-Banner, wants details of the shooting, so I repeat the story a little crankily. When he's satisfied, Granger tells me Mawby is in intensive care, listed as critical. "That doesn't mean much," he says. "Everybody in intensive care is considered critical."

"No visitors, right?"

"Just family. He was hit just below the left shoulder. An inch lower and the only visitors would have been at the mortuary."

Trying to get back to sleep doesn't work out. It's too hot, the sheets are sticky, my mind's in gear. I choke on the first acrid taste of cigarette, then walk to the open window next to one with an ancient air conditioner that's so noisy it hasn't been turned on in five years. Downtown is shrouded by a dirty-dishwater haze. A gunman lurks somewhere out there under it, but when the sun burns the mist away he'll still be hidden. Finding him is police business, but I decide that doesn't entitle the police to know what story a newsman is working on. Maybe it's the wrong decision, but I've made it.

From seven thirty to nine every weekday morning, a large round table near the entrance to the hotel dining room is occupied by city

124

officials. When one leaves, it isn't long before another shows up to take his place. With them every morning is Bert Simon, city hall reporter for the News-Banner. He's had the beat ten years and knows it like a cabby knows the city streets. That doesn't offset the fact that he's too cozy with his sources. He's considered one of the boys, which means he settles for handout material. He never asks probing questions unless ordered to by Jake Richards. Of course, Jake knows Simon is in the administration's pocket. His attempts to switch Simon to another beat have always failed, though, because Simon has always gone over his head to ward them off. When Clint Mawby exposes some wrongdoing in The Lens, Simon shrugs it off as unsubstantiated. If it does prove otherwise, if the story becomes a nine-day wonder, Simon pursues it relentlessly and reports details even Mawby missed.

I watch from my favorite table in the corner until the gathering is about to break up, then catch Simon's eye and nod for him to come over. He ambles across the room and slumps down in the chair beside me. "What's the good word, Hal? Heard you had a little excitement last night."

I grind out a cigarette and nod. "Mawby got under somebody's skin. Any idea whose?"

He chuckles. "Could be half the town. Mawby's always had plenty of enemies."

"I hear he's been spending lots of time at City Hall lately."

"No more than usual. He always spends a lot of time at the hall."

"Anything out of the ordinary going on there?"

Simon's bovine expression of innocence doesn't change. Either he's the least curious reporter I've ever encountered or he's a shrewd actor who knows it sometimes pays to keep your eyes averted. "Nothing, Hal," he says. "Not a thing. Just the usual hot weather routine. No one doing a thing they don't have to."

He takes an antique gold watch from a pocket of the vest he refuses to discard despite the heat, flips open the cover, and pushes back his chair. "Gotta go, ol' buddy. The Board of Works is ready to meet."

I drop a quarter under my saucer and say, "I'll tag along."

The Board of Works meets every Wednesday morning in the old city courtroom on the third floor. A cheerless room with too much dark mahogany and dingy yellow walls. Formality is acceptable only in small helpings in a Hoosier city of eighty thousand, so I am greeted with remarks that aren't very funny but call for a grin in response. Eddie Lang, the feisty little city attorney, assumes a look of mock apprehension and says, "Oh-oh, boys, hide the good stuff. That keyhole columnist just walked in."

Walt Durkee quits shuffling papers and glances along the table. "Where's the agenda? Must be something big on tap to get Blinn down here."

Even Sam Whitlow, the less affable city controller, pitches in with, "To what do we owe this honor, Hal?"

I reply in kind, as expected, then look around. A dozen spectators have seated themselves as far from each other as possible. Half are regulars at any public meeting. A watchdog from the League of Women Voters, pen poised above a yellow legal pad on her lap, catches my eye and waves.

Like most governmental meetings, this one is a study in boredom. Maybe that's the idea, make them so dull a citizen seldom comes back for a second dose. When the merciful end finally arrives, I start making the rounds of the offices.

I'm acquainted with many of the people at the Hall, but have few intimates. The Morning Sun mentioned that I witnessed the shooting, so everyone asks for the gory details. A few are genuinely shocked. Most fake it, betrayed by the glint of excitement in their eyes. It's an ideal door-opener, an excuse for me to ask questions about Mawby without raising the subject myself.

It doesn't lead to anything, though, until I run into Min Stivey on her way to a coffee break. I offer to buy and lead her to a small hole in the wall place around the corner on Mulberry, then to a secluded booth. Min is one of the party faithful who drift from office to office, from City Hall to the courthouse and back again, depending on who holds office at any given time. An angelic face hides a satanic mind. She knows everything about everybody and is always willing to deny them the benefit of the doubt. Angelically, of course.

She devours every detail of the shooting, which I embellish in the telling. A few of the embellishments are prefaced with, "I haven't told this to anyone, but. . ." Min reacts with feigned horror, straining toward me to get every word on the recorder whirring in her mind. Later it will be edited and further embellished.

Then I switch tactics, become the bumbling outsider lost in the intricacies of city government. A bewildered guy searching for a helping hand, knowing Min's is reaching out. Knowing, too, that she believes most of what she tells me won't be remembered or even comprehended. Without the Min Stiveys of the world, a newsman's life would be much harder.

I lead her through a few decoy questions, then say,"Mawby was spending a lot of time at City Hall lately. I've been wondering why, but nobody seems to know."

Min makes a sniffing sound. "That's not hard to figure out. He and Luella Rachline have a thing going."

"Who?"

"Luella Rachline in the controller's office. That gawky bookkeeper with the thick ankles and droopy eyes. A real sweet kid."

"But Mawby's married."

Min smiles pityingly. "Oh, Hal. So is Luella, but when did that ever stop certain people? Take it from me, they're a hot item."

"You mean really..."

"I mean really."

I mull it over on the walk back to City Hall, three stories of art deco in ivory-toned brick. People have been saying for years that Clint Mawby gets many of his stories in bed. It could be, so I head for the controller's office. Luella Rachline must have been waiting for me because she comes from behind the counter when I walk in and leads me down a hall to a cubbyhole stockroom.

After shutting the door she leans back against it, both hands behind her. There's a sick look in her eyes but they don't droop and she must have had her ankles fixed since Min last saw her. She asks, "Have you heard any news about Clint?"

I repeat what Granger told me, then answer her questions about the shooting. "Was he conscious?" she asks. "Did he say anything?"

"He told me he was working on a story about kickbacks involving Walt Durkee. I think he wanted me to follow up on it, but the ambulance crew interrupted us before he could finish. That's why I came to see you. I understand you and Clint are close."

Her face reddens a little, but she doesn't say anything. "I think he'd want you to fill me in on what's going on."

She shakes her head. "I don't. That wouldn't be like Clint."

I give her one more chance. "If the story doesn't come out, whoever shot him may try again."

Her head keeps shaking. "Unless Clint tells me ... "

Fat chance, I think. But without meaning to, she's confirmed that I'm on the right track.

A couple of tedious hours sifting through contracts, purchase orders, payment vouchers, and whatever other records I lay hands on makes me wonder if I wouldn't have been better off in some other part of town when Mawby was shot. Then something looks familiar and I backtrack until I find it again in slightly different form. Suddenly the first step is clear, the one that opened the door to the kickbacks.

Under Indiana law, any purchase or project costing fifteen thousand dollars or more must be put out for bids. Certain department heads, in this case the city engineer, can award purchases or contracts for minor jobs without going through that lengthy procedure. Otherwise even fewer potholes would get filled than is the case, which is few enough.

So certain local firms or contractors supply goods or services that may not amount to much individually but can add up to a hefty sum over a year's time. If it's handled at all fairly, there's nothing wrong with the system because it keeps things moving. But when contracts for the same project are awarded piecemeal, it's obvious someone is out to circumvent the law. In the case I've come across, Walt Durkee contracted with Bessemer Construction Company to repair a bridge in three stages, each costing fourteen thousand nine hundred and fifty dollars. Joe Bessemer's outfit had repaired the east end, then the middle, then the west.

A little additional digging reveals more of the same on street projects, all involving Bessemer. I haven't covered everything when I quit after writing down sixteen jobs totaling two hundred and four thousand dollars. It doesn't prove kickbacks were involved, but you'd have to be pretty naive to believe otherwise.

A rumble from within tells me lunchtime has come and gone, so I walk to Horner's for a bowl of spicy chili and a beer. Then I cross the street to the News-Banner and hack out a quick column. A real potboiler using whatever material came in the mail along with a few comments on the heat. Granger wanders in while I'm at it and tells me Mawby's condition is stable. His wife and a high school kid who helps him at times have finished the job of pasting up pages, so The Lens will appear on schedule.

That makes me wonder if Mawby intended to write the kickback story last night and run it this week. Or was it still incomplete? I go back to Horner's to try to think everything through, wishing for once that Grady Driscoll was around rather than off somewhere on vacation. Just like him, I think to myself, to leave town right at the time I need a colleague willing and able to kick ideas back and forth across the table. His shoot-from-the-hip attitude can be annoying, but we have a knack for clearing each other's heads.

Jake Richards is at the bar when I walk in so I tap him on the shoulder and say, "I need to talk, Jake. Come on in back and I'll buy you a beer."

He turns and looks at me from watery, red-streaked eyes.

"Dammit, Hal, I don't want another beer. It's time to go home and fix supper."

"Come on, Jake, it's important."

He sighs long and piteously, but eases the skinny body that has seen sixty-two years' hard service off the stool, clutches the small of his back and groans, then follows along, muttering under his breath. When we are settled, he glances around the empty tabletop and says, "Well, where the hell's the beer?"

I go back out front and get a couple, then tell him the whole story, including the questions in my mind. He frowns now and then, shakes his head a few times, gives an exasperated snort every so often. When I finish, he says, "My God, but you've got a muddled brain."

"In what way?"

"First, Mawby himself gave away what he's working on, so that puts it up for grabs. Second, he was going to write it last night so it would have been in The Lens tomorrow. That means a week's grace but we can't wait that long because somebody else might get wind of it. Third, it should be Bert Simon's story but he won't do anything with it, so you go ahead. But it's page one stuff, not column material. Fourth, it's not the business of the police to know what story a reporter is working on."

He pauses a moment, then says, "Well, in this case maybe it is their business, but let Mawby tell 'em if he wants to, which he won't."

I sit nodding my head while he empties his glass. "The kickback story is the big one, Hal, but you need proof. Talk to that woman again, whatever her name is, and get it. Without the kickback angle, the cheating on bids is drab stuff.

"Finding out who shot Mawby is secondary. If you should come up with something, tell that cop friend of yours about it, but for God's sake, try to do it on our time, not The Morning Sun's. As I see it, the gunman could have been Walt Durkee, that contractor Joe Bessemer, somebody one or both hired to do the job, or a party unknown who has nothing to do with the kickback story."

He stares at his empty glass almost wistfully so I reach for it, but he shakes his head and gets up. "I'm going home and fix supper. Honest to God, Hal, I can't figure out what your problem was."

Neither can I, now. Except that none of this really fits in with the way I had planned to spend the next few days. But like it or not, I'm stuck with it. And Jake was wrong, Greg Staley is Driscoll's cop friend. I just know him.

By chance I run into him when I stop in the Backstage Bar on the way to the hotel for dinner. "You're not working on the Mawby shooting, are you?" I ask him.

"No, Hanley and Caproletti are on it. Did you know they found the car? An '81 Buick stolen from a factory parking lot, then returned before the owner got off work at midnight. He reported it anyway because he knew somebody had driven it. The seat was closer to the wheel than he keeps it, and he had filled the tank and set the trip odometer on his way to the plant, but instead of one mile it had gone seven."

"Sounds like it was a spotted car, one a pro had on his list for safe use during a given time."

"Right, but from what I've heard it wasn't a professional job. The guy was too quick on the trigger. A pro would have taken his time and done it right, and he would have used a silencer. The whole thing was amateurish, aside from using a safe car."

So scratch the idea of a hired killer. Unless Durkee or Joe Bessemer found a dumb one or talked a friend into doing the job, which isn't likely.

During dinner I try to think of a way to talk to Luella Rachline again without waiting till morning. I give up on it after deciding I can't very well knock on the door while she and her husband are watching TV and say I want to discuss the affair she's having with Clint Mawby. But it does give me a tool to apply a little pressure with.

After coffee, I walk back to the paper and into the library. The file on Durkee is bulky and I skim over it quickly. Bessemer's is light. All stuff related to business and most of it about his activities in a contractors' organization and the East Side Kiwanis Club.

The Rachlines' is even skimpier, just a pair of clips. One tells of her being named a party secretary two years ago. The other is an announcement of her husband Clifford's being promoted to production superintendent at Clay Brothers International, a transmission plant at the east end of town and Midland's largest industry. That one's dated 1977.

I cross the hall to the newsroom, eerie in its nighttime loneliness. Beyond the wall The Morning Sun crew is in high gear. That only adds to my feeling of being in a mausoleum. After a couple of puffs on a cigarette I grind it out, dissatisfied, but without a cure in mind. A few lethargic moments pass, then I get out the phone book and jot down four numbers. No one answers at any of them. I didn't have a real plan, was just going to wing it, so I don't care because at least I tried.

Gusts of wind are scattering debris when I leave the building, stinging my eyes with particles too small to see but big enough to feel. An empty beer can clatters along the sidewalk. The air carries the scent of a prairie storm, and as I turn west onto Main, the horizon flashes yellow and white and thunder rumbles in the distance.

I lean into the blow and quicken my pace. When I get to the corner, the lights are on in the old drive-in that now is The Lens. Mawby's wife, or a woman I assume is his wife, bends over a desk in the second window.

I bang my fist against the metal door, get no response, so keep at it until it swings back abruptly and the woman stands scowling out at me. She's big, both in stature and because she's carrying twenty pounds too many. Her sandy hair is tousled, her print housedress dusty and wrinkled. Yet an animal attractiveness emanates from her, hard to define but magnetic. Even her impatient scowl and harsh "Yes?" don't diminish it.

I'm not sure why I've come, so I hesitate. While I'm trying to frame some lame excuse, her features relax and she says, "You're

Hal Blinn. I know you from your picture. Ought to, it's in the Banner every day." She steps aside and motions me in.

I follow her through a small outer office and into another that's not much bigger and is amazingly cluttered. I don't have to be told it's the one where her husband does his writing. Beyond it is a large room with upright racks for pasting up pages, tall stacks of back issues of The Lens, and library tables piled high with tools of the trade and plain junk. Among other things, Clint Mawby is a pack rat.

She pours two cups of coffee from an urn and hands me one without asking. She sips from the other, eyeing me all the while.

"Well?"

"Any news of your husband, Mrs. Mawby?"

"He'll live. And the name's Fern. Now, what's really on your mind?"

I grin a little. "Maybe I just wanted to be neighborly, Fern. See if everything's going okay."

"Maybe pigs fly after dark."

"Not a Hoosier, are you? New York? New England?"

"Try New Jersey. Sniffing around after the story Clint was working on, aren't you? Don't try to con me into believing otherwise; my dad was a reporter so I've been around your kind all my life. Sorry, but I can't help. The white knight in dirty linen doesn't let me in on his escapades, business or personal."

"I don't really know Clint very well, but I learned a few things today."

She looks at the window, where the first big drops of rain splatter against the glass. She's tough, but not as tough as she pretends to be. Something more than the shooting is bothering her. I have an idea she needs somebody to talk to, but I would bet there aren't many of that kind in her life. I'm not much help when it comes to that, but I say, "Problems, huh?"

"Everybody's got 'em," she says, shrugging. Then she smiles at me, a warm smile tinged with hurt. "Relax, Hal, I'm not going to unload my troubles. Clint's just Clint. Getting shot isn't going to change that. He could have been a good newspaperman, a good man in general, if he didn't have this constant need to prove something to himself."

"Maybe it's that way with all crusaders."

"And philanderers."

"So you know about that?"

"I've always known, every time. I quit caring a long time back. It's just been a silent, unspoken part of our lives until last week. Then there was a phone call and, to coin a fresh new phrase, it was the last straw."

"A call tipping you off?"

"Uh-huh. One of those 'You don't know me but . . .' calls. Anonymous, of course. Having her put it into words woke me up, though. I just decided that's it." She laughs without warning and, in a cheerier tone, says, "Hey, I said I wasn't going to tell you my troubles. Really, now, did you have something in mind when you came down here?"

I shake my head. "Look, if you'd like a drink ..."

She runs a hand across her hair, looks down at herself, and shakes her head, too. "Thanks, but not tonight. Now if you ask again in a few days ..."

I tell her I will, and when I'm back on the street again, realize I meant it. The rain didn't amount to much but left even more humidity in its wake. I try a couple of the phone numbers again when I get to the newsroom, still get no answer and decide to call it a night. On the way to the hotel I wonder how much real trouble is caused by the Min Stivey types.

I'm waiting when Luella Rachline walks into the lobby at City Hall in the morning. I fall into step beside her, tell her I think we'd better have a cup of coffee, and am a little surprised when she agrees without argument. We start for the hole in the wall on Mulberry, but I change my mind and lead her to the hotel so we can have more privacy.

The time has passed for the gentle approach, which didn't work anyway, so when the waitress leaves I get right to it. I tell her I have the kickback story worked out and she has three choices: tell me what she knows, tell the police and prosecutor, or find herself playing a major role in a cover-up story.

She surprises me a second time by saying, "I'd already decided to tell you if you came back again."

"Smart idea. Go right ahead."

"You know where the engineer's office is and those two little storerooms just to the north of it?"

"I don't recall the storerooms, but go on."

"Well, the engineer uses one of them but the controller's office keeps old records stored in the other. I think they used to be part of the same office because there was a window or just an open space connecting them and it's been covered with plywood. It doesn't fit tightly any more, so you can see part of the other room from the controller's side. I was looking for something up there one day when Walt Durkee and Joe Bessemer went into the other room."

"How did you know it was them?"

Lowering her eyes, she blushes and says, "I peeked. I was quiet, so they didn't know I was there. They talked about different jobs and Durkee told Bessemer he would get a couple of good ones that are coming up. Then Bessemer handed him an envelope and said, 'Here's the rest of your twenty for Elm Street.'

"I thought he meant twenty dollars but Durkee opened the envelope and took out a thick bundle of large bills. Then I realized what was going on. Bessemer had meant twenty percent. So I told Clint. He did a lot of checking and the story was going to be in The Lens today."

Even using my arithmetic it doesn't take long to figure that twenty percent of two hundred and four thousand means more than forty thousand dollars in Durkee's pocket. Tax free, and there could be more.

I ask her, "Did Durkee and Bessemer know Mawby was working on the story?"

"I don't know. Clint was digging into things for several days, though, and I know he talked to Durkee a couple of times."

"Does your husband know about you and Mawby?"

The color drains from her face. "Good heavens, no. And it's finished, I swear. He doesn't have to be told about it, does he?"

"I don't know, Luella. Who can tell where this will lead?"

"No one, I guess," she answers softly.

It's mid-afternoon by the time I finish combing the records again. This time I make sure I have everything and carry it back three years. The next step is talking to Durkee and Bessemer, if they have anything to say, but it will have to wait until late evening or early morning when the danger of The Morning Sun's picking up on it is past.

There won't be time to write a column so I pull one from my reserve bank and file it for tomorrow. That will make two dogs in a row, but it can't be helped. Then I go ahead and write the kickback story so all I'll have to do in the morning is add the comments of Durkee and Bessemer, or their "no comment." When it's finished, I stash it safely away.

After dinner I go upstairs and dial Durkee's home number, figuring it's too late for The Morning Sun to do anything. His wife answers and tells me he's at a meeting of the party central committee and won't be home till late. "That's the third night this week," she says testily.

"What were the others?" I ask, suddenly curious.

"Monday he was in Indianapolis for an engineers meeting, Tuesday he was out late at a planning commission meeting."

I thank her and dial Joe Bessemer's number. "He isn't available. Can I help you?" his wife says. I tell her who I am and ask when she expects him home. "Not until Sunday, Mr. Blinn. He's at a convention of contractors in St. Louis."

"How long has he been there?"

"He left last Sunday morning."

I make another call to verify that Durkee was at the planning commission Tuesday night, find he was there until ten thirty. Then I go downstairs to the bar and think about it over a drink. Halfway through it I walk out to the lobby and buy a News-Banner, read Granger's follow-up on the shooting again, and confirm that the car was stolen from the lot at Clay Brothers Plant One.

Then I try to remember where my own car is. When I do, I walk a couple of blocks to where I left it Tuesday afternoon, nearly fifty-five hours ago. It's there, parked next to a one-hour parking sign. Without a ticket.

Luella Rachline is at the central committee meeting – I have made sure of that – so her husband comes to the door after my first ring. Instead of the rangy, rugged type I'm expecting, Rachline is well under six feet, weighs one-fifty tops, combs his thinning hair carefully to cover as much area as possible, and still has a necktie on and neatly knotted at ten o'clock at night. He peers at me through wire-rimmed bifocals. The News-Banner trails toward the floor from his left hand and my photo stares out at me from the upper corner.

"Yes?" he says, then quickly adds, "You're Hal Blinn, aren't you?"

I tell him I am and ask if I can talk to him a minute. He leads me to a living room so neat it seems no one really lives there. I wonder where in the world I'm going to begin. For some reason, confronting this meek little man has thrown me off stride, makes me wonder if I'm making a big mistake. Again I wish Driscoll hadn't left town when he did. He's better than I am at this sort of thing. It's not my style, but I decide his blunt approach is the only one to use.

Rachline has offered me a chair a few feet from his own, so I sit on the edge and lean toward him. "Mr. Rachline, I know you shot Clint Mawby."

He blinks a couple of times, nothing more, and says, "Why do you think that?"

"Last week you got an anonymous phone call telling you what was going on between Mawby and your wife. You probably checked it out because you don't impress me as a man who'd go off half-cocked. You felt compelled to do something, but at the same time you didn't want to upset the routine of your lifestyle.

"Then you did some further checking on Mawby, found he always works late Tuesday nights, pasting up pages to take to the printer the next day. You decided that would be the time to take your revenge. I think you planned to drive up, shoot him through the window, and then go on, but something changed your mind. Anyway, you didn't want to risk using your own car so you took one from the plant parking lot, one you knew wouldn't be missed till the shift ended."

His expression doesn't change as I spell it out for him. He quietly measures me a moment, almost smiling from one side of his mouth. At the same time he tamps tobacco into a pipe from a glass humidor on the table beside his chair. When it's filled, he searches his pockets for a match, doesn't find one, and pulls open a drawer in the table. Rather than coming out with a match, though, his hand holds a gun.

When it's only a few feet from your nose, the bore of a .38 looks awfully big. The tableau – Man with Gun and a Fool – goes on with neither sound nor movement far too long to suit

136

me. Finally Rachline says, "I had no intention of shooting Mawby from outside the window. I was going inside to tell him who I was and just why he was going to die. That was very important to me."

"What changed your mind?"

"Circumstances. I parked down the street, which seemed the safe thing to do, planning to walk the rest of the way. When I got to the corner, though, he was locking the door, and then he came toward me. He passed no more than a foot away and even nodded to me."

Recalling it seems to upset him, so he pauses a moment. "I've never been involved in anything like this, Mr. Blinn. I was girded to go inside, but having him come out that way unnerved me, I'm afraid. I turned and watched him go into that bar across the street from where I had parked; then I went back to the car and waited. He was in there nearly an hour. Apparently I'm not cut out for this sort of thing because the longer he remained inside, the more tense I became. When he finally came out, I just picked up the gun and fired."

"Did you intend to kill your wife, too?"

He looks surprised. "No, of course not." He adds, "But now I'm afraid you've given me no choice but to kill you."

"Don't be a sap, Rachline. I'm surprised the police haven't been here already, and you can bet they will be before much longer. Mawby's going to live, so you don't even face a murder charge."

"That isn't the important thing. Whatever the charge, my life would be over. I'm really sorry, Mr. Blinn, but I'm going to have to do it."

"Look, Rachline, under the circumstances why don't you stop calling me mister? So where do you intend to shoot me, here in your living room?"

"No, that wouldn't do at all. I think we'd better go some-where in your car." He motions with the gun for me to walk to the door.

For a few seconds I consider just leaning back in the chair, maybe throwing him off stride again, but decide it's not such a hot idea. He's already on his feet so I get up, too, and start edging toward the door sideways, still facing him.

He really isn't good at this sort of thing. No more than a yard separates us, and the hand with the gun is extended toward

137

me. As often as I've seen it done in the movies, I still have qualms about trying it myself, but I lash out and knock his arm down and away from me, then grab his arm with one hand and the gun with the other. The struggle is brief and probably would be comic on the screen. Just as I wrest the gun from him, he uses his free hand to crown me with something very solid.

I drop to my knees, conscious but with an eight-martini feeling inside my head. I stay there, mouth open like a bird that found a sheet of glass in its flight path, until a car starts near by. Then I risk moving and discover it's still possible. Not comfortable, but possible. Rachline is gone, which suits me, so I look around for a phone and eventually discover it under the hand I'm using for support. Trying to remember whom I intended to call comes next. When I do, I feel quite pleased with myself and catch sight of my reflection smirking at me from a large mirror. On the third try I hit the nine-one-one buttons in the right order, then slur a few sentences into the mouthpiece.

I'm only vaguely aware of being driven back downtown in my own car and have a dim recollection of winning an argument with a policeman about going to the hospital. Once I'm seated across a desk from Greg Staley, things begin to clear a little. I look at my watch and smile because The Morning Sun deadline has passed.

I had insisted on talking to Staley. In the middle of explaining everything to him we are interrupted by another detective, Caproletti. "Rachline's on his way in," he says. "He flagged down a state police car out on 1-69 and gave himself up. Said he decided there was no place to run to."

Caproletti sticks around to hear the rest of my story. Every so often he and Staley look at each other and make clucking sounds about withholding evidence. But when we've finished, Staley walks me across the street to the hotel and buys a genuine martini for me.

In the morning I add two lines to my story: "unavailable for comment" for Bessemer and "no comment" for Durkee. Bert Simon writes a sidebar with comments from the mayor and a little political analysis. Granger does the story on Rachline's arrest. Jake grouses about having too much local copy to deal with, but no one is taken in. He's really beaming, it just looks like a scowl.

By evening, dull gray clouds have moved in from the west, and it has begun to cool off. I'm alone at a table in Horner's back room, debating whether to call Fern Mawby to see if she's ready for that drink, when Driscoll walks in. He's wearing a green-striped sport shirt with matching shorts and his face is sunburned.

"You look like a tomato on top of a watermelon," I tell him, but he ignores it. When he's settled with a beer and a Bushmills in front of him, he says, "Anything happen while I've been gone?"

So I tell him. He pretends it isn't very interesting, but I can tell he's mad because he missed the fun. When I finish, he yawns and says, "Probably nothing will come of it."

"Nothing come of it?" I begin ticking things off. "Mawby's in the hospital, shot. Mad, too, because he missed his big story. His wife, Fern, is filing for divorce. Walt Durkee has resigned. The grand jury convenes Tuesday to take up the kickbacks involving him and Joe Bessemer. Clifford Rachline's in jail for attempted murder. His wife Luella has quit her job, quit her position with the party, and gone into seclusion. Nothing come of it!"

I add, "Oh, yes, and Bert Simon got a note from the publisher praising his in-depth analysis in his sidebar."

Driscoll leans back in his chair and stretches noisily, then looks at his watch and yawns again. "So what else you been doin' while I was gone?"

THE TOWN CLUB MURDERS

To enter the tavern you climb six concrete steps worn smooth by the comings and goings of countless pairs of feet. Once inside, there is little enticement to remain. On the street or in the building you feel that air of weariness that is as much a part of any factory district bar as the neon beer sign in the window.

That's under favorable circumstances. Now, on a dank September night when fog hides the wilted stalks of corn and decrepit industrial areas on the flatlands of central Indiana, it is bathed in a misty red that doesn't come from the Budweiser emblem over the back bar. Someone armed with a sawed-off shotgun has used it on a man and woman seated in a booth to demonstrate why they call it a scatter gun.

I turn away after one look, revolted. So does Greg Staley. He pulls a handkerchief from his pocket, wiping his face with it as he says, "No matter how much you see of this kind of thing, you never get used to it."

Then, because he is a detective and it is his job, he turns again for a closer look. I walk back to where four men with parchment faces stand huddled together near the front of the bar. The tavern's aptly named *The Before and After*, a place to buy a drink so you can face up to another day in the sweat-shop, and another drink when you have gotten through it. Or two or five.

"What happened?" I ask, taking my notebook from a side pocket of the worn corduroy jacket I have decided should be good for one more season of cold weather. At the time I bought it, corduroy was the cheapest material on the racks. Now it has become fashionable, and replacing the jacket would cost more than I normally pay for a suit. It doesn't matter; no one trusts a well-dressed newspaperman.

The men look at each other, each waiting for someone else to answer my question. Finally one of them, from appearances the bartender, says, "You're Hal Blinn, right?"

I nod, so he says, "I didn't know you covered this kinda thing."

"I don't," I tell him. "I was at the police station when the call came in and tagged along. What happened here?"

Suddenly everyone is eager to talk. "They was just sittin' there when this guy comes in and cuts loose," says a man with the gaunt look and penetrating eyes of a young John Carradine on the midnight movie.

"Right," agrees another, nodding a round head that rests on wide shoulders without much neck between. "Never says a word, just walks back to 'em and blasts away. He was wearin' one of them masks ... wha'd'ya call 'em?"

"A ski mask," says the most intelligent looking of the quartet. "Black or navy blue with two white stripes. He did say something, though, just before he pulled the trigger. Just a few words so low you couldn't hear them up at the bar, and I was sitting just a few stools away."

No-neck turns a skeptical eye toward him. "I didn't hear nothin.'"

The other, a rangy man with a face weathered by year-round sun and wind, smiles patiently. "He wasn't talking to you, Joe. He didn't mean for you to hear."

"Oh," replies No-neck, accepting the explanation.

I look at the weathered man and say, "What happened after he shot them?"

Before he can respond, the bartender says, "He just turned and walked back out. Calm as could be, like nothin' had happened."

"Nobody tried to stop him?"

"It was too fast," the weathered man replies. "Too much of a shock. By the time any of us reacted, he was gone."

I nod, understanding how it must have been. I move my head toward the booth where Staley and two other detectives are still busy and say, "Does anybody know who they were?"

Heads shake and the bartender says, "They come in a few times in the past but kept to themselves, never said nothin' to nobody I can recall." As an afterthought he adds, "'Cept to order

142

drinks, but they never drunk much and mostly stuck around only about an hour."

Staley walks over, frowning at me. He doesn't say anything, but he is obviously displeased because I have been interrogating witnesses before he has had the opportunity. I step back a little, not feeling guilty but preferring to avoid annoying him more than necessary. As I do so, the front door is opened by the patrolman stationed there and Steve Granger, the *News-Banner* police reporter, walks in.

He is surprised to see me and unless I misread his reaction, not happy about it. If he thinks I am crossing his beat, he should know better. I greet him coolly but then take him aside and give him what information I have gathered. He is welcome to it. I want nothing more than a fast trip back uptown, a warm bar, and a tall drink.

The lobby of the old Delaware Hotel is crowded when I walk in. A meeting has just broken up, and politicians are everywhere. Under the best of conditions I want as little to do with them as possible. The present circumstances make the glad-handing and boisterous talk more than I can stomach, and the thought of seeking refuge in my third-floor rooms crosses my mind. But I want a drink and this is my home, so I refuse to let them take it over. I head for the bar, nodding curtly to those who greet me and refusing to allow anyone to swerve me from my course.

It conies as no surprise to find Driscoll lounging on a stool, a glass of Bushmills in front of him. He is the *News-Banner*'s court reporter, and ordinarily I enjoy his company. I am keyed up, though, and say, "What are you doing here, Grady?"

He glances around, feigning bewilderment. "It's a public place, isn't it?"

He is at the hotel because I have not turned up at Horner's Tavern. Trying to tell him there are times when a person feels like being alone would be a waste of breath, so I sag down on the stool beside him and give the bartender a signal he has come to know means a double martini on the rocks.

Driscoll recognizes the other signals I am giving off and pumps me until he has all the lurid details. Still he wants more, and nothing short of the killer's name, motive, and whereabouts will satisfy him. I grow surly and soon he is belligerent. "I know," he growls, "you just want to hold the details for 'Around Town with

Hal Blinn.' You think that column of yours is the first thing people turn to. Well let me tell you something, big shot, that doesn't—"

"Oh, shut up, Grady," I tell him, relaxed by his predictable outburst. Driscoll is angry, the world is back to normal.

Two days pass without an arrest being made. The victims were a Daniel Collins and Roberta Dillard. Both had nicknames. Collins' was "Red" and it appeared in the newspapers. The woman's was "Anytime Roberta," and it didn't. They were married, but not to each other, and had been meeting clandestinely for several months. Collins worked on the shipping and receiving dock at the wire mill, was a union steward, had three kids ranging from seven to seventeen. Anytime Roberta was a daylight waitress at a downtown Greek restaurant and the mother of two teenage children, each born to separate previous marriages. Her latest husband is a stun man at the meatpacking plant and both exes live in Midland. The obvious motive has leaped to all minds, and no one seems much interested or concerned.

Steve Granger comes into the backroom of Horner's while I am having a late lunch of hot chili and beer, pulls out a chair, and calls to Jack Horner to bring him the same. When my bowl is empty I say, "Where does the investigation stand?"

"Right where it began. They've questioned the woman's husband three times, but his alibi is solid as a rock."

"Maybe he hired someone to do it. Or what about the man's wife? Maybe she hired someone."

Granger looks up from his chili, a quizzical expression on his face. "Why does it matter to you?"

"Well, it wasn't the most pleasant sight I've seen lately. Aren't you a little curious about the reason for it?"

"Not really. Somebody's always getting shot in a south side bar."

Driscoll has come in and immediately takes the offensive. "That's the trouble with you, Granger. You've been on the police beat so long you're starting to act like a cop. Somebody gets blown away in a south side bar, so who cares, right? Keep it on the other side of the tracks and nobody's going to get too excited."

Granger goes on eating, undismayed by Driscoll's outburst. He has been on the receiving end of such tirades before and won't allow anything so commonplace to interfere with his lunch. Driscoll turns away in disgust, unable to comprehend anyone willing to pass up the opportunity for a good argument.

I crumple up my paper napkin and toss it in the empty bowl, then walk out front and pay the check. People, it seems to me, have been at their worst the past few days, and I have had enough of them. For the first time since childhood I feel an urge to go to the zoo in search of more compatible creatures. But a zoo is just one of many things not to be found in Midland so I settle for going back to the newsroom, which comes closer to being a zoo than anything else available.

When I leave at five o'clock I have had the place to myself for two hours, but that hasn't inspired any desire for company. The evening sun has the pale glow of autumn and is pleasantly warm as I walk two blocks east on Jackson to the Delaware. After checking the mail and as usual finding the box empty, I go to my favorite table in a quiet corner of the dining room without first taking the time to climb the stairs to my rooms.

I am halfway through my second before-dinner martini when Granger and Staley come in together. Granger walks over when he sees me. "Another murder," he says a little excitedly. "Do you know Fletcher Stout?"

"No, but I know who he is." Everyone in Midland knows who he is because Fletcher Stout is president of The Commercial Bank and Trust Company, a member of numerous boards, one of those men involved in every do-good project that comes along if it offers the chance to have your picture in the paper.

"Somebody shot him from a car as he was leaving the country club," Granger continues. "Right on the front steps with half a dozen people around, but not one of them got a look at the killer. One of the bystanders took a bullet in the leg, though."

"An epidemic," I say halfheartedly. "An epidemic of murder in Midland."

"Believe me, this one is going to shake up the town. Fletcher Stout, it's hard to believe."

"Why is it hard to believe?"

He looks at me as a teacher might look at a not-too-bright first grader. "Come on, Hal, a prominent citizen killed on the front steps of the country club. Things like that just don't happen."

Without intending to, I laugh. Not because someone has been murdered but because Granger's reaction is so out of phase with his response to the murders at *The Before and After*. I say, "Then Driscoll was right, keep it on the south side. God help us when it spreads to the country club."

Granger curls one side of his mouth and shakes his head pityingly. He thinks I have had one drink too many and walks away without saying more. I am not sorry to be rid of him.

He was right, of course. The citizenry is outraged. I hear his words repeated a dozen times or more after Midland awakens to *The Morning Sun's* account of the murder – things like this just don't happen. Murder in New York or Chicago or south of Conrail's tracks is to be expected, but not among the nice people of Midland. They have forgotten, because it is convenient to forget such things, that only two months ago murder struck the town's leading family.

Driscoll also reacts predictably. I find him having a Hoosier lunch of ham and beans with cornbread at the Green Door. He looks up as I pull out a chair at his table and says, "So help me, if you start in on how terrible it is about Fletcher Stout, I'll slug you. That's all I've heard all morning."

"Then you disagree?"

"I don't necessarily disagree, I'm just sick of hearing about it. How many people did you hear talking about the murders the other night?"

"You didn't expect anything different, did you? One is acceptable, one isn't. Murder at the country club isn't looked on as being the same as murder at the town club."

For a moment he looks puzzled, then he grins. "That's pretty good. You ought to use that in your column. Compare the reactions, and don't forget to say that after Stout was killed the police dumped the town club murders in the bottom desk drawer."

It isn't a bad idea. After thinking it over I decide to follow up on it, and I try to recall another of Driscoll's suggestions I have ever put to use. None comes to mind.

There are times when a newspaperman, particularly a columnist, can judge the quality of his work by the number of people he has made angry, and who those people are. Using that as a criterion, Driscoll's idea was sensational. The *News-Banner* has been on the street no more than two hours the following

146

afternoon when Granger stalks into the newsroom, livid. The people of authority at the police department, particularly Greg Staley, reacted with fury to my suggestion that Stout's murder is receiving more attention than the others. Although he had nothing to do with it, Granger bore the brunt of their wrath because he was handy. He passes it along to me in a way that leaves little doubt he sides with them.

I have hit on the truth, but Staley and the others do not see it as the truth. Perhaps they do deep in their subconscious thoughts but will not allow the realization to surface. But when I leave the building and see a uniformed patrolman I know, he winks and says, "Goring the right oxen again, huh, Hal?"

Of course Driscoll is elated when I join him at Horner's. Jake Richards, who has been city editor longer than the two of us together have been in the business, listens without comment as we discuss the reaction to the column. He sits bent over the table because years of bending over a desk reading copy have rounded his thin shoulders and given him a stoop that never goes away. A stranger seeing the frayed coat two sizes too large that hangs on him like something a farmer might drape over a scarecrow, the watery gray eyes that shine now after several beers, the outdated necktie twisted to one side of his collar, probably would put Jake down as a man of little consequence. That stranger would be wrong.

When Driscoll and I quiet down, Jake settles his eyes on me and says, "Mind you, Hal, I'm not saying you're wrong. In fact, I know you're right, and it's a thing that needs pointing out now and then. But don't forget – and this goes for you, too, Grady – that along with calling attention to a thing we may know isn't right, it's our job to tell people all we can about what it is that interests them. Right now they're interested in the murder of Fletcher Stout more than anything else, and don't think the police aren't aware of that, whether anyone down at the City Hall will admit it or not. So you might say they're doing the same thing we are, giving the people what they want."

I get as far as, "I know, Jake, but—"before he raises a hand for silence.

"What you're going to say, Hal, is that it still isn't right and the murders of a couple of obscure people are just as important as the murder of a prominent citizen at the front door of the country club. And you're right, your town club

147

murders as you called them are every bit as important. And it's funny but I've seen it before and it could be that way in this case that over the long haul they'll have a lot greater effect on people and on the town than the other one. But right now that doesn't change things, so we're going to keep playing the Stout murder and the police are going to keep concentrating their efforts on it. Nothing's going to alter that."

He's right, but then he nearly always is. Driscoll knows it, too, and neither of us says anything. Jake finishes his beer and gets up, mumbling something about going home and fixing supper, then going to bed. I know he's usually in bed at his apartment by seven because he's out on the street at three in the morning. But sometimes when I look at his frail body I wonder if he really bothers about the supper he is always going to fix.

Driscoll sits quietly after Jake has gone, a dour expression on his face. Then he nods determinedly and turns to me, suddenly alert again. "Let's see what we can dig up on your town club murders," he says.

I return his stare, but mine lacks his enthusiasm. "Such as what, Grady? And then what will we do with it?"

He shrugs away my questions. "Let's talk to the widow and widower, see where it leads us."

"I know exactly where it will lead us and it's not where I want to go. I'm going to drive out to *The Bird* and treat myself to the biggest steak in the place, a carafe of burgundy, then a cognac or maybe two, and the longest, fattest Garcia & Vega I can lay hands on."

"Fine, it's right on the way," he replies, pushing his chair back and standing up. "I'll drive, but we'll hold off on the cognac till later."

"Now wait a minute, Grady," I protest, but he is halfway to the door, so I sigh and reluctantly follow.

The meal is not at all what I had in mind. Driscoll talks constantly, getting more and more wound up as he goes along. As usual he gulps his food, then watches every forkful on its way to my mouth, checking his watch between bites. Before I can finish chewing the last one, he is ushering me out the door. We cut south on Batavia, cross the tracks, and within five minutes have parked in front of the Widow Collins' house on West Eighth in the part of town they call Avondale.

If Hettie Collins feels any joy at seeing us, she does a remarkable job of concealing it. Her first words are, "that paper of yours was all wrong about them things you said about Red. He hadn't been meetin' no woman regular like it said, especially that one. I have a good mind to—"

"You knew Roberta Dillard?" Driscoll interjects.

She makes a contemptuous sound. "No, I never knowed her. What give you that idea?"

"The way you said it—"

"I meant Red never had no truck with that kinda woman. He had what he wanted right here at home."

"Uh, Mrs. Collins," I say after seeing the neighbor to the right come out to sweep the nearest side of her porch, "why don't we step inside for a minute so you can tell us a little about your husband. How did he spend his free time?"

She stands aside and motions with her head. Without bothering to offer us chairs she says, "Red never really had no free time. When he wasn't workin' he was busy with union business. 'Course he bowled and went fishin' some, things like that, and had a beer with the boys now and then. Not our boys, I mean the guys he worked with."

"Did he have any enemies?" Driscoll asks, then gets the customary answer, of course.

"Who were his closest friends?" I ask her.

She gives a little shrug, turning the ends of her mouth down at the same time in a way that doesn't do a thing for her looks, which aren't too hot to begin with. A hairdresser, a little less makeup, losing thirty pounds wouldn't hurt her a bit. She thinks about my question a moment, then says, "Prit near everybody Red worked with was his friend, and lotsa others, too. I guess you could say Ed Dubravitz and Tommy Cline was his bes' friends, though."

We don't stay long and when we are cramped into Driscoll's old VW beetle again I say, "Well, are you satisfied? Can you tell me one thing we learned from that?"

He turns a scathing look on me and shifts gears violently. "What were you expecting, that she'd tell us the name of the killer?"

Across town on the far east side of Midland is a neighborhood of small frame houses the developer had the audacity to label ranch style. Standard equipment at each is four kids, two dogs, a pickup truck, at least one car that hasn't run for more than a year, and a couple that have but shouldn't. Running north and south the blocks seem endless because the developer didn't want to use land for anything that wouldn't put money in his pocket. In the middle of one of them is the house Roberta Dillard won't be coming back to any more.

Fred Dillard is doubled under the raised hood of the inevitable pickup, parked inside a lighted garage because darkness has settled quickly. He straightens up at our footsteps, a bear of a man although no more than five ten. His arms and chest, exposed by an unbuttoned flannel shirt, are covered with black hair that matches an unruly shock half covering his ears and almost meeting a pair of shaggy eyebrows. He scowls at us and says, "Wha'd'ya want?"

I tell him who we are before Driscoll can say something antagonizing, then ask, "Can we talk to you a minute about your wife?"

"What about her?" he growls from deep in his diaphragm.

"Any idea who killed her?" Driscoll asks without giving me a chance to lead up to it gently.

"No. Why should I?"

"Well, what we've heard is—"

I dig an elbow into Driscoll's side and say, "What we've heard is that in cases like this an ex-husband or old boyfriend often is involved. Did Roberta have any contacts like that?"

"You mean they come knockin' on the door invitin' themselves to supper, no. How do I know what she done when I ain't around?"

"Any ideas at all about what happened?"

He taps the long crescent wrench in his hand against the other palm. "Why don't you just come out and ask if I done it?"

"Did you?" asks Driscoll.

"No," he answers, his voice surprisingly subdued. "No matter what ya heard, Bertie was okay." He stares down at the floor a few seconds, and when he raises his head, moisture glistens in his eyes. Even more quietly he says, "I loved that woman." Then in more of a growl again, "I don't have no idea what happened and maybe it's just as well I don't."

150

I murmur an apology for disturbing him and lead Driscoll away, convinced we will learn nothing. Back in the car I say, "He didn't do it and he didn't get somebody else to do it. Scratch that thought."

A nod is Driscoll's only reply. When we are back on East Jackson headed for town, he says, "Let's talk to Molinari next."

"Grady, the one I want to talk to next is the bartender at the Delaware. Who the devil is Molinari, anyway?"

"The ex-husband. Her first ex."

I sigh quietly, wishing I had driven. But the Molinari house on Beacon Street is dark and my spirits lift until Driscoll says, "We'll try Beckett."

"I suppose Beckett is the second ex-husband. Grady, how do you remember these people and where they live?"

"Looked 'em up and wrote 'em down."

"When?"

"At Horner's before you came in. I figured we'd do some checking."

I scrunch as far down in the seat as I can, sighing again.

Lights blaze in the Beckett house on Royale, a street in the northwest part of town. As I grudgingly twist my way out of the underdeveloped car, Driscoll says, "Either this guy has come up in the world since he dumped Roberta or she took a big step downward."

I think of several reasons why he could be wrong but forget about them when the front door opens before we get to it. A tall man in a white shirt with sleeves rolled once and necktie loose at the collar is highlighted by the light behind him. He says, "Hi, I'm Bob Beckett," grinning broadly as he says it.

The affability seems premature, and I wonder if he's running for public office. But in Indiana "Hi" means "How are you?" and the correct response is "Fine" so I say, "Fine. We're from the *News-Banner*. This is Grady Driscoll and I'm Hal—"

"I know who you are. Recognized you from the picture every night." He swings the storm door aside and motions us in. "What can I do for you? How about a cuppa coffee or a drink?"

Driscoll and I look at each other, then shake our heads in unison. The man has to know why we're here, I think to myself, so why the old-buddy routine? He even anticipates that question, although I wasn't going to ask it, and says, "It's about Roberta, isn't it? A real tragedy. I'm all cut up about it. Greg Staley was out yesterday talking about it."

"You know Lieutenant Staley, do you?" Driscoll asks, as turned off as I am by Beckett's charm.

"No, not before yesterday. A nice guy. Sharp. Real sharp. But you want to know, my thoughts on Roberta's death, right?"

"Right, and—"

"I have no idea who would want to kill her. In fact I'm certain in my own mind that the man was the target and Roberta was the innocent victim."

"From what we hear she wasn't so innocent," Driscoll says.

Beckett smiles magnanimously. "Come now, gentlemen, are any of us really in a position to judge the actions of another? Roberta may have had her faults, but who doesn't?"

"Then why did you divorce her?" I ask.

"Divorce her?" he says, raising his eyebrows. "I didn't divorce her, she divorced me."

When we are back in the car I say, "Chalk one up for Roberta. Anybody'd divorce a guy like that couldn't have been all bad."

Driscoll sits without moving for a moment, then starts the engine. "Amen. Buddy, we need a drink after that. Let's head back to Horner's."

I sigh again, contentedly this time. "No. Make it the hotel."

The usual crowd has gathered for morning coffee at the Backstage Bar. Only Driscoll is missing.

I am curious about his absence but don't say anything. Granger announces that the police are close to making an arrest in the Stout case but chooses to remain secretive concerning details. Gloria Thompson is cheerful again after nearly a month of lamenting the opening of the schools. Now the initial crises are past, a routine has been established, her beat is under control, and she has remembered how to smile.

She has grown impatient with Granger's heavy-handedness, the smugness he doesn't attempt to hide because his beat makes him privy to information unknown to the rest of us. She uses a small mirror in applying fresh lipstick, makes a smacking sound when satisfied with the result, then says, "I hear Fletcher Stout wasn't as goody-goody as he pretended to be."

Granger casts a skeptical glance in her direction but I say, "What have you heard?"

"That he wasn't above a little playing around on the side. Only with women in his own circle, though, not with us commoners. I understand he scored pretty well with the country club gals, including the wives of some of his so-called best friends."

"Where did you hear that?" Granger asks, scowling at her.

She makes a pixyish face and says, "I have my sources," then gets up and walks out, leaving Granger glaring after her. I wonder for a while if she's really heard anything or was just baiting him, but don't come to a conclusion.

I linger on after the others, not ready to start on a column but without anything else in mind for the morning. While I'm contemplating a fourth cup of coffee, Driscoll bursts in the front door as he always does, making heads turn to see if someone is in pursuit. He has a self-satisfied look and there is the usual air of excitement about him.

"Where have you been?" I ask.

"It's my day off, remember?"

"Why would I?"

"Let's get rolling, and wait'll you hear what I've come up with."

"What do you mean, get rolling?"

"We've got people to check out. And get this, Roberta Dillard had another boyfriend along with Collins. His name's Lee Tierney and he worked on the loading dock with Collins."

I motion to the waitress and hold up my cup, determined not to rush into the street with him. As she refills mine and pours a fresh cup for Driscoll I ask, "Where did you find this out?"

"From Molinari."

"Let's see, Molinari is the first ex-husband, right? So how did you happen to be talking to him?"

"I went out to the house early, before he left for work. He's a clerk in the shipping office at the wire mill, and that's how Roberta got to know both Collins and Tierney. She'd stop by to see him at work once in a while, something about child support."

I shift around in my chair, trying to get rid of the heartburn that has come on suddenly. When it eases I say, "That's some place out there. More action than any singles bar in town."

Driscoll gulps his coffee in three swallows. "Molinari looks clean to me. Remarried and has two kids by the second wife. Swears the only times he's seen Roberta since the divorce were about child support. Guess she was always after him for something extra."

"So he says so, that doesn't make it true. By the way, I looked up Beckett in the city directory. Mr. Wonderful sells real estate."

"Forget him," Driscoll says assertively. "Molinari, too. Neither of them had anything to do with it."

"You know that for sure, do you?"

He nods and says, "Let's go, we've got a lot of ground to cover."

"Don't forget I've got a column to write. Where are we going, to the wire mill?"

"Not yet. We're going to see Tommy Cline." He sees my puzzled look and adds, "One of the friends Mrs. Collins told us about."

Cline is daytime bartender at a place called Stretch's Tavern far out on East Main. I don't bother asking Driscoll how he tracked him down. A few men I assume are part of Midland's growing number of unemployed sit scattered around the long and dark room, drinking beer in heavy-hearted solitude.

The man we have come to see is about forty, heavy around the waist and jowls, friendly enough but not really communicative. Short answers to questions tell us little we didn't already know. Cline has kind words for Collins but doesn't portray him as the saint his wife described. The police have not talked to him, however. Perhaps Mrs. Collins neglected to tell them about Tommy Cline, or they may not have gotten to him yet.

I decide we are wasting time and by way of parting say, "So you can't think of anyone with a reason to kill Collins? He didn't have any enemies?"

Cline begins wiping the bar mechanically, looking up and down it to see if anyone is within hearing. Satisfied no one is, he says, "Red didn't have what you would call enemies, but sometimes there was trouble with people at work. Union business mostly. He was a steward and you know how the boys sometimes get heated up over things. Once in a while they get to arguing in here, and Red was never one to sit on the sidelines. He took the union very seriously."

"Who specifically did he have trouble with?"

Cline rubs his jaw contemplatively, then laughs tersely. "If you call that trouble, just about everybody at the mill, one time or another. You know how it gets when they're heated up. It's not exactly a meeting of the board of directors, but I don't think you could call it trouble."

"So you can't think of anyone in particular he didn't get along with?" I ask.

"No, but I'm not really part of it, understand. Why don't you ask Ed Dubravitz? He and Red were buddies and worked together out on the dock."

Driscoll says, "That's where we're headed," and starts for the door.

The wire mill is a collection of shabby brick buildings, most dating back to the turn of the century. It stands close to the river and is enclosed by a high link fence with rusted barbed wire on top. Not a good advertisement for the product, I think to myself, although not certain they manufacture it. How we will get to the loading dock concerns me. It turns out, though, that no one pays attention to our presence, and we have the run of the place.

The first person we ask points out Dubravitz as a rangy but muscular man in navy stocking cap and flannel shirt at the far end of the dock. When we introduce ourselves, he turns on a broad smile, revealing perfect rows of sparkling teeth, and gives each of us a bone-crushing handshake. But there is an almost mocking glint to his eyes, a look I can't quite fathom, and I decide he isn't a man I would care to tangle with.

Dubravitz leads us to a secluded spot a short distance inside the building, cocks one leg over a packing case, then answers our questions in precise phrases that indicate he hasn't spent his entire life at manual labor. He strikes me as an enigma, a man who would interest me even had we met under other circumstances and one whose background I would like to know more about.

After the usual preliminaries Driscoll asks, "Who do you know that might have had a reason to kill Collins?"

"A reason or a desire?"

155

"Either or both."

"Then you think it was Red the killer was after?"

"We don't know," I tell him. "What do you think?"

"From what I've read in the papers and heard around, I would have bet on the woman. But a lot of people didn't like Red. He was abrasive and could be bullheaded once his mind was made up. If somebody had picked up a crowbar on the dock and done the job, that I could understand. But what happened wasn't a flash of anger, it was cold-blooded, calculated well in advance. Whoever did it had plenty of opportunities to change his mind along the way."

"Know anyone with the personality to fit?" Driscoll asks.

Dubravitz stares out over the dock for a moment to where a large truck is maneuvering for position. He grins, or smirks, because the driver has all but jackknifed the rig. Then he turns back to us and says, "Check Vie Russo."

"Who's Vie Russo?" I ask.

"He worked here a few years but was fired two months ago for drinking on the job. Red was his steward so he wanted him to intervene. Russo thought the union should get his job back, but Red didn't agree."

"And they fought?" I ask.

"They didn't fight, not physically, but some hot words were exchanged a few times. Russo would wait outside the gate at quitting time and they'd go at it. The last time he told Red he'd get him, but that was six weeks ago and to my knowledge they didn't see each other after that."

"So what makes you think it might have been him?"

"His nature," Dubravitz replies. "Russo is your classic loner. A brooding, taciturn man."

"What about Lee Tierney?" asks Driscoll.

Dubravitz stares at him a second or two, then puts his head back and laughs. "Who told you about Tierney? Tierney is a big, not-too-bright guy who is gentle as a pup and practically worshipped Red because Red was good to him. Tierney is the one person I know who you can cross off your list and be sure you're not making a mistake."

"I heard he ran around with Roberta Dillard, too."

Dubravitz laughs again. "Tierney? Once, and that was all, he met her in the parking lot across the street because Red was

156

tied up and asked him to. Tierney drove her to Stretch's to wait for Red and somebody saw them and jumped to the wrong conclusion." He motions with his head toward the office where Molinari has his desk. "And I'll bet I can tell you who it was."

"Have you told the police about Russo?" I ask.

"The police haven't talked to me. They were out here the day after and talked to a few people, but not me." He looks at his watch and says, "I've got to get back to work."

We thank him and start to walk away but he calls after us. "You forgot to ask me one question," he says, flashing his white teeth again.

"What's that?" I ask.

"Where I was the night of the murders."

He turns away without saying more, but in doing so rolls his cap down so it is a navy blue ski mask with a single white stripe. Although I can't see his face, I can visualize the smirk.

It is after eleven, the morning has slipped away. Knowing I have a column to write, Driscoll points the snout of his ugly little car toward town and we ride a few blocks without either of us speaking. Then Driscoll says, "That Dubravitz is a strange bird."

"An intriguing one, I'd call him. I'd like to know more about him. Who he really is, what he did before the loading dock."

"Think he might have killed his buddy?"

"It wasn't his style. He would have done it when he and Collins were alone somewhere. With provocation I think he'd kill, but it would be a personal thing with him and he wouldn't involve anyone else. That's my opinion, anyway."

Driscoll mulls it over, then says, "Agreed. We'd better look up this Russo. Meet me at Horner's about two."

I sense the excitement when I walk into the newsroom. Everyone is busy, so I stop at Jake's desk. "What's going on?" I ask but he doesn't look up from the copy he's reading on a screen, just waves a hand and tells me to go do something.

Gloria has been watching and now she grins, so I go to her desk and repeat the question. "They arrested Stout's killer," she replies.

"That's what I figured. Who is it?"

"Remember that little auto parts store that used to be out on Granville, the one that never had much in it? The owner, a man named Hastings, he killed Stout."

"Why?"

"He blamed Stout when the business went under. He thinks Stout was responsible for his loan application being turned down."

"Doesn't seem like much of a motive. Things like that happen every day."

"Yes, but this Hastings has been a hothead all his life. I don't know any of the details, though, so you'll have to ask Granger or wait till the paper comes out."

She goes back to whatever it is she's writing, but I have learned as much as I need to know. I comprehend it but don't understand it. Had it been a jealous husband as Gloria hinted earlier, it still would make no real sense, but this seems preposterous. Of course, deliberately making a bad situation worse always is.

Fortunately I have several letters that will help me hack out a frivolous column, the kind readers seem to enjoy more than something with a little meat to it. At times that is the most discouraging feature of the business. Now, however, I am glad to do a fluff piece that can be gotten out of the way quickly and requires little thought or effort.

I arrive at Horner's well before the appointed time, but find Driscoll waiting impatiently. He has come up with a. little information on Vie Russo, including his address and, although I can't at first imagine how he knows, the fact that the police plan to question him later in the afternoon. I ask and he tells me he had lunch with Greg Staley. As a result he also learned all the details of the arrest in the Stout case and passes them along while watching me hurry through a bowl of chili.

I insist on driving this time. Once we are headed for Russo's house in a sparsely settled area in the southwest part of town I say, "Won't Staley be teed off when he finds out you've jumped in ahead of him? He's already mad at me, you know."

Driscoll shrugs. "He didn't tell me not to. I told him we might drive out that way."

"I imagine he thought you meant after he'd been there."

Driscoll looks at me and grins.

Russo lives in an old frame bungalow, the type popular in the 1920's. It is the only house along a winding unpaved street, a monument to an untimely dream called Prairie View Addition that died aborning on Black Friday in October of 1929. Someone puts in a lot of hours keeping the house and yard immaculate, but it seems a little incongruous, sitting alone as it does among the scrub growth and weeds.

As we pull up, a woman carrying a folded canvas shopping bag descends the five wooden steps from the porch, then walks across the grass to an old Granada parked in the driveway behind an even older Firebird. She dallies when she sees us, obviously a bit suspicious but not wanting to show it. Like the property, she is well-preserved. Somehow I feel certain she moved into the house as a little girl when it was brand new and has lived there ever since.

Driscoll is out of the car ahead of me. By the time I get to where they are standing he has turned and headed toward the house. The woman smiles tentatively and I return it the same way, then follow Driscoll. She has aroused my curiosity so while Driscoll pounds on the door I watch her drive away, then ask him if he found out who she is. "Russo's mother," he replies just before the door opens.

Vie Russo carries muscle on his five ten frame, but his complexion is pasty and dark pouches hang loosely below pale eyes that size us up with unconcealed distrust. He is no more than thirty-five, probably younger than that, and I would bet you could use your fingers and a few toes to count the number of times he has smiled during those years.

He stands motionless and silent as Driscoll tells him who we are and asks if we can talk inside. Then he pushes the screen door open a few inches, turns away, and nods for us to follow. Driscoll raises a brow as our eyes meet and I respond with a shrug, then lead him on through a living room that is the width of the house. It opens only into a dining room separated from it by a wide arch. Russo has continued on down a hall with doors to two bedrooms and a bath standing ajar at the left. The hall ends at a kitchen with a back porch beyond. Russo has halted beside a round table that occupies most of the space not taken by appliances, cupboards, and a sink.

He nods toward the two chairs at the table, then gets a third for himself from the porch and places it so he sits with his back toward the door. On one shelf of a door-less cupboard to his right is a loaded revolver, a stubby .38 Colt Detective Special. I glance around as unobtrusively as possible and am relieved at not seeing a shotgun.

A half-empty coffee cup is on the table in front of me, and Russo reaches for it, studying me as he does so, then sips from it before saying, "So wha'd'ya want?"

"We hear you didn't get along with Red Collins," I reply, barely getting the words out before he snaps, "So what?"

"So we're looking for his killer," Driscoll says testily. "You seem like a good prospect."

I shudder a little at his abruptness. Russo just stares at him from across the table, but it seems to me the pupils of his eyes are dilating, giving him a predatory look. I want to divert his attention from Driscoll's words so I ask, "What caused the trouble between you and Collins?"

Russo turns slightly so he faces me. He draws a deep breath, but my question hasn't eased the tension. "He coulda saved my job if he wanted," Russo says, "but he did nothin'."

"What was it all about?" I ask.

The right side of Russo's mouth twists in a sickly grin. "I went down the street and had a beer with a coupla guys."

"When you were supposed to be on the job?"

"Sure. People do it all the time."

"And you took a six-pack back with you?"

"Sure, why not? So they fire me and do nothin' to the other guys. And Collins, insteada actin' like a steward, sits on his can and lets 'em get away with it. He's on the grievance committee and carries a lotta clout, but he does nothin' for me, nothin' at all."

Driscoll leans toward him a little. Russo turns back to face him. Driscoll stares across the table, his eyes two chips of steel-gray flint. "What I don't understand is why you killed the woman. She didn't have anything to do with the trouble between you and Collins."

Russo grins again from one side of his mouth. "She just happened to be there."

Without warning he pushes away from the table, then lifts it upward and shoves at the same time, sending Driscoll sprawling to the floor. Russo takes a step backward, still wearing the twisted grin, and reaches for the revolver on the sideboard. I sit watching him, too surprised to react.

Driscoll curses under his breath and tries to extricate himself from the tangle of table, chair, and coffee cups. Russo waves the gun at him, backing toward the door at the same time and saying, "Better stay right there, newsie."

When he is past the door, he kicks it shut behind him. Driscoll has managed to get to his feet and starts in pursuit, but I grab him as he goes by. "Hold it, Grady, he's got a gun and he'll use it."

He hesitates, glaring at me, then wrenches his arm free and goes on after Russo. I get up and follow, not in any hurry about it. A car starts in the driveway beside the house, tires squeal, then there is a shot. As I push aside the screen door and step warily out onto the back porch, there is another, and I see Driscoll leaning over the side rail, a gun in his right hand. He draws back just before there is that distinctive crack of a bullet passing closer than I care to hear one.

Surprising me with his agility, Driscoll vaults the railing, landing on his feet in a crouch with the gun in firing position. He squeezes the trigger and there is the sound of glass shattering, then a car door slamming in the distance. Driscoll runs forward and reluctantly I peer around the corner to see what is happening.

Greg Staley and a detective I recognize as Caproletti are running up the driveway from the street, guns drawn. Driscoll is standing beside the old Firebird and behind the myriad of broken glass that had been the windshield I see Russo slumped over, holding his bleeding right shoulder.

Jake sits opposite me at one of the round tables in the back room of Horner's Tavern, shaking his head and repeating, "I don't see how we're going to handle this, I don't see how we're going to handle this." His eyes are streaked with red, a cigarette burns in the ashtray in front of him, and another is in his hand. "So what's to handle, Jake?" asks Driscoll. "Let Granger write it like any other police story."

Jake scowls fiercely but Grady just smiles, either not recognizing the danger signs or ignoring them. Jake opens his mouth to reply, then goes into one of his violent coughing spells. When it ends he says, "So what's to handle? Write it like any other police story? A *News-Banner* reporter guns somebody down instead of doing his job of reporting the facts, and we're supposed to just casually pass over that like it's an everyday occurrence, is that what you're saying?"

"Grady didn't exactly gun him down," I tell him. "They were exchanging shots and he hit Russo in the shoulder."

Jake snorts derisively. "Exchanging shots! Since when is it a reporter's job to exchange shots?"

I turn to Driscoll, suddenly remembering that I have not asked him about the gun. "Why didn't you tell me you were armed? How often do you go around carrying a gun?"

He doesn't answer, just keeps on smiling.

"Grady, I don't like being around people with guns."

Still smiling, he says, "You have the answers to your town club murders, don't you?"

He is right, of course, but I believe I had the answers before the shooting began. Another question comes to mind. "How did Staley happen to show up just at that time?"

"Actually I figured he'd get there a little sooner than he did."

None of his answers satisfies me. Nothing can be done about any of it now, however, so I finish my drink and signal Jack Horner for another. While waiting for it I say, "Strange, isn't it?"

"What's strange?" Driscoll asks.

"The similarities. Except that someone who wasn't the intended victim died in one of them, what real difference was there in the murders?"

Driscoll shrugs uninterestedly. "There's a world of difference in the country club and the town club."

"Is there, really? You believe that, do you?" Jake drains his glass, then bangs it down on the table. "You know what really burns me up about this whole thing? Why is it the two of you usually manage to time your hijinks so *The Morning Sun* gets the first story?"

Driscoll straightens up in his chair, the color rising in his face. "That's not true, Jake. You think about it and . . ."

The rest of whatever he has in mind is lost for me in a sudden, overwhelming desire for the peace and solitude of the old hotel down the street.

VIGILANTE LAW

The pale October sun smiles warmly on the flatlands of Indiana, but the thoughts swirling through my mind lack even the hint of warmth. Instead there is a cold fury directed at Jake Richards. I turn from the window where I have been standing, looking out but seeing nothing. "Jake," I say to him, "you know how I feel about this sort of thing. I don't appreciate being told what to put in my column. Anyway, I'm a week ahead and have enough material for another, maybe longer."

Without warning Jake slaps his palm flat against the top of the city desk. "Get off your high-horse, Hal. How often does anybody tell you what to write? Never, and you know it."

He studies me smugly from eyes red-rimmed by the day's quota of cigarette smoke drifting up from both his mouth and the ashtray that overflows onto the desk. He is right, and knowing it only adds to my annoyance.

"But this is different," he continues. "It's perfect material for 'Around Town with Hal Blinn.'" He pauses again, a smirk playing at the corners of his mouth. "Besides, I don't know what else to do with it."

He has touched a match to a short fuse. Of course Jake intended it that way. "Fine," I cry, "just fine. You don't know what to do with it because it's not material for a real story so you dump it off on good ol' Hal – let him bore people with it. Right, Jake, am I right?"

He doesn't answer, just sits looking up at me, grinning, so I say, "Anyway, it was an accident. Granger brought out every sordid detail in his story, so what more is there to say?"

163

Jake straightens up from his slouch, hackles raised. "What more is there to say?" he growls from deep in his throat. "Some poor S.O.B. walks in off the street to buy a tube of toothpaste and gets gunned down by this wild-eyed shopkeeper and you ask what more there is to say?"

"For Pete's sake, Jake, be reasonable. It was unintentional, he was shooting at a holdup man. Those things happen, but it doesn't mean the vigilantes have taken over the town."

Jake abruptly swivels his chair and begins reading copy on a video display terminal. "Do the column, Hal. Just do it."

After reading Steve Granger's story of the incident a second time, then tracking him through half the taverns in Midland to ask a few questions, I find I know nothing more than I did at the start. The victim, Okla T. Lenfestey, was a resident of Flintville, Tennessee. So far his reason for being in Midland has not been established, aside from the fact that Flintville sends half its native sons here to work in the factories. But Lenfestey was forty-three, operated a one-man television repair shop in Flintville, and not a factory in town is hiring. He wasn't job hunting in Midland.

Shortly after eight in the evening, he entered a store on the south side of town, a convenience store of sorts owned by a Kurt Sideris. According to Sideris, he was alone in the store when Lenfestey entered and began looking at a display of toilet articles just to the right of the counter. Within a matter of seconds a young black male followed Lenfestey into the store, walked to the counter, and pulled a gun from under his jacket.

Sideris, who had been robbed several times before, reached under the counter and came up with a gun of his own, a snub-nosed .38 revolver, loaded and cocked. The bandit, Sideris told police, slapped the gun Sideris was pointing at him, and it went off. The bullet struck Lenfestey in the chest, killing him instantly.

At that point the bandit fired at Sideris but was wide of the mark, and the bullet lodged in a wall stud behind the counter. Sideris then shot him between the eyes.

The dead bandit was DeWon Mitchem, a twenty-year-old native of Midland who lived six blocks from the small store on South Madison, a street which at that point is the dividing line between black and white neighborhoods. Mitchem had no police record, worked part time for the Midland Community Action Agency, and was a student at Indiana Vocational Technical College, a trade school better known as Ivy Tech.

It surprises me to find the store open and Sideris behind the counter only twenty-one hours after the shooting. I guess his age to be forty as he studies me with disfavor from narrowed gray eyes above high cheekbones, a hook nose, and thin lips that barely move as he says, "I've already told the police and reporters everything there is to tell."

I nod understandingly. "I'm sure it's been an ordeal for you." I turn a little and look around the store for a moment. More to myself than Sideris I murmur, "Why do you suppose Lenfestey stopped here?"

"The same reason anyone else does. He needed something."

"But apparently he just arrived in town. At least the police haven't found a hotel where he was registered, and if he was staying with anyone, they haven't let it be known."

Sideris lays aside the tool he has been using to stamp prices on the tops of cans. "What are you driving at?"

"Nothing, just wondering. Funny how things work out, isn't it? All the places he could have stopped, but at just the wrong moment he walks in here for the first time and... it was the first time, wasn't it?"

"It was."

"But I suppose the place gets crowded sometimes, so you can't be sure."

"I'm sure. It was the first time he was here."

'Then you had never seen him before?"

Sideris makes an impatient sound, shaking his head as he does so.

"How about the gunman – Mitchell, was that his name?"

"Mitchem. No, I never saw him before, either."

"That's strange, he only lived a few blocks away."

Sideris looks at me as he might look at a child asking stupid questions. "Would you expect him to try to hold up a place where he was known?"

I grin sheepishly, say, "Guess you're right," then hand him a quarter and nickel for a roll of mints before heading for the door.

The white residents of the section of Midland known as Industry began their exodus shortly after the Second World War. It was completed in a few blinks of the eye. One by one in the years that followed, the factories bordering the neighborhood shut their doors until now only empty shells remain as a reminder of more prosperous times. DeWon Mitchem lived in the heart of Industry on South Hackley, a street of substantial old homes shaded by tall oaks, maples, and sycamores.

I drive slowly past the Mitchem house without stopping, then turn back to Madison where a small building that is mostly gymnasium serves as a community center. There is laughter and shouting in the gym as half a dozen young men wearing "Each One Teach One" T-shirts instruct small boys on the fundamentals of basketball.

Several of the men nod or wave a. hand in greeting and one – slim, rangy, and older than the others – walks over to the doorway where I stand watching. Along the way he picks up a towel draped over the back of a folding chair, wipes his face and hands, then extends his right one. I greet him by his Muslim name, thinking back for an instant to the time when as Harry Evans he led Midland Central to a state championship. Seven thousand people crowded into the high school fieldhouse for home games then, cheering his every move. Today few recognize him on the street. Most of those who do look on him as a problem rather than seeing him for what he is, an important part of the solution.

He leads me into a small office. We sit down and I ask him about DeWon Mitchem. For a moment he lowers his head, shaking it slowly. His eyes glisten when he looks at me again and says, "No matter what the police say or what the newspapers say, DeWon Mitchem wasn't a holdup man. Not DeWon, and no matter how much wind they blow uptown, they can't make him one."

"What about the gun?"

He laughs tersely, without humor. "Ask anybody, ask any brother on the street if ever, even once, DeWon Mitchem so much as touched a gun. I mean ever, man. Not because he was black – you know me well enough to know I'm not saying it just because he was black – but that was the best-hearted, most gentle man you're going to find in this town."

166

If I didn't believe what he tells me, I wouldn't be talking to him. We both know that, but he hasn't told me what I expected to hear, so I'm confused. For a moment we sit quietly, then he says, "I don't know what happened. I wish I did because some of the brothers are upset and I don't know what to tell them. But I know one thing for sure, DeWon Mitchem wasn't carrying when he walked in that store last night."

On impulse, rather than returning uptown, I drive west past rows of gray, two story buildings – Midlandia Homes to most people but "the project" to those who live there. Half a dozen men stand arguing in front of a tavern at "the low end," a ramshackle part of town carefully avoided by most white Midlanders. When I pull to the curb, the hot exchange of words and gestures ends. All eyes turn to me, fury still flashing in some but quickly giving way to curiosity.

Two of the men recognize me. One laughs and says, "Blinn – wha'd'ya doin' down here?"

"Just asking around. Know DeWon Mitchem, Eddie?"

An angry murmuring, most of it unintelligible, is followed by a longer silence than I care for. At last it is broken by someone saying, "Why you wanna know, bright skin?"

Eddie grabs the speaker's arm and says, "Hey, man, watch your mouth. This's my friend."

Quickly, before another argument can start, I say, "I hear DeWon wasn't a man with a gun."

There is a louder exchange among them, then Eddie says, "You better believe it, my man."

"He was what you might call upright," a slender man I don't know says in the cultured tones of a West Indian.

Isiah Racker, the second of my acquaintances, crouches so his face is level with mine and no more than eighteen inches away. "They're right, Hal. I knowed DeWon since he was a babe, and his daddy and momma 'fore then. Don't you believe what they're saying uptown."

It is after eight when I finish checking the files in the newspaper library. There is none for either Sideris or Mitchem, which comes as no surprise. It does, though, to find Grady Driscoll working at his desk when I walk into the newsroom. He tells me the jury has just reached a verdict in a rape trial he has been covering. He is writing the story so it won't be waiting for him at seven in the morning.

While he finishes it, I stand at a window overlooking an empty street, mulling over what I have heard. Then we walk the two short blocks to the Delaware Hotel and exchange stories of the day's events at a table in the dining room. He is amused, when I say Jake is growing more autocratic by the day, but listens skeptically as I tell him what I have heard about DeWon Mitchem.

"Sure you aren't getting fed a line, Hal?" he asks when I finish.

"It's not a line. That's not saying they couldn't be wrong."

He pushes his chair back and stands up, patting the rubber tire that causes his shirt to gap above his belt. "Let's walk across the street, see if Staley's in his office. Maybe there's some new developments."

I follow him, but without enthusiasm. Greg Staley looks up from his desk as we enter the dingy detective's room in the police station at City Hall. His shirtsleeves are rolled just below the elbows, and his tie hangs loosely below an unfastened collar. He slides the papers he has been studying into a file folder, yawns, and checks his watch.

"Break time," says Driscoll.

"Break, hell," Staley mumbles, "I'm heading home." His thin features are drawn, fatigue has glazed his eyes.

Driscoll nods in the direction of the hotel. "Have a drink on the way."

Staley takes his jacket from the back of his chair arid slips into it without bothering to unroll his shirtsleeves. He says, "Just one and that's it."

As we talk quietly at a table in a dark corner of the hotel lounge, it gradually comes across that Staley is far from satisfied with the case. The chief is satisfied, however, and wants him to wrap up the loose ends as quickly and cheaply as possible. Staley won't be specific about what it is that bothers him, and even Driscoll can't get him to theorize on what might have occurred if the story told by Sideris was off the mark.

Finally he grows weary of Driscoll's pestering and says, "Look, you people can speculate all you want. I have to go by facts, by solid evidence and information."

"But you have theories, don't you?" Driscoll counters.

Staley looks at me and sighs. "What I'd like to do is go down to Flintville, but the chief nixed the idea."

"Why Flintville?" I ask him.

"You know, don't you, that Mrs. Sideris is from there?"

"No, I didn't know. That wasn't in the newspapers."

"We just found it out this afternoon. I've checked down there by phone and the Flintville police don't know of any connection between her and Lenfestey, but they told me about another accidental killing he was involved in. A year ago he thought there was a prowler in the house and took a shot at him, but it turned out to be his own wife. She was killed."

Driscoll whistles softly. "Now that's *some* coincidence."

I tilt back in my chair, think about it a moment, then say, "Almost too much of one. Two accidental shootings, the man with the gun in one, the victim in the other."

Staley stares into his empty glass, then pushes it aside, arching his eyebrows. "Things like that happen. The chief thinks so, anyway, but I'd like to go down and check it out myself."

Driscoll turns to me and says, "Let's do it for him."

I study him over the rim of my glass, wondering if he's serious. He is, I decide, but it's a good time, not work, that he has in mind. I shake my head and say, "For God's sake, Grady, you don't think the *News-Banner* is going to be any more willing to pay for a trip to Tennessee than the City of Midland, do you?"

"We've both got vacation time left."

"And I intend to spend mine with both feet propped up on the end of the couch. I *am* going to talk to Mrs. Sideris in the morning but that'll be it."

Sideris is stacking canned goods near the front of the store when I drive by shortly after nine in the morning. I continue south to Twelfth Street, then turn east and go more than a mile before coming to a 1920's bungalow that is the Sideris residence.

Fern Sideris, wearing a frayed and faded housecoat, hair up in rollers, looks older than her husband. Like him, she is thin, but in her case it borders on emaciation. When I have explained my reason for being on her porch, she invites me into a small living room so clean it looks unlived in. I settle on the edge of a chair, and she brings coffee.

After a few preliminaries I say, "They tell me you're from Flintville."

She nods her head, then sips coffee.

"But you didn't know Okla Lenfestey?"

"I didn't know none of the Lenfesteys. They lived a little outside town, I think." She talks in a monotone, and it comes across that her life probably matches her voice.

"Then you didn't know Lenfestey's wife?" She shakes her head, so I say, "Did you know he accidentally shot and killed her a year ago?"

"No, I didn't know about that." The news doesn't jar her from the lethargic frame of mind, which apparently is a constant thing.

"Where did you meet your husband?" I ask her.

"Down there. He stayed at the hotel where I worked, so we got to know each other."

"How'd he happen to be in Flintville?"

"Business. He was just out of the army and was selling ... let's see, it was some kind of hardware supplies. It didn't work out, and after we got back here – I mean back to Indianapolis, where he was from – he went to work for a supermarket."

"You came back with him?"

Her cheeks flush slightly. "We got married while he was in Flintville."

I decide not to press it further, sensing it is a sensitive subject that might make her withdraw completely. "That would have been about when?" I ask.

"Let's see, 1969. It was July and Mr. Sideris had only been back from Vietnam two weeks,"

"Found a job pretty fast, didn't he?"

"Mr. Sideris has never been one to lay around much."

Calling him mister as she does makes her sound like the wife of an educator. It could be a habit of Flintville women, but I have never noticed it in others from there. I set my empty cup on a tray she has placed near me, then stand up. "I understand your husband didn't meet Okla Lenfestey while he was in Flintville."

She gets up, too, running her hands along the sides of her housecoat. "Oh, no, the Lenfesteys weren't in the hardware business."

As I walk to the car I wonder if Mr. Sideris was.

170

Driscoll watches me expectantly when I walk in the newsroom. I light a cigarette and then sink down in my chair, ignoring him while I contemplate my next move, if there is to be one. After a moment or two I grind the cigarette in an ashtray and go over to him. "Okay, how soon can you go?"

"Right now. I'm clear."

We approach the city desk together. Jake looks up, sensing a conspiracy, then goes into one of his coughing spells when I say, "Jake, we're going on vacation."

When the cough is under control he says, "Now wait a minute, you two, you can't just walk over here and say you're going on vacation, you know that."

"We've got it coming," I reply. "I'm a few columns ahead so you won't run out."

"And now that the trial is over, there won't be anything doing in the courts for a few days," Driscoll tells him.

Jake grins unexpectedly. "What're you up to now?"

"We're driving down to Tennessee – Flintville – to check out a few things about those shootings at the convenience store. You told me to do a column on it, remember?"

"And you're not asking the company to send you?"

"No."

"Or expenses or anything?"

"No."

He shakes his head, bewildered. "Okay, if you're crazy enough to spend your own money, be my guest. Jeez, I'd think you'd at least have asked."

"Well how about it, then?"

He makes a snorting noise. "Forget it. Have a nice vacation."

Driscoll naps as we travel south on Interstate 65. It is our second trip to Flintville, and on the last one Driscoll pulled a disappearing act. I glance at him suspiciously as he sleeps open-mouthed, wondering where he spent his time and if he intends to vanish again. Probably, I decide, thinking it explains why he was so eager to return.

We arrive an hour after dark. Nothing has changed in fifteen months, not even the characters who appraise us from a bench in front of the only hotel in town. The man behind the desk remembers us, even gives us the same room with twin beds.

Then we walk down the street to the same restaurant we had eaten at before and are served by the same waitress, a skinny, hard-bitten woman with a chalk-on-blackboard voice.

"Hey," she says, "I remember you two. From up in Midland, ain't'cha?"

"You called it," Driscoll replies. "Man from here was killed up there the other night. Did you know him, Okla Lenfestey?"

"Sure I knowed him, everybody did. It was in the paper about him. Seems like somebody from Flintville's always gettin' killed up there. Must be some town. I keep tellin' my brother he oughta come back."

"Trouble happens everywhere," I say to her. "We heard Lenfestey had some of his own right here not long ago."

She purses her lips, nodding. "Yeah, that was too bad. Just one of those things, I guess. She was a nice lady, all things considered, and Okla was all broke up over what happened."

"Like what things considered?" I ask.

"Well, her bein' from up north and all. I'll give her credit, she fit in better'n most."

"Where up north was she from?"

"Don't rightly recall. Now what'll you fellas have?"

Just as I anticipated, after breakfast in the morning Driscoll tells me he has a few things to do and heads off somewhere by himself. It dawns on me that being in Flintville with him could be dangerous if he has met a woman with attachments. In hill towns, discovery means cutting or shooting.

The morning sun quickly warms the crisp air; the hills guarding Flintville from the outside world are adorned in their autumn finery. Reluctantly I leave the outdoors for the dank corridors of the courthouse, an ornate old building that looks better outside than in. The first item on my list is to learn the maiden name of Mrs. Sideris, something I neglected to ask her. Knowing the month and year of her marriage simplifies the task, and within minutes I learn she was Elizabeth Fern Keeney and, as I suspected, is six years older than her husband.

The sheriff's office is in a separate building on the courthouse square, a decrepit, two story brick structure that also contains his living quarters and the jail. I find Arlo Crockett going over the previous night's reports in his narrow private office that was once a front porch. A muscular man about six inches above six feet, wearing khaki pants and a sport shirt of burnt orange, he has a brusque air of competency.

After I remind him that we met several years earlier when he testified at a trial in Midland, we spend a few minutes talking generalities before I ask if it was his department that investigated the death of Mrs. Lenfestey.

"We did – they lived a mile south of the city limit."

"Was there any doubt about its being an accident?"

"Of course. There always is when there are no witnesses to a killing. He was tried, but it took the jury only eleven minutes to acquit him. Can't say I disagreed with their decision."

"Then you think it was an accident?"

"There was nothing in the way of evidence to indicate otherwise, not even the usual stories that they hadn't been getting on. There had been a rash of break-ins prior to that and people were edgy at the time. Lenfestey was awakened by a noise in another room, so he picked up a gun he kept under the bed and went to investigate. When he got to the door of the other room, a figure was outlined against the window, so he fired."

"He hadn't checked to see if his wife was in bed, and he didn't call out before he shot?"

"Negative to both. They slept in twin beds, and he assumed she was in hers. Trigger happy, a damn fool trick in my opinion, but unintentional as far as we could learn."

"Ever find out why she was standing at a window in another room?"

"No," Crockett says with a shake of his head. "Who was there to ask?"

"Did you know them well?"

"I didn't know her at all. I knew him to speak to."

"What was her first name? And I understand she was from up north, do you know where?"

"Her first name was Ruth." He gets up from his swivel chair with the quickness of a mountain cat. "Come on, I'll check the other."

I follow him to another, more formal office and wait near the door while he gets a folder from a file cabinet. He flips through pages, reads to himself for a moment, then looks up and says,

"Ruth Ann Lenfestey, thirty-seven. Maiden name Williams. Born Indianapolis, Indiana."

As he walks with me to the outside door, I ask Crockett if he knew Fern Sideris. He shakes his head, then says, "If I was investigating Lenfestey's death in Midland, there are a lot of coincidences I'd want explained."

The Flintville phone book, little more than a quarter inch thick, reveals only one Keeney. A woman with a tired voice answers when I dial the number. Yes, she tells me, Ken Keeney is her husband and the brother of Fern Sideris. I can find him at work at the lumber company just south of town.

He is pointed out to me, and I walk through the yard to where he is working between high stacks of lumber. He looks up, scowling, then extends his hand, thinking I am a customer with an order form to fill. When I introduce myself, his scowl deepens, and in a monotone similar to his sister's, he says, "So wha'd'ya want with me?"

"Just thought I'd look you up while I was in town. Ever get up to Midland to see your sister?"

He shakes his narrow head, then brushes back strands of brown hair cut with long sideburns in the style of the hills. "Just once. Never hit it off much with him." He gives a curt laugh, then says, "He never brung her back once since they got married up. She even come alone when Momma died, and Daddy, too."

"From what I understand, they got married kind of sudden, didn't they?"

His eyes narrow around the scowl. "That's been a long time now. No point draggin' up old trouble."

"There was trouble?"

"Look, mister," he says turning away, "I got work to do."

I find Iva Delroy, sister of Okla Lenfestey, at home in a big, unpainted, Victorian-style house two blocks from downtown. I had gotten her name from the *News-Banner* story on her brother's death and her address from the phone book.

She admits me hesitantly, and I follow her into a musty room crowded with furniture dating back to the early years of the century. Faded blue drapes are closed to the sunshine, and what little light there is comes from a forty-watt bulb in a table lamp

174

with a stained glass shade, She waves me to a massive rocker with over-stuffed arms that, when I sink down a little tentatively, rise nearly to my shoulders.

She settles on a matching couch across the room, patting lifeless hair pulled back and knotted behind her head. There is a frail look about her, probably from lack of fresh air, and I estimate her age at fifty, give or take a few years. After expressing my condolences, which she accepts without comment or change of expression, I ask if she knows why her brother traveled to Midland.

"Said he had somethin' to attend to up there, that was all. I think he got a letter, but it wasn't out to his place when I looked yesterday so maybe he took it along with him."

"Had he ever been to Midland before?"

"Not that I know about."

"Did he know anybody there?"

"Naturally he did. Everybody in Flintville does, but nobody close to him."

"His wife was from up that way, I understand."

She shakes her head, correcting me. "Not Midland, it was Indianapolis. That's some distance away, isn't it?"

"About sixty miles. How did they happen to meet?"

"Okie was in the army up to Fort Harrison in Indianapolis and met her in town." She laughs softly, reminiscing. "He was a real operator with the ladies back then, Okie was. Could have had his pick of about any in town, but he didn't want to tie himself down to just one. Then he went off to the army and come back a few years later with a wife. Pretty little thing, too, and just as sweet as could be."

For a few seconds we sit silently, then she says, "Here now, I'm forgettin' my manners. Let me get you some coffee."

I welcome the chance to think for a moment without interruption. When she comes back with a tray, I take a cookie, mushy stale, and then the cup she has filled with rancid coffee. When she is on the couch again I say, "Did your sister-in-law – Ruth, wasn't it? – have many visitors from Indianapolis? Family or friends?"

"A few, right at the beginning. Then her parents died about a year apart, and after that I think her brother come down just once, and that was years ago. That's all she had, one brother."

"What was his name?"

She studies on it a moment, then says, "Chris, I think it was. He was kind of a strange one, if you ask me. Didn't even come for her funeral 'cause Okie didn't know how to get in touch with him."

"Did any friends ever visit her here?"

"Not that I heard about." She pauses to, sip from her cup. "If any had, I would of heard."

"When was your brother at Fort Harrison?"

"Well, he got out during the summer of '68 and had been there a little better'n a year."

"Did he serve in Vietnam?"

"Never left the States. He worked in electronics, that's how he come to go into TV repair."

"And he and Ruth never had children?"

Her body stiffens, shock clouds her face. "Oh, yes. You never heard about that? Two boys, the sweetest you ever seen." She hesitates, her features contorting. 'They was walking along the highway south of town – it was in '77 when one was seven and the other eight – and was killed by a hit-and-runner."

For a moment we sit without speaking as she sags back on the couch, head shaking slowly. Then I say, "Did they ever catch the driver?"

"Not to this day. It just tore Okie and Ruth all up. She always was a quiet soul, but after that the life just seemed to drain right out of her."

I set my cup aside and stand up, wondering just how much tragedy can be heaped upon one family. I thank her, then at the door turn and say, "Did you know Fern Sideris when she lived here? She was Fern Keeney at the time."

"By sight, that's all."

"How about the man she married, Kurt Sideris?"

Her head shakes again. "He wasn't from these parts."

The last thing I expect to find when I return to the hotel is Driscoll sitting on the bench out front. He gets up, saying a goodbye to the three regulars as if they are old friends, then turns to me, frowning. "Where've you been all this time?"

I say, "Around," and start walking toward the restaurant. Driscoll falls into step beside me. "I went down to the drugstore for some blades and smokes," he complains, "and when I get back you're nowhere to be found."

"You mean you've been sitting on that bench all morning?"

"So what else is there to do in Flintville? What did you turn up, anything?"

I contemplate him suspiciously, but fill him in after we're seated at a table next to the window. He listens without comment, then says, "Did you hear about the shotgun wedding?"

"What shotgun wedding?"

"Kurt Sideris and Fern Keeney. The old man next to me back there told me all about it. Would you believe he's nailed down that seat for thirty years? Except in bad weather; then the boys move into the lobby."

"Get to the point, Grady."

His lips curl in a biting grin. He is determined to make me pay one way or another for going off without him. "You never have time for an old fellow like that, do you? All you ever care about are your own selfish interests, right?"

I sigh resignedly, stare out at the street a second or two, then turn to him again. "Okay, Grady, I lack your feeling and compassion. Now about this wedding..."

"Well, the old man knew Fern Keeney because she had been chambermaid at the hotel for years. A real frigid piece of cake, he called her. Thought every man that came along had designs on her body, but the truth was she never had a date in her life. The joke among the fellows around town, what they called her behind her back was "Blowtorch" because it would have taken one to thaw her out enough so she'd even say hello."

"Very funny. She's no beauty, grant you, but—"

"Knock it off, Hal. Anyway, the old man remembers Sideris because he stayed four nights at the hotel, which comes close to being a record."

"Four nights? How many hardware stores did Flintville have back then?"

Driscoll laughs scoffingly. "He wasn't selling hardware or anything else. The old man says he never could find out what Sideris was up to, but it wasn't anything good. For a while he thought Sideris was an outlaw casing the bank or something like that, but decided he was just spying around for some reason, as things turned out."

"Now we're coming to the good part, right?"

He pretends not to hear. "One day Sideris was out drinking early and came back to the hotel about noon, feeling no pain. So pretty soon Fern goes in to make up his room, not realizing he's there, and he must have made a grab for her. She screams just once, so the desk clerk – not the one there now, an old guy who didn't move too fast – went upstairs to see what was going on, and the other old fellow, the one I was talking to, followed along. They didn't set any speed records getting there, but even so nothing much had happened except Fern apparently had changed her mind because she had just removed the last of her clothes. When they opened the door she really started screaming – so loud that Sideris, who was halfway passed out on the bed, raised up a little and asked what was going on.

"Fern put her clothes back on, yelling all the while because the old guys are standing there grinning. By the time she finished, a crowd had gathered, and she went running out of the place.

"An hour or so later, her father and brother arrive and go up to the room where Sideris is sleeping it off. They grab him and drag him out, with him still too drunk to know what's going on, let alone resist. When he comes back that night, Fern's with him and they're married."

I sit silently, letting it soak in. Finally I say, "What about a waiting period?"

Driscoll laughs derisively. "Hal, you think of the craziest things. Under the circumstances I don't imagine the father and brother had much trouble getting it waived, if they even bothered. What difference does it make?"

"None," I concede. After a few minutes spent concentrating on rubbery hamburgers I say, "I think we've done all we can here. What we have to do, we have to go to Indianapolis. If we're going to find an answer, if there's even one to find, it's going to come there. That's the only thing I can see that Sideris, Lenfestey, and Ruth Williams have in common — Indianapolis."

Driscoll swallows his last french fry, washes it down with coffee, then says, "Let's go."

Clouds roll in from the west as we retrace our route along a narrow highway that twists around and over the Tennessee and Kentucky hills. The temperature drops, and a chill autumn rain begins soon after we reach the interstate at Glasgow. I switch on the heater as we cross the Ohio River at Louisville. Dusk falls an hour ahead of schedule, and when the rain becomes mixed with snow, I pull off at Franklin. We check into a motel beside the interstate, then pass the gloomy evening in the lounge, reviewing what we have learned, speculating on whether any of it will eventually make sense.

Frost sparkles in cold sunlight when we leave in the morning, but the snow hasn't stuck to the ground or pavement. In less than an hour we stop at a branch library on the south side of Indianapolis, where Driscoll jots down names and addresses as I read them from old city directories. Twenty minutes later we are headed north on Meridian Street toward the neighborhood bordering Pendleton Pike where, fifteen years ago, the Sideris and Williams families lived only nine blocks apart. The main gate at Fort Benjamin Harrison is a short distance away.

The house where Kurt Sideris grew up stands among others just like it in one of those projects that mushroomed everywhere after the Second World War. A home to call their own for everyone, that was the goal, and it didn't matter how many were crowded together on minuscule lots, how cramped they might be inside, or that those called ranch-style resembled nothing ever seen on a ranch. The project is in a bedroom community adjoining Indianapolis, but a stranger would never realize he had passed from one to the other unless he noticed the city limit signs.

The young woman who answers our knock at what had been the Sideris home has lived there only three years and knows nothing about the family. She directs us to a house three doors south on the other side of the street, where an elderly woman greets us with the eager cordiality extended by the lonely. She tells us that of course she remembers the Sideris family because like her and her late husband, Mae and Fritz Sideris moved in when the houses were new.

"But they've been gone for years now," she says, "and we haven't kept in touch. They moved to Florida – Venice, I think it was – and for a few years we exchanged Christmas cards, you know how you do. I'm ashamed to say it, but I don't even know if they're still alive."

"They had a son, didn't they?" I ask.

Her face lights up again. "Yes, just the one, Kurt. He was the jolliest little boy you ever saw, and he stayed that way, too, even through high school when some turn unpleasant. Kurt, he always had a smile on his face and a pleasant word for everybody. A sunny disposition no matter what, and a hard-working boy, too. Always shoveling snow or mowing lawns or whatever he could to earn money. And he delivered the *Star* in the morning for years – the best paperboy we ever had. The one we have now, why you never know if he's going to come at all, and when he does he's always late."

"Kurt didn't move south with his parents, did he?"

"Oh, no, he was grown and married before they left. He had been in Vietnam, you know. It was so sad, how he had changed when he came back."

"In what way?"

"Just about every way you could think of. He was still polite, of course, but gloomy and not wanting to be around people. You would of thought he forgot how to smile while he was away. It hurt Mae and Fritz, believe me. Kurt couldn't help it, I'm sure, but he was there a long time in the infantry and must have had some terrible experiences because he just wasn't the same boy at all."

"You haven't kept in touch with him, either?" Driscoll asks her, even though we both know what her answer will be.

"No, he didn't stay at home long after he got back. Just a few weeks later he got married, which was another shock for Mae and Fritz because they didn't know about it until it was over and they didn't know the girl at all. She wasn't from around here, I remember that. For a while they had an apartment in town but would hardly ever visit his folks. Then they moved away someplace – Kokomo or Marion, one of those towns up north, I think. Soon after that Mae and Fritz went to Florida so I never did see Kurt again."

"Did you know a girl about Kurt's age named Ruth Ann Williams?" I ask her. She thinks a moment, then shakes her head.

When we are back in the car Driscoll tells me to stop for coffee. He also had bad experiences in Vietnam, but managed to adjust well to civilian life once he returned. The story has bothered him, though, and for some time he sits quietly staring out the window of a fast food dining room. Finally, without looking at me, he says, "I knew some people who had that happen. Still do know some, I guess."

He is silent again for a few minutes, then finishes his coffee, grins at me, and says, "We'd better be moving along, buddy. Know where that street is that Ruth Ann Williams lived on?"

We find it in an older development built when the town was a little distance from the city and had an identity of its own. Ruth Williams lived on a pleasant street of two story houses under tall trees. The city directories had told us her father was an accountant with an insurance company based in Indianapolis and that her brother was attending Butler University while she was in high school.

We have a difficult time finding anyone who remembers the family and end up going house to house knocking on doors. Eventually we find another elderly woman halfway down the next block who was a friend of Caroline Williams, the mother. She repeats what we learned in Flintville, that Mrs. Williams outlived her husband by only nine or ten months and that both have been dead more than a decade.

Ruth had been a pleasant, pretty girl, she recalls, but the brother comes across as another type altogether. Obviously the woman was not taken with Christopher Williams, who as a boy apparently was the exact opposite of Kurt Sideris – taciturn, arbitrary, lazy. Her nose seems to turn up as she tells us that to her, for one, it came as no surprise when he became a hippie while in college. "Long-haired, filthy, and foul-mouthed," are the words she chooses to describe him.

"Oh, but you should have seen him after his parents died and he had a little money," she says. "By then the hippie phase was fading, so overnight he turned into a three-piece-suit man and somebody was always telling me about seeing him in a fancy restaurant or going into one of those cocktail lounges."

"Whatever became of him?" I ask.

"He had a good job with his father's old company. Sold insurance, he did, and from what I hear, did well at it, but then decided-to open his own agency out in some small town – Rushville, I think. Underneath, though, I'm sure he never changed."

"Of course you know about Ruth," I say.

"Yes, just one terrible tragedy after another." She sounds almost pleased in saying it, as if tragedy is just fine so long as it is somebody else's. "Of course you can expect things like that when you marry a soldier."

"How did she meet Okla Lenfestey, do you know?"

"Isn't that a terrible name, Okla Lenfestey? So, so ... oh, you know what I mean. Anyway, she met him at a dance somewhere, and after that he was always hanging around the Williams house, mooching meals and God knows what else."

"I take it you didn't care for him?"

"I never laid eyes on him, thank goodness."

"How about a boy named Kurt Sideris, did you know him?"

She looks up, closing her eyes and repeating, "Sideris, Sideris." When I've had about all of it I can take, she opens her eyes again and says, "No, I never heard the name before."

As we walk down the driveway Driscoll says, "Whee-ouu. A nice sweet old lady, huh?"

I laugh, then tell him to watch for a phone booth. We stop at the first one; I dial Rushville information and ask for the number of the Christopher Williams residence and insurance agency. A curt voice snaps out both. Driscoll watches as I write them down, then we look at each other. Without saying anything we return to the car, head south on the interstate to U.S. 52, then southeast toward Rushville.

The drive takes less than an hour, but it is past noon when we arrive. Rushville is a typical Hoosier county seat, a picture-postcard town of large, well-maintained residences fanning out in three directions from an old fortress of a courthouse that stands imperiously on a downtown square. Most businesses close on Wednesday afternoon, and only a few storerooms stand empty. Change is accepted reluctantly in Rushville, and individuality takes a back seat to conformity.

We discuss our approach to Christopher Williams over lunch at a small but busy restaurant on a downtown corner. The result is a mental list of several points we would like cleared up for our own satisfaction, but only one question that truly matters. Both of us, I think, know the answer, yet want to hear it spoken.

Christopher Williams' insurance agency occupies a new brick building where two highways part company at the south end of town. A receptionist, long of tooth and suspicious of eye, sizes us up as poor risks, then says, "I'll see if Mr. Williams is in." After a brief phone call she motions with her head toward a hallway and says, "Last door on the right."

Williams has left his desk to greet us at the door on the off chance we may be customers. The vest of his three-piece gray suit bulges a little at the waistline. His hair is thin on top and his eyes are calculating, but he greets us like a true salesman. Any trace of the hippie youth has long since vanished. That other lifestyle, I decide, was quickly discarded and forgotten once it ceased to be convenient.

His eyebrows lift when I tell him we are checking out the circumstances surrounding the death of his brother-in-law. "I didn't know he was dead," he says, but doesn't bother to ask how Lenfestey died. After that he listens without comment or emotion as I tell him what we have been doing the past two days. I finish by saying we heard he didn't attend his sister's funeral.

"For only one reason, no one bothered to tell me of her death until long after the fact," he says, putting a little feeling into his words for the first time. After a short pause he adds, 'To. be honest about it, Ruth and I were never close. She was four years younger than me, and we lived in different worlds, really. There wasn't trouble between us, understand, but our lifestyles, our values when we were children, were at opposite ends of the poles."

"One of your old neighbors said she was a sweet girl, and pretty."

"Oh she was." He hesitates, then laughs harshly. "That's how everyone, thought of Ruth – always sweet and good. I'm not saying she wasn't, I'm not downgrading her, but it did get a little tiresome always being compared unfavorably. Everyone thought she could do no wrong, so it struck me funny when she threw over her childhood sweetheart to marry a smooth talker from the army base."

Driscoll and I exchange glances. He says, "We hadn't heard about the childhood sweetheart."

After all the years that have passed, Williams still seems to relish what to him was the showing of his sister's true colors. "From the time they were in the sixth grade they had this attraction for each other, and through high school she rarely dated anyone else. After graduation he went into the service, and they had an understanding that when he came back . . .but then

183

Lenfestey showed up and her old sweetheart got a 'Dear John' letter while he was in Vietnam."

"What was the sweetheart's name?" Driscoll asks softly.

"Didn't I mention it?" Williams says. "It was Sideris. Kurt Sideris."

We pass the hour it takes to drive to Midland in silence. Driscoll, I know, sees it all from a viewpoint different from mine. I understand his feelings, his empathy for Sideris, because Driscoll also experienced Vietnam. My thoughts center on someone else, DeWon Mitchem.

I pull into the parking lot of a tavern far out on South Madison, the street that takes us uptown. When the bartender has drawn two beers, we carry them to a booth, where our silence resumes. Finally I say, "It seems to me this is where we turn it over to Staley."

Driscoll nods uninterestedly. Then after a moment he returns to the present with a start, saying, "But I think we're entitled to go along when he talks to Sideris."

It has been dark two hours, and a fierce wind rattles signs and blows debris along the streets when we set out to find Staley. We have been in no hurry because we want the story, assuming there is one, to break on *News-Banner* time, which means after *The Morning Sun* midnight deadline. With that in mind we have tracked down Steve Granger, the *Banner*'s police reporter, and told him to remain available.

The search for Staley goes on for an hour, which fits well with our time schedule, and then it takes the better part of another to relate our story. Driscoll ends it by telling him we want to go along when he talks to Sideris.

Staley strokes his chin, frowning, then says, "Considering what you've told me, I don't have any choice but to arrest him and read him his rights immediately. I doubt if there'll be any talking after that." He glances briefly at the digital watch on his left wrist. "He'll be closing the store in fifteen minutes. I guess you can go along, you deserve that much, but stay in the background and keep your mouths shut."

We park near the curb and wait in the car until Sideris walks to the front door to lock up for the night. Then Staley and another detective he has taken along walk quickly to the door and on inside. Driscoll and I follow a little distance behind. By the time we enter the store, Sideris is being patted down by Caproletti, the second detective, and Staley is starting to read to him from a card.

Sideris smiles wryly, his eyes on me, until Staley finishes. Then he quietly says, "The right to remain silent? For what? I have an idea you know all there is to know, anyhow. In a way I'm kind of glad it's over."

He pauses, looking around the store for what he knows may be the last time. Satisfied, he fixes his gaze on Staley and says, "You know what he did, don't you, that Lenfestey? Not only ruined her life but killed her, too. Ruth deserved the best, but she got the worst, she got Lenfestey. So I lured him up here on the pretext of knowing something about the death of their two boys years ago. I planned to take him somewhere and kill him for what he had done."

Forgetting Staley's orders, I ask, "But why did you have to involve DeWon Mitchem?"

"Because Lenfestey started getting nasty and I knew I'd have trouble getting him off by himself. That's when the kid came in and I changed plans. It was just Mitchem's bad luck, that's all. I took care of Lenfestey first, then when it was all over I locked the door arid pulled the shades. After that I went out the back way and got an old gun I kept in the glove compartment, one I bought years ago on the street and knew couldn't be traced to me. When I came back inside, I lifted the kid so he was standing, stuck the gun in his hand and fired one shot, then called the police."

For an hour or more Driscoll and I sit quietly at a table in the nearly deserted lounge at the hotel, lost in our private thoughts. Then Staley joins us. Still no one has anything to say. There is none of the excitement, the feeling of accomplishment that usually goes with the completion of a job. Staley finishes his drink, pushing his chair away from the table and getting up at the same time. Driscoll follows his lead, but stands looking down at me from eyes glassy with fatigue and drink.

"Tragedy on top of tragedy," he says softly, then kicks the leg of the table and laughs bitterly. "No matter how high a wall you build, it still gets through to you. All these years now, but that war, it just keeps coming back. It just won't let you alone."

I stay where I am for a moment or two after they have gone, then get up and slowly climb the stairs to my rooms on the third floor. My body is tired, but not as tired as my mind. Even so, sleep is out of the question until certain thoughts are expurgated. It can be done only one way, by putting them on paper.

I retrieve the old portable Royal from the back of the bedroom closet, take it into the other room, and shove papers aside so there is space for it on the desk. Then, with a glass from the bathroom and a bottle from the bottom drawer close beside a stack of yellowed copy paper, I am ready.

The story I write is one of childhood love. A complicated first love filled with the exhilaration of youth, but also the uncertainty that tempers that exhilaration. The love of a happy-go-lucky boy forced to become a man, a killer, overnight. A love that was the one good thing, the one sane and reliable thing remaining in a world that to him had gone mad. A focal point that made it possible to retain some portion, however small, of the qualities and values that once had been dominant, that had formed his character. And then it, too, was taken from him.

Jake looks up, frowning through a cloud of smoke, when I lay the three typewritten pages on his desk.

'What's this?" he asks, beginning to read.

"My column. Substitute it for the one scheduled today."

"You didn't do it on a VDT?" He glances at the clock. "It isn't in the system?"

"I wrote it last night at home. Let them set it in the composing room."

"I don't know, Hal, it's getting late and—" He trails off as he goes on to the second page, then the third. When he finishes he looks up, shaking his head a little. "It's maudlin, Hal, but if it's the best you can come up with ... "

I walk to the window and for a moment stare out at the leafless trees spaced along the opposite sidewalk. The clouds are low and dark, there is a chill look to everything. Jake is right, it's a maudlin story. Right from the very beginning. Right to the very end.

A DEBT TO BE PAID

The old man awoke with a start. He peered around the veranda, his eyes blinking rapidly as they skipped from one empty chair to another. Satisfied he was alone, that he had not been observed by any of his cronies, he sighed with relief.

He struggled to his feet, using both hands and arms to hoist himself out of a wicker chair. Once up, he remained still a moment, giving his blood a chance to start circulating through his shaky legs. When the tingling eased he reached out to the long wooden railing and used it for support until he got to the stairs.

He walked down them, across a wide lawn and past a barn with *County Home* lettered on its cupola. He continued on to a small woods cut in half by a brook flowing along a rocky bed.

He stopped when he reached his favorite hideaway, a huge gray boulder close beside the stream. Its smooth surface was imbedded with small pebbles and he traced a pattern from one to another of them with a bony forefinger. After a few seconds he eased around the side of the boulder and faced the water, coming to the small ledge that was his usual seat. Once settled, he bent and picked up a loose pebble, tossed it in the brook, and wondered what he was going to do about the dream.

He had easily coped with it when it interrupted his sleep only three or four times a year. Then it began bothering him more and more often. Once a month, twice a month, every week until finally now it had become a nightly occurrence. It had invaded his afternoon nap for the first time a week earlier. Twice he awoke with a cry to find the others on the veranda staring at him. Had he been talking in his sleep?

187

The dream started to take shape in his mind just as it did in his sleep. A swirling white mist and then suddenly a vivid picture. He angrily pushed it aside. Bad enough seeing it in his sleep without letting it take over his waking hours. But after a minute or two it crept back again and this time caught hold. He sat glassy-eyed as it unfolded.

The train was creeping into a dark freight yard as he dropped to the ground from an open boxcar door. A light rain, hardly more than a vapor in the air, dampened his face. He turned up the collar of his red-and-black plaid jacket in a futile attempt to ward off the intermittent gusts of cold wind from the west. He didn't know where he was and didn't care. The important thing was the railroad bulls were preparing to sweep the train and it was time to find shelter elsewhere.

He had jumped from the south side of the train, so he headed south. Cautiously he picked his way across half a dozen tracks to a street that ended at a guard rail where two large warehouses faced each other. He considered each of the buildings as a place of refuge but rejected them in turn. Watchmen with clubs would surely be inside.

He walked on, coming next to a long row of ramshackle houses. In the following block, the houses began to show improvement and after two more blocks he was in a neighborhood of well-maintained bungalows. Most had garages, so maybe he'd be lucky and find one with an unlocked door. The third knob he tried was unlocked.

He slipped inside, softly closed the door behind him, and stood quietly in the blackness. He reached out a tentative hand, touched a car, a sedan. It also was unlocked, so he opened a rear door and silently climbed inside.

The seat was soft. Not wide enough to stretch out full length but a lot more comfortable than his usual bed, the ground or the floor of a boxcar. Best of all, the car was warm and dry.

He reached in a jacket pocket and pulled out half a sandwich wrapped in wax paper. He chewed slowly, savoring every bite, making it last as long as possible. When the final crumb was gone he rooted around in another pocket until his fingers closed on the butt of a cigar. He put it in his mouth, withdrew a flattened box of matches from the same pocket, struck one, and drew on the dry cigar. When it was burning he relaxed on the soft seat, exhaled the smoke, and sighed contentedly.

It was October, time to think about heading south. Maybe find a job somewhere. Conditions were improving, or so they were saying around the hobo jungles. He had seen little sign of it himself but it would be nice if it were true. Life on the road seemed harder at thirty-two than it had even a year earlier. Yes, it would be nice if he could find a job, rent a room of his own, eat regularly … The cigar slipped from his fingers as he slept.

The florid face was only a foot from his own. Bulging eyes, bulbous nose, thick lips spread wide as angry words poured from the man's mouth. For an instant he was bewildered, disoriented, but then he sprang from the seat and out the door on the other side of the car.

The man continued to berate him. "You no good bum! You dirty, rotten bum, I'll teach you a lesson you won't forget!"

Too late he moved toward the open double doors. The man had grabbed a heavy spade, cut off his retreat, and was advancing menacingly. As the spade descended toward his head he made a desperate lunge for the handle, wrenched it free, and kicked at his assailant's groin.

The man gasped and sank to the floor. Instinctively he raised the spade and struck. Again and again he lifted it and brought it down. At last he stopped, recoiling in horror from the bloody heap on the floor. He dropped the spade, looked around wild-eyed, and ran out into the gray light of early morning

Once outside he hesitated, caught sight of a woman's face watching him from a window of the house, and fled down the driveway. Again he halted uncertainly when he reached the sidewalk. A man stared at him in surprise from a porch across the street, so he began running. North this time, back toward the railroad tracks.

The run was like miles instead of blocks. When at last he arrived at the warehouses he slipped out of the blood-splattered jacket and tossed it under a loading platform. He hated to part with it – he would miss its warmth and protection; but it was too distinctive, too easy to spot.

He resumed his run but after crossing several tracks he slowed to a walk and struck out east. He was nearing a dense patch of tall weeks when he heard the first siren. He re-crossed the tracks, stumbled over the last rail, and fell headlong into the tall protective weeds.

The wailing of the sirens seemed interminable. He lay shivering among the weeds and knew it was not from the cold alone. At last he heard a train and carefully parted the foliage. An eastbound freight was moving through the yards, slowly gaining speed. He ran for or it, climbed aboard an open gondola, and dropped down among pieces of tarpaulin-covered machinery.

He jumped from the train when it slowed just west of Cleveland, hid in a woods until darkness fell, then stumbled wearily along the tracks to a hobo camp. An old man offered him the remains of a stew and after gulping it down he slept fitfully, cold, lonely, afraid. In the morning he realized he didn't know where the nightmare had taken place. A good-sized town somewhere east of Indianapolis, but it wasn't important. He was on the run and what did it matter where the pursers had taken up the chase?

The dream faded and the old man slowly focused on the present. Damn the dream, he thought. It was becoming an obsession. Why? Why now, after forty-two years? If only it really were a dream, but of course it wasn't.

He rummaged through his pockets until he found a battered old pipe bound together at the stem and shank with friction tape. From a roll-up pouch he tamped crumbling flakes of stale tobacco into the bowl, struck a match, and puffed until it was burning well. He watched the smoke curl skyward and meditated. If he walked away from the County Home he wouldn't be able to return. Others had done so and found themselves at the end of a long list waiting for admission.

He had to do it, though, he had known that for days now. Conscience, that must be it. A feeling after all this time that he had to clear the record before it was too late. There would be no worry about getting back into the County Home – he would have a new home behind high walls. At least he would be able to sleep again and that made all other considerations unimportant.

He'd leave in the morning. There was money the authorities didn't know about, concealed long ago near the gray boulder and added to from time to time. Not a lot but enough for a bus ticket west, food, a few nights in cheap hotels.

After breakfast he gathered his meager possessions together, slipped out a side door, and walked to the highway. He raised his thumb and the fourth car pulled over.

The public library in town was his first stop. A librarian directed him directed him to a large atlas showing railroad lines. With a gnarled finger he followed the old New York Central mainline east from Indianapolis. Anderson was the first possibility, then Midland. Winchester was too small. So were Union City, Sidney and Bellefontaine. Marion, Ohio? Big enough but too far east. No it had to have been Anderson or Midland.

Shortly after noon he boarded a Trailways bus. The ride was long and tiring, so he kept reminding himself how much more comfortable the seat was than the floor of an empty boxcar. Still, it would be nice to stretch out. He changed buses twice, arrived in Anderson the following morning and went directly to the library.

The librarian placed the reel on the machine, showed him how to focus it and center the pages of the *Herald* on the screen. Laboriously he studied headline after headline, page after page. Hours later, eyes burning, he switched off the machine. The librarian came over, put the reel back in the small cardboard box labeled *October 1937*. He stood up, flexed his legs and walked slowly to the door and outside into the nippy autumn air. No, it hadn't been Anderson.

He bummed a ride to the edge of town, hitched another on to Midland. Rickety stairs led him to a flophouse over a tavern near the tracks. When the dream jerked him awake hours before dawn it had been even more distinct, more intense than usual. Despite his weariness he was unable to sleep again.

A bowl of oatmeal and a cup of coffee in a greasy restaurant was his breakfast. When the library opened he was waiting on the wide steps outside, the grocery bag containing all his earthly possessions under his arm. He pored over microfilm again until noon, then stopped when his eyes could take no more. He had covered the pages of the Midland *News Banner,* from the first to the fifteenth of the month without finding what he was looking for.

The first nagging doubt entered his mind as he got up and wandered outside. What if he had made a mistake? Suppose it hadn't been the New York Central between Indianapolis and Cleveland? But it had been, he was certain of it. Still, the knot in the pit of his stomach grew steadily larger. What if he couldn't find it? His money was getting low. Where could he go, what could he do?

He ate a sandwich, drank another cup of coffee. He wanted to lie down and rest his burning eyes, but he forced his legs to climb the steps to the library again. He had to find the place, he couldn't give in to the fatigue that engulfed his body.

It jumped out at him twenty minutes after he returned to his seat at the machine. Page one, October 17, 1937.

South Side Man Murdered, Transients Questioned

A 42-year-old Midland man, John J. Squires, was beaten to death early today in the garage at his home, 614 S. Dudley St. Police immediately began a roundup of transients.

The victim's wife, Anna, told police her husband went to the garage shortly before seven o'clock this morning. Several minutes later, not having heard the car start, she went to a rear window and saw a man run out of the garage.

Mrs. Squires went to the garage and found her husband lying beside the car. He had been badly beaten, apparently with the blade of a garden spade. Mrs. Squires called an ambulance and the police. Her husband was pronounced dead at the scene by Coroner Ralph T. Taylor.

Mrs. Squires said the running man appeared to be a transient. She told the police he was about 30 years old, 5-10, and 150 pounds. He was wearing a gray cap, black trousers, and a red-and-black plaid jacket.

A neighbor, Frank Edwards, 613 S. Dudley St., also saw the man run from the garage and then north on Dudley. He confirmed Mrs. Squires' description of the killer.

Police theorize the man sought shelter in the garage and was surprised by Mr. Squires. By noon more than a dozen men had been picked up and questioned at police headquarters.

Mr. Squires, and 18-year employee of Clay Brothers Company, also is survived by. . .

The old man leaned back in the wooden chair, sat quietly for a moment, then read the story again. When he reached the end he rewound the film, placed it in its box, and walked to the service desk.

The librarian looked up and smiled. "Finished?" she said.

The old man nodded his head. "Where's the jail?" he asked. The woman told him and he walked away.

He pressed the button beside the pair of heavy steel doors and looked around, puzzled, when a voice asked, "Can I help you?" Above and to the left of the doors he saw a small television camera. He looked at it and said, "I want to see the sheriff."

"What? " This time he realized the voice came from a square grating above the button, so he repeated, "I want to see the sheriff."

"He's up at the courthouse. Can I help you?"

The old man shook his head and turned away. He had passed the sprawling modern courthouse walking down from the library, so he retraced his steps and entered the white structure. He crossed the lobby to a directory, studied it a moment, then turned to the elevators. When he got off at the third floor he looked around uncertainly, finally saw a small black sign reading *Sheriff*, and shuffled toward it.

A woman seated at a desk behind a counter smiled and said, "Can I help you?" but he ignored her and walked to the open door of a small office at his right. A portly, ruddy-complexioned man in a brown uniform looked up from his desk.

"Hello," he said. "What can I do for you today?"

"You the sheriff?"

"You called it." The man stood up, walked around the desk, and extended his hand. "Joe McAuliffe. What's on your mind?"

"I killed a man."

The sheriff drew back a little and studied him from surprised eyes. "Better tell me about it, old-timer. Who'd you kill?"

"A man named Squires. John J. Squires."

"Where'd this happen?"

"At his house. 614 South Dudley Street. In the garage."

"It would be a city matter then, but I should of heard about it. Did you just come from there?"

The old man shook his head, so the sheriff said, "You're sure you killed him? How'd it happen?"

"I hit him with a shovel. It killed him all right."

"John J. Squires, you say?" The sheriff scratched his head, then shook it from side to side. "Funny, I don't remember it. When exactly did it happen?"

"October 17, 1937."

The sheriff dropped down in his chair, hard. He frowned a moment, then his face broke into a grin. "Are you putting me on, old man? That's better'n forty years ago."

"I know it. Want to get it off my chest."

A frown creased the sheriff's brow again. He studied his visitor intently for a minute before picking up the phone, dialing a number, and saying "Detectives." After a short pause he said, "That you, Charlie? Joe McAuliffe. Do me a favor, will you. See if you've got an open file on a John J. Squires." He spelled the last name, looking at the old man for confirmation, and then, "A murder victim."

The sheriff drummed two fingers on his desk and continued to stare at his at his visitor while several minutes passed in silence. At last he said, "You don't" No, don't bother. Thanks, Charlie."

He cradled the phone, took two cigars from a shirt pocket, and held one out to the other man. "They don't have a file on it, Pop. Think maybe you made a mistake?"

"No mistake. Not by me, anyway."

The sheriff removed the cellophane wrapper from his cigar, rolled the tip of it around his lips, and struck a match. Through a haze of smoke he said, "I don't know what to tell you, old-timer. What do you want me to do?"

"Lock me up. I told you , I killed a man."

McAuliffe chuckle a little.

He picked up the phone again, dialed, and said, "This is the sheriff. Is Phil there?" A short delay and then, "Phil, I need some help. Can you come down to my office a minute?"

The two men sat without speaking until a dark-haired man of about 30 attired in an expensive suit entered the door. The sheriff stood up again and walked to the man, put a hand on his shoulder. Turning to the old man, McAuliffe said, "This is Philip Cosgrove, the county prosecutor," and then, to the other, "Phil, we've got a little problem. My friend here says he killed a man out on South Dudley back in 1937 but the city hasn't got a file on it."

The prosecutor laughed. "Did you say 1937?" He turned to the old man and said, "That's forty-two years ago and you're just getting around to reporting it?"

"Like I told the sheriff, I want to get off my chest."

"Better explain it."

"I was on the bum. That was back in the Depression, you know. It was cold and I needed a place to sleep, so I hid in a garage. In the morning this man found me, came at me with a shovel, and I took it away from him and killed him with it. I hopped a freight a little while later and they never caught up with me."

The prosecutor looked at the sheriff. "You say there's no record of it?"

"No active file at the city. That's all I checked."

The prosecutor looked at his watch, glanced at the old man, and shrugged his shoulders. "Okay, lock him up. It's too late to do much about it now but we'll check it out in the morning. No hurry, I guess, after forty-two years."

The old man leaned back in his chair and sighed. For the first time in days he smiled.

He was given a cell to himself. It was warm; the bunk suspended from a wall was comfortable and the evening meal was tasty, better than the ones served back at the County Home. After dinner he stretched out on the bunk, lit the cigar the sheriff had given him, and reviewed it all in his mind. He had made the right move, he was certain of it. Now he was content. After a time the cigar went dead and he slept soundly, untroubled by dreams.

Late the next morning a turnkey unlocked his cell, said, "The sheriff wants to see you," and led him out of the block and down a hallway to a small room.

Joe McAuliffe was leaning back in a chair, feet on a table, a cigar in his mouth. He took another from his pocket and held it out. The old man put it away to enjoy later.

"Sit down, Pop," the sheriff said and grinned at him as a clock on the wall loudly ticked away seconds that extended into minutes. Finally he said, "What's the story, old timer? Need a place in out of the cold with winter coming on, is that it"

The old man stared at him, bewildered.

The sheriff swung his feet to the floor. "Why don't you try the Mission down the street? They could put you up for a night or two. Don't you have relatives somewhere, kids or anything?"

The first tremor of fear shook the old man's body. Haltingly he said, "I don't get you sheriff."

"I hear you were checking the old newspapers down at the library before you came in to see me yesterday. It was a good try but you didn't read far enough."

His fear intensified. "I still don't get you."

"That murder took place, all right. Just like you said but they caught the guy the same day. If you'd read one more issue you'd've known that and saved us both a lot of trouble."

The room seemed hazy before the old man's eyes. He ran the back of a hand across them but it made things even less distinct.

"But –" he began, then he hesitated, groped for words. "But I did it, I told you that. What do you mean they caught the guy? They couldn't have."

"They did, old timer. A fella named George Prescott. Caught him in the railroad yards about six blocks away. Two witnesses identified him." The sheriff flipped the pages of a file on his desk. "An Anna Squires, the victim's wife, and a Frank Edwards."

"But how could they? It was me."

"Positive identifications. Picked him out of a lineup."

McAuliffe took a paper from the folder and read, "George Prescott, twenty-seven, no known address. Five-eleven, one hundred seventy pounds. Brown hair, brown eyes. Wearing blue denims and a red and black plaid jacket."

The old man brought his fist down sharply on the table. "That was it, the jacket? I threw it away under a loading dock. I knew it would be too easy to spot. He must have found it."

The sheriff grinned at him. "Give it up, Pop. Everything you know about it could have come from the newspaper. The case was closed a long time ago."

"You're not saying they convicted this Prescott?"

McAuliffe nodded.

"But how could they? He was innocent." The old man sat down, shaking his head, staring with haunted eyes at the tabletop. Suddenly he jerked his head up and said, "What about fingerprints? On the shovel or in the car."

The sheriff leafed through the papers. "Nothing in here. No mention of finding any at the scene. Prescott's are on file, of course."

"But there had to be prints! Can't you check?"

McAuliffe chuckled. "I have checked." He pointed to the file and said, "This is it. What do you expect after forty-two years?"

The old man slumped in his chair. "This Prescott, how long did her serve?"

"Six or seven months."

"That's all?" The old man's face brightened. Thank God for that, at least.

"Yep," the sheriff said. "He got the chair in May of thirty-eight."

A deputy was holding smelling salts under the old man's nose when he came to. The sheriff handed him a cup of coffee and said, "Drink this, you'll feel better."

When the cup was empty, McAuliffe gave him the bag containing his possessions and walked him to the double steel doors. "How you fixed for money?" the sheriff asked and when there was no reply, took a ten-dollar bill from his wallet and pressed it in the other's hand. He unlocked the door and gently nudged the old man outside.

He turned then and murmured, "I thought only one died, but –" The door clanged shut behind him.

The old man remained standing there, confused, uncertain. After a time he slowly descended the stairs and shuffled away up the street. A misty rain had begun to fall. With fumbling fingers he turned up the collar of his jacket, but the cold October wind found its way inside. The frail old body trembled.

Also available by Dick Stodghill

**THE CASE FILES OF CRIMESTOPPER JACK EDDY
VOLUME ONE**
Eight stories featuring Jack Eddy, an assistant manager of
Wellington's National Detective Agency, and newspaper reporter
Bram Geary, narrator of a long running series in Alfred
Hitchcock's mystery magazine. ISBN: 978-0-6151-3508-3

NORMANDY 1944 – A Young Rifleman's War
The Battle of Normandy, neither glamorized nor sanitized as seen
from ground level during the bloody summer of 1944 – the
personal experiences of an 18-year-old 4th Infantry Division
rifleman. A true, highly acclaimed account of one of history's
great battles. ISBN: 1-4241-4913-4

Books available at Amazon, Barnes&Noble, other online
booksellers and many local bookstores.
Visit website: **www.dickstodghill.com**

www.ingramcontent.com/pod-product-compliance
Lightning Source LLC
Chambersburg PA
CBHW050532260626
47157CB00004B/1575